POLICING UTOPIA

Policing Utopia. Copyright @ 2026 by Alex Mell-Taylor

Published by Jabber Jabber LLC
Library of Congress Cataloguing-in-Publication Data has been applied for.
ISBN 9798988038597 (print) | 9798988038559 (Ebook)

First Edition.

Cover designed by David Colón.

POLICING UTOPIA

ALEX MELL-TAYLOR

CONTENT WARNING

Policing Utopia is a story about murder, dysfunctional queer relationships, grief, and abuse. As such, it is filled with examples of negative self-talk, gaslighting, manipulative group dynamics, and charged language.

PROLOGUE

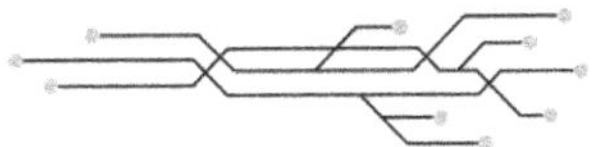

As she entered the Royal Boardroom, Three-Seven bowed at the Lord Directors, lowering herself as humbly as her back would allow. The Directors ignored her, too wrapped up in a heated conversation. Her supervisor should have canceled this shift, but she had learned young that it was better to accept her supervisors' failures than to challenge them.

Her knees buckled, and she waited until an HR Compliance officer waved her inside. She dragged her plastic cart with her, its creaky wheels almost snagging on the black carpet. She permitted herself the smallest of looks at one of the Boardroom's many windows before beginning her task. Every window here had a view of the murky Atlantic Ocean, a rarity in the Eastic, or at least a rarity among non-Premium Members like her.

She decided not to use her heavier machinery. The noise undoubtedly would be considered a nuisance to the Royals. Instead, she opted for a small hand-sized vacuum, whose hum was hardly noticeable amongst their bickering. She bent over, her back already sore from her prostration, and pushed the device along the edges of the conference room's carpet, making the quintessential vacuum impressions along the way. She only needed to look like she was cleaning for about 15 minutes or so, and then Three-Seven could leave and come back in an hour to finish the job for real. With a machine, she could sit in rather than break her back.

It was her custom to disregard the words of the Royals—gossipmongers were not treated very kindly—but they were being so loud and, strangest of all, direct.

"You are a damn fool, Jane," said Lord Manager Benison, a portly yet spry gentleman with perfectly coiffed black hair. Three-Seven couldn't see him, but she had seen the face of Eastic's Security and Development Director every day for the last two decades of her life. She saw his sculpted face on posters and screens, and in information videos, telling her to report anything suspicious.

Three-Seven had to stop herself from gasping at his boldness. She would hear the occasional muttered curse between Royals, but those were said from a distance or away from prying ears and recording devices. Worse, he had said these words to Her Majesty CEO Jane Smith for all to hear. The minutes from this meeting were recorded and technically public for Premium Members. It was sacrilege. She knew she shouldn't, but Three-Seven found herself listening in.

"It's what we are doing," Her Majesty cut, straightening out her white suit as if his objection bored her. "Our contacts have assured me that the secession movement is still underway. I am not going to throw away years of planning just because one member of the fucking Restoration decided to get in our way. Fuck those hippies."

"It could mean war," a nervous Director said, out of reach from Three-Seven's vision. "The other corporate holdings would hardly defend us against the Restoration's federated forces."

"And you are not even having the decency of increasing our shares in the venture," Benison chastised.

"Careful," Her Majesty cautioned, tapping the table with her finger.

Three-Seven realized she had been vacuuming the same spot for over a minute and received a nasty look from the HR compliance officer. She returned her hand vacuum to her plastic cart and emptied the dust into a bin before resuming her move along the room. She wasn't sure what the Royals were talking about now, something about agricultural yields and housing developments, but things had appeared to have gotten less heated.

"If we increase interest by...."

She tuned them out. It was better that way. Besides, if there was one thing she hated more than bending her back to clean the floor, it was the banal way her lords talked about the realm. The way they described the world had never made sense to her. Everything was about projections *this* and outcomes *that*. She had thought, naively perhaps as a child, that numbers didn't rule the lords like they ruled her. The debt on her contract and the debts of her children were a constant concern. Why would Royals want that fear, too? But she had been wrong. Numbers were everything they cared about.

She concentrated on her goal of lapping the hand vacuum around the conference room, but her knuckles were sore and cramping. Three-Seven had never recalled a point when her calloused hands weren't aching. Her contract was not an easy one, but for today at least, she only needed to do two more laps before she could bow out of this performance and sneak a quick break in the supply closet, three levels down. The one with the glitched-out camera that no one seemed to have reported.

As Three-Seven made her way back to her cart to empty out her hand vacuum yet again, she heard a pop. The air filtration system must be on the fritz again. She bent over to retrieve a screwdriver so she could check out its interior before she got yelled at by a lord directly.

She then heard a scream. Three-Seven turned her head to face the noise and couldn't quite process the scene before her. Her Majesty, CEO Jane Smith's head was lying on the conference table, with what seemed like blood pouring out, drenching the black keyboard and tablets beside her. Lord Manager Benison had a gun, a black thing he held unsteadily, still pointed in the direction where her majesty was...where her majesty had been.

"What the hell are you doing?" Screamed a director.

Lord Manager Benison shot him too, and then another lord, and another, before turning to the surviving members and saying with a bit too much relish, "Luckily for you, I do have a plan. Any objections to...."

Three-Seven hadn't comprehended that she had run out of the conference room until she registered the clanking sound of her feet hitting the metal grating of the stairwell. There wasn't a lot of time. Her parents had experienced a coup. Her father had not survived it. She looked at the painted number beside the door she had just darted past. Floor 52. She had to get to her kids at the Career Development Center on level 26 before Benison started liquidating Jane Smith's former property, which included people like her and her children.

She sprinted down the stairs, her heart pounding, trying not to think about how, at this speed, one slight misstep could cause her to start tumbling down. At 47, she felt like she could reach her goal in an instant, as if all it took to get her children was a short sprint downward into the bowels of the Eastic. At 35, she felt exhausted, sweat dripping down from her brow. At 30, all she could think of was her boy and girl. That morning, she had dropped them off in their Her Majesty-branded uniforms like any other day. It couldn't be their last. She wouldn't accept it.

She reached the thick black door and pulled the bronze handle that had greened from years of being so close to the sea. It wouldn't budge. She screamed. The lockdown had already begun. She heard an alarm blaring from the other side, more screams, and what sounded like a piece of equipment malfunctioning, but what she knew had to be gunfire. Three-Seven pounded at the door.

"Open up, goddamnit," she screamed.

Yet, as the gunfire got closer, she stopped. She couldn't help but shake intensely. She heard various children's cries rippling into nothingness. As fear permeated every part of her body, she stepped back from the door. Her kids were brilliant. She had told them what to do during coups—to run and to hide. They were fine; they had to be, but she would die here if she stayed.

Processing for the first time that she had carried the screwdriver in her hand down dozens of flights of stairs, she scanned the stairwell for a vent she knew from years of observation was here. It took her no time to unscrew it and crawl inside. That was the easy part. Screwing it back in from the opposite side was slightly more complicated, but the most challenging thing was stopping herself from crying as the guards entered the stairway and joked about the screams "non-premies" made when they died.

She waited for them to pass and then eked forward to the first grate, separating the first section of piping from the next. She could hear the sea not 80 yards away, but this grate was locked, possibly a consequence of the lockdown, maybe just a feature of the Eastic. She withdrew her screwdriver, positive that her work had just begun.

ONE

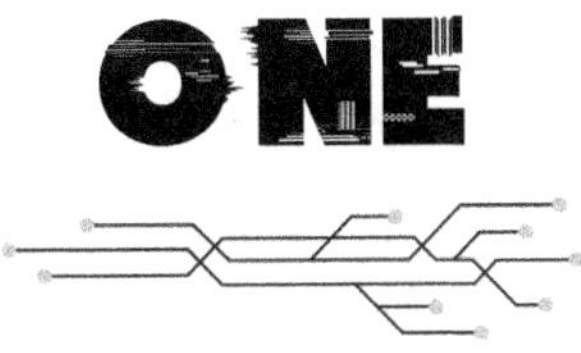

ROWAN

PUBLIC COAR DOWNLOAD/Book/The Restoration Is A Paradox/Author Hosa Liu/3-8-2094

-> *'Collective-bound' are an interesting phenomenon in the Restoration. About 90 million people roam in three different types of 'herds.' These are 'Reclaimers,' charged with mitigating environmental damage; 'Forest Sprouters,' who lay the groundwork for food forests; and 'Maintainers,' who ensure these great ecosystems continue.*

-> *Yet 5 million (and growing) live in stationary communities, or 'collectives' that do work that cannot easily be moved: medical clinics with patients whose conditions prohibit their transportation, repair facilities for complex machinery, and places of learning whose study requires a stationary life, such as astrophysics, geology, or the observation of a particular ecosystem. When someone moves from a herd to a collective, they are known as 'collective-bound.' Their herd celebrates, and their loved ones mourn their departure, which is some-*

*times temporary but increasingly more perma-
nent.*

*-> Some see this demographic shift as the defin-
ing problem of the Restoration as it...*

TIME: 6:45 PM
DAY: SUNDAY 5-15-2101

Rowan watched her wife Úna observe the theater troupe pantomime a murder on the amphitheater stage. She loved this part. The jester character had just pushed his lover out of a window. "Now that's what I call a goodbye," Rowan mouthed wordlessly, watching happily as her adorable wife let out a hearty belly laugh.

It was not the first play she had written, but it was her best work so far. She switched to watching her son Haldan, a twenty-four-year-old sourpuss, slouching beside her on the resined log they were seated on. He surprisingly had laughed, too. His brilliant, black braids slapped against the back of his head.

"Good job, Mom," he said, squeezing her hand.

She squeezed back, placing her arm around Haldan to give him a sideways hug. He had gotten to see her best work before leaving. Trash, he was leaving because she and Úna had decided to be so fracking 'supportive' and let him go off to the Bangalore Collective to study bioengineering. Not that she could've stopped him. Haldan, like his mothers, did what he wanted. Gaia, she wanted to punch something. She removed herself from the hug, retrieving a piece of string inside one of her suit's many seemingly invisible pockets, and began unraveling it, a fitting metaphor as any.

The jester finished their monologue, only for 'shepherd' characters to emerge from the audience. They had heard his out loud confession, a tick established in the first act.

"Oh well," he said mischievously, "I guess the joke is on me."

Cheesy but effective. The band in the back played the scene out, a comedic tune with a frantic energy that the characters matched by moving with tiny stomping footsteps. The lead gave their final monologue, a beautiful bit about justice and the need to resist violence.

"Violence begets violence," they cautioned. "We restore, not fight."

There was more applause, and then the play was done. The floating apparatus of spores the theater troupe had sprayed around the outdoor theater to control the lights around them faded away, allowing the dying evening light to eke in. The characters lined up, taking off their holomasks (thinly weaved pieces of fabric that projected a false image for the show) so you could see their real faces before they bowed. There was uproarious applause. The audience especially loved the Jester, played by a petite woman named Tulip, a relative newcomer to Salem who Rowan had not enjoyed working with, but her talent was undeniable. The Jester had not been the most prominent role, but Tulip had stolen the show with it.

"You really are improving," Úna commended. "Much better than the last one."

"Yes, Mom, you did well," smiled Haldan.

"I have to mingle, but shall we go for a walk after?" Rowan asked of Úna and Haldan, her simple family of three; maybe the last time they would ever be one.

"Well, you see...." Haldan cast his gaze at a man sitting not too far away. Peter, a muscular man his age, with a snowy hue and a crooked smile. He was in Haldan's polycule. They'd met years ago at a theater camp. Haldan was giggling, just looking at him.

"I know you want to say your goodbyes," Úna put delicately. "But we have a whole party later tonight for that."

Haldan didn't argue, nodding before getting lost in the rush of people coming up to Rowan to congratulate her. She was brief, accepting praise and gentle criticism with thank yous that didn't prompt further conversation. Many aspiring Writers' Cooperative members not so subtly tried to ask questions about the process. One, an exo who had settled into Salem just this rotation, had even asked directly if she could inquire about his ranking on the waitlist, to which she gave a stern stare and a simple no. It took her ten minutes to extricate herself from the crowd and find her way back to Úna and Haldan, who were chatting about nothing in particular, not too far away.

"You love being at the center of attention, don't you?" Úna laughed.

"No, no, well, yes, parts of it. It's hard to explain."

"Strange for a writer to be at a loss for words," Haldan teased.

"Bullies, the lot of you," Rowan chastised facetiously, smiling widely.

They strolled away toward the forest. In the distance, she could hear the roar of camp, which was abuzz with activity. Herd members were putting on events like Rowan's play to say goodbye to their collective-bound, some of which they would never see again.

"You excited for Bangalore?" Úna asked.

"I'm excited for the mentors there and for the classes. BPC's workshops on genetic sequencing are so frackin' advanced. I'm competent with DNA modification, but there are so many complexities that need to be worked out."

"We're very proud of you," Rowan managed to say, although all she wanted to do was cry.

They parked themselves on the sands of the shore. The Cods Archipelago had so many islands scattered about, sheer sandstone walls emerging from the ocean like the fingers of Gaia testing the waters. On top of them were green trees and shrubs that had clung to the rock like little hats. It was a stunning sight to behold.

The only break in this vista of natural beauty was a massive dome-like structure bobbing above the surface. It was one of the corporate Baronies called the Eastern Shore Trading Combine. It was an old structure that some Fallen billionaire had set up when the former United States collapsed. Before even the Corporate United States of America had emerged and fallen. Before the Second Great American Civil War. Before the revolution.

It looked like someone had cut a gray marble in half and affixed it to a string that kept it more or less in place, but not perfectly so. A sinking fortress. It was hard to believe that people still lived there.

Yet Rowan didn't want to think of those tiny people and their small ways. She focused instead on her son as he stared outward at the endless sea. He appeared so incredibly happy. He'd been so miserable for years. Herd life didn't suit him, she'd suspected. She would hear Haldan complain about the inefficiencies of Herd life. He bemoaned their chaotic self-organizing, their spontaneous trades, and longed for the more scheduled life of the Collectives, making it a habit to map out every Collective on their Herd's route since he was at least twelve.

As he made preparations for the Bangalore Bioengineering Collective these last few days, however, he'd seemed so happy, and she couldn't begrudge him for pursuing his happiness. Not for long, anyway.

"Hey, Haldan," called out Peter's confident voice.

Rowan saw that Peter and Tulip were by the threshold where the sands of the beach collided with the tree line. It was strange seeing those two together. Rowan remembered Tulip having left Haldan's polycule after a pretty nasty breakup. She supposed goodbyes could cause people to forget a lot. They did have some history together, after all.

Haldan was beaming. "Would it be...could I...?"

"Yes, go," Rowan swallowed. "Have fun."

"Thanks, moms," he shouted excitedly, kissing Rowan and Úna on the cheek as he darted over to Tulip and Peter.

She watched him leave, disappearing into the tree line. Rowan had wanted this walk to last just a little bit longer. She had wanted it to never end.

"Now don't pout like you usually do, but I will need to head to the celebration too," Úna said softly. "Our Representative is making an appearance as well. Trying to get everyone to support the amendment he's pushing, and I need to diffuse the situation if it gets," she paused. "Tense."

"Stay with me just a bit longer," Rowan pleaded softly.

The two of them sat on the sands, watching the dying rays of dusk dance over the waters. There was never enough time.

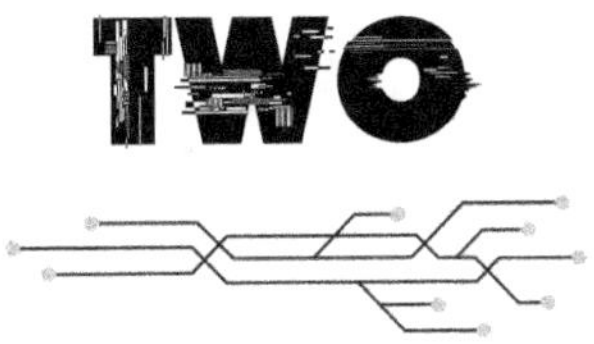

CALISTO

PUBLIC COAR DOWNLOAD/Article/The New Workers Collective/Author Garykillsfascists/5-14-2101

-> *Is this the scandal that will finally end the Groundwork Party for good?*

-> *For years, the Groundwork Party has spent social capital trying to centralize the Community Repair Specialist Delegation so that 'Delegate-approved' people from outside of a herd (i.e. peacekeepers) can help assist with murder investigations—something critics like myself have said reminds us eerily of Fallen cops. And now rising party star Calisto Tremblay has gone on a rampage and killed five people while on the job. The Peacekeeper program was already controversial, as all centralized authority should be, but with so much blood on their hands, the GWP doesn't look as impenetrable as it once seemed.*

TIME: 7:37 PM
DAY: SUNDAY 5-15-2101

"I am so thrilled to be accepting this award tonight," Calisto smiled.

The smile was a lie. Calisto didn't want to be here. Murderers shouldn't get awards. They shouldn't be able to stand on a stage and smile as their peers clapped at their pre-written speech. Some hackneyed thing about resilience, written by a party member Calisto had never met, or if they had, had left no impression.

The room was Mishigami's theater space, a large auditorium with comfortable chairs made of upcycled leather and wood. It was where the collective held shows, comedy skits, plays, sacred ceremonies, and other significant events. A place Calisto had seen again and again since they were a young child, but tonight, the GWP had booked it for their Awards Ceremony. It was technically for the Community Repair Specialist (CRS) Delegation, rewarding members of its Peacekeeping Program for a third successful year, but only party members had accepted such invites because only party members were *really* invited.

"As our program goes through growing pains," Calisto said, almost choking on the lie then and there.

They wanted to ask the Party Leaders in attendance if five dead people were the growing pains referred to in this speech, but they held their tongue.

Not now, the voice of their mentor, Sirius, said inside their mind. *Wait for a better moment.*

They remembered his kind face. The way his eyes widened in excitement whenever talking about their duty to the law and the Party. He had looked younger than his forty years let on, even as he had been gunned down. His creamy cheeks had beamed back at them. Until, well, they hadn't.

Calisto swallowed their pride and repeated the words of the speech with a removed enthusiasm. They smiled when the speech called for them to smile. They winked when it asked them to wink. They thanked whom it said to thank. And they felt nothing for it. They then returned to their seat, thunderous applause following them as they went.

Calisto sat next to their wife, Colibri, whose one-piece suit shimmered a radiant red that swirled about like a storm prepared to break landfall.

"That was excellent, Cal," she smiled. Colibri spoke Québécois French, the complexities of which Calisto still hadn't mastered orally, even after years of marriage to her and despite their father being from the former nation of France. They could understand it well enough, though they had to occasionally have their suit pipe in a rough enough translation into their ears.

Calisto nodded, feeling too disgusted to disagree with her.

Many more speeches continued after theirs. Nearly half of the CRS Delegation was part of the Groundwork Party, and all its members enrolled in the CRS Delegation were here, repeating their pre-written speeches and receiving their uniform applause.

The last speech was delivered by Comrade Chair Roxane Chapman, a petite woman who had switched her suit's color to pearl white, which contrasted beautifully against her golden tan skin. She gave a speech extolling the virtues of the CRS Delegation. "It's hard to believe that even six years ago, the

Delegation didn't exist," she stated, "That herds didn't coordinate matters of justice between themselves. Someone could be removed from their herd and just relocate, and except for word of mouth, their new community would be oblivious to the harm done."

There were murmurs of agreement and even one or two 'shames' shouted by enthusiastic members.

"And with the Peacekeeper Program, we're accelerating this trend. Providing outside support for the most difficult repairs to the herds that need it the most. All of you seated here this evening should be proud. Give yourself a round of applause."

There were woos and shouts. Roxane then smiled and said the same thing she said at the end of every meeting: "We are the light, held up by the collective. A beacon guiding the Restoration against both internal and external threats. May you shine brightly in this struggle."

"May you as well," The auditorium repeated in unison.

And with that, they were dismissed, everyone rising from their seats. There was nothing officially scheduled after the celebration, but seeing as long speeches tended to drain even the most resolute of party members, most everyone in attendance went to the cafeteria for a late dinner. It had once been described to Calisto as overly plain, like the barracks you see in old Fallen movies on the COAR. It was a long, low-hanging room with rows and rows of mismatched tables and chairs.

The cafeteria was open most hours, though staffing varied depending on when people wanted to cook and what they wanted to serve. Tonight, tacos were made from corn tortillas filled with black beans and squash, the latter browned with sugar. Calisto was positive that the sugar had to be refined from sugar beets left over from last season. This was a treat this late in summer that the GWP had no doubt haggled for with the collective's cooks and quartermasters.

Colibri and Calisto sat alone, picking at their tacos in silence. Few were inclined to approach them. Even as the party said nothing about the murders, all their peers still treated Calisto like the plague, as if they would get contaminated by Calisto's past through the sheer act of talking to them.

"They keep staring," Calisto whispered bitterly. "If they're going to pretend we aren't here, they should stop making this so frackin' awkward."

"Ignore them," Colibri hissed, "The Party has kept you in the CRS delegation. You're still a Peacekeeper. This will pass."

Calisto had given up on eating, nervously shredding apart their tortilla. "That's easy for you to say. You don't have blood on your hands."

Colibri rolled her eyes. "You're being so dramatic. You aren't responsible for the extreme measures you must take on duty. Roxane has been over this in her COAR posts."

"Has she now?" Calisto said. They were being sarcastic, but their wife was either too oblivious or too stubborn to acknowledge it, instead reciting a diatribe Roxane Chapman had written about the special allowances that should be made for peacekeepers in the CRS Delegation. They let her drone on, too exhausted to respond. They weren't even sure they disagreed. Why did they want to push back against logic that only helped their career?

"Great speech."

Calisto looked up to see the sand beige face of Dela Feinberger-Wu, their liaison, who in a pre-Fallen world may have been referred to as Calisto's boss, though the lines in the Restoration were blurrier. She was more of a glorified task manager than anything else. A layer insulating Calisto from the inner wheelings and dealings of Party leadership, and they preferred it that way.

She also, for some reason Calisto still didn't understand, really liked them. She said it was because they completed more cases than anyone in the Delegation, but Calisto had difficulty believing that. Case numbers were not officially ranked competitively, as it was considered bad form to set a timeline for a community repair when no two were ever the same. But the GWP was 100% tracking the time it took to close cases, which meant the Delegation was too.

"Thank you, Dela," Colibri chimed in after a beat of silence. "An excellent suggestion to use Stanley as a speechwriter."

"One of our best," she smiled. "May I?" she said, gesturing to the table.

Colibri nodded, and Dela sat down.

"Trash, Cal, frackin' smile will you. Do you want all of Mishagami to hate you?"

"Don't they already?"

"Listen, I won't get into a spat with you. I came to warn you, Cal. Roxane is gunning for your membership."

"In the GWP?" They said, more out of reflex than anything else. Even after everything, it seemed so far removed from the realm of possibility. Anyone could technically call for someone's removal, but it required a plurality of votes among the membership, and after the GWP fought so hard to keep them in the CRS Delegation and remain a peacekeeper, they didn't think they would have to fight to preserve their

Groundwork membership, too. Calisto wanted to scream, but all they could manage was a hoarse: "She has the votes?"

Dela nodded her head yes. "Maybe. She thinks you're a liability to the Party. Wants to distance us from the incident and make the Peacekeeper Program less about the GWP."

"But it is about the GWP," Colibri stated, a tad surprised. "We fought for it."

Calisto stared at their wife and realized her statement had everything to do with pride.

"Yes," Dela continued, "but she doesn't want it to look like a GWP thing, but more of a general Restoration program. Optics, you understand."

"What do you want, Dela?" Calisto said bluntly.

"Nothing," Dela said quickly. "It's just," she paused, stumbling over her words. "Don't make a scene, Cal. Keep your head down. Let me handle it."

"Roger," Calisto said, plastering a broad smile on their face as they gave a thumbs up.

"Good," Dela smiled and walked away.

Calisto felt numb from the interaction. They wanted to sink to the ground and cut themselves off from the world, but Colibri became even more animated, entering into a long, one-sided conversation about how, upon rethinking some of her COAR posts, this was the type of narcissistic behavior she could see Roxane Chapman doing.

Calisto said nothing as they watched the many eyes in the cafeteria darting away from them. The party had been their home since before they could remember. Even when they'd not been an official member, they'd grown up on the party's cookouts and picnics, chasing other excited children through the halls, always imagining what they would do when they would become a member and serve the Party.

When Roxane Chapman had called on Mishigimi to flood the CRS Delegation, Calisto had taken it as a point of pride that they had been one of the youngest volunteers at seventeen. They would be one of the youngest again when she made a similar call for the emergent Peacekeeper program. They had always been on the frontlines, willing to sacrifice for their community, and that enthusiasm had touched Sirius so much that he had taken them under his wing.

We have a world to win, he had said the first time the two of them were assigned to a distant herd on the fringes of Turtle Island. *And we will win.*

The party was all they'd ever known, and they were going to lose the vote to be a part of it.

THREE

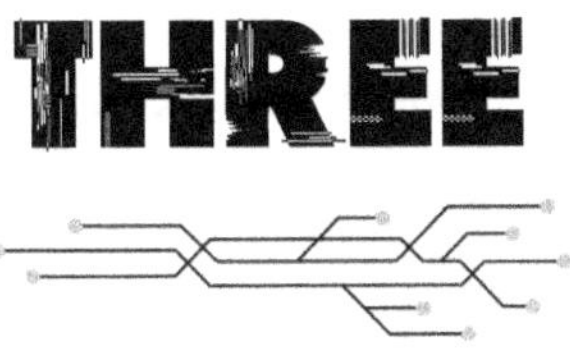

ROWAN

PUBLIC COAR DOWNLOAD/Article/Musings on the In-
doors/Author Haldan Kramer/8-20-2100

-> *The biggest benefit to living in a collective
is safety. I've been in a herd my entire life,
and as much as I love parts of it, you're surrounded by death all the time. A predator will
swoop in on its prey in front of you. A person
will get lost in the woods and never be seen
again. Someone will take a tumble and fall and
never get back up. We're more integrated into
nature, and with that comes death. It's something you just get used to.*

TIME: 11:40 PM
DAY: SUNDAY 5-15-2101

Rowan awoke to the sound of screaming: a loud gut-tural shriek that echoed across the night, amongst the trees and wind. It startled her upright from her sleeping mat, an alertness honed over years spent in nature, so close to the cycle of life and death. Úna had been cuddling beside her and was jostled awake by Rowan's sudden movement. Her wife opened her eyes, saw that it was still dark outside, and groaned.

"Trash, why are we up so early?"

"By Gaia, did you hear that?" Rowan asked.

"No, my little overreacter. I heard you, grumpy bear, just you."

"There was a noise."

"It's probably a coyote. It ain't coming to camp. There are hundreds of us here."

Rowan didn't think it was a coyote. They sounded like yipping dogs. This scream had pierced through the night like on the cusp of a word. An 'ah' or an 'oh' that had not quite gotten out of whatever or whoever had screamed

"I heard something. And I live in these woods too, Head Shepherd," Rowan protested.

"Things in the woods scream, Row. Animals kill each other."

"But..."

"Please, Row. Come back to bed."

Rowan sighed, indignant. She had heard something. At least, she'd thought she had heard something, but her wife was right. The more Rowan thought about it, the less certain she felt.

"Fine, but if we die, by Gaia, I will be so upset."

"I can live with that," Úna smirked.

Rowan slowly lay back down, kissing her wife on the back of her neck as she spooned her from behind. It might seem strange to an outsider that the ever-strong Head Shepherd of Salem loved being the little spoon, but Úna had always been a softy at heart. She sank into Rowan as her wife enveloped her.

"This is nice," Úna yawned.

Rowan felt herself falling into the twilight of consciousness, almost ready to shut down. And then there was rustling outside, and Rowan couldn't help but jolt awake.

"Again," Úna hissed.

"Moms, I heard one of you screaming," whispered their son's voice from outside their tent.

They hadn't kept track of where he'd ended up that night, not that they ever really did. Herd children tended to go where they wanted, and Haldan was well past childhood, anyway.

"Ugh, will we ever go to sleep?" Úna complained.

"I just got the jitters, sweetie." Rowan assuaged.

"Could I?" Haldan paused, his deep voice breaking for a second as he considered his question. "Could I sleep with you tonight?"

"You're twenty-four," Úna groaned.

"Of course, you can," Rowan said, ignoring her. "You're never too old to sleep with us."

"Come in," Úna groaned.

Haldan walked in quietly. "Thanks, moms," he panted.

Úna and Haldan shared a look as he entered. His suit's shoulder pad was torn, and there was a messy substance on his hands that he quickly wiped away before they could see it. Úna immediately noticed, pointing at it with her eyes.

"Just a scratch. The wind was howling tonight."

Úna started to cry at this. "Smog, you never were careful." She sobbed, not small tears either, but the kind of ugly trickle that runs down your cheeks when you can't control it. "Such a clumsy piece of trash."

"Honey," Rowan said sweetly. "That's not nice."

"Sorry, Hal. It's been a long day."

"Let's sleep," Rowan suggested, gently squeezing her wife's hand.

Haldan lay down beside his two moms, sandwiched between them. He hadn't slept with them since he had been a late tween. He'd had an auntie, someone who died from cancer a few years back, whom he had spent nights with as a child instead, because he claimed she'd smelled better. They'd not contested this preference; he was a person, after all, and childcare wasn't something people in Salem were particularly precious about, but a selfish part of her had always resented missing those cuddles. She wished she could go back in time and have more of these moments.

"I'll miss you," Rowan whispered.

"I'll miss you too," he replied.

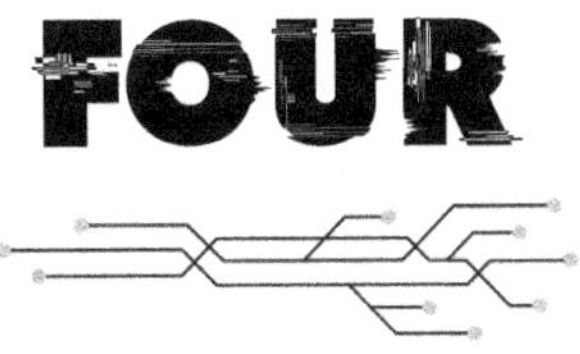

CALISTO

PUBLIC COAR DOWNLOAD/Book/The Restoration Is A
Paradox/Author Hosa Liu/3-8-2094

-> Every collective and herd makes its own
rules on how to govern, even if they are merely unwritten norms of when and where meetings
occur and how consensus is achieved. Some herds
use direct democracy. Others select leaders by
elections or sortition. One or two even do so
by a council of elders. Politics is involved in
every single one of these methods, and only a
fool would think otherwise.

-> In fact, political factions were and have
always been an inevitable aspect of our government. While most herds are always moving, their
populations are relatively stable. In some of
them, political factions can dominate so much
that being alienated from them can feel like the
same thing as being alienated from your herd or
collective.

TIME: 8:45 AM
DAY: MONDAY 5-16-2101

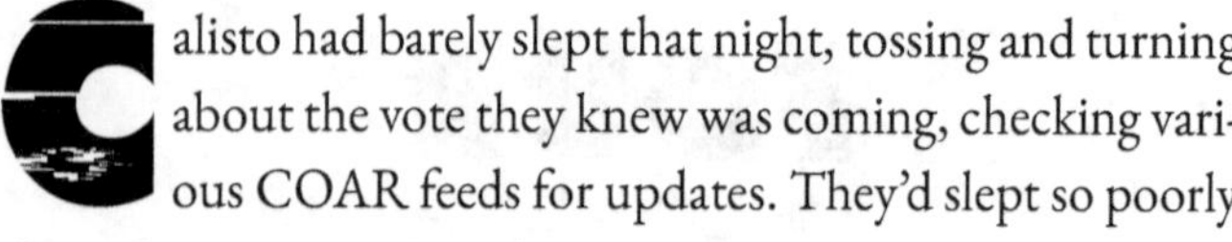alisto had barely slept that night, tossing and turning about the vote they knew was coming, checking various COAR feeds for updates. They'd slept so poorly that when a ping popped up on their wrist informing them that the vote had been scheduled for that morning, all they had to do was open their eyes to skim the information, groaning as they did.

Roxane—because let's face it, this was her doing, regardless of who cosponsored the resolution—shouldn't technically have been able to schedule the vote this quickly. The bylaws were very clear about the amount of notice required before such a vote could take place, but Calisto was positive she'd taken advantage of some technicality. After several seconds of scanning the COAR and monitoring a debate on their membership unfold in the feed, they learned that the vote had been *technically* scheduled over three weeks ago, tucked away at the bottom of a weekly bulletin that few had read.

They don't know why the interaction hurt so much. It was how the GWP operated. As their enemies often joked, some groups had conversations; the GWP had procedural maneuvers. Calisto had always assumed that those who made such complaints were simply sore losers, unable to accept the process, but being on the receiving end of such a maneuver didn't make them feel warm and cuddly about it. Every three months or so, a member would rage quit the GWP after dealing with something similar, and the pit at the bottom of their stomach made them empathize with such 'losers' in a way they never had before.

This frackin' sucked.

They called Dela, the person who'd promised to 'take care of this,' but she did not pick up. They called her a second, third, and fourth time and still got nothing. This makes sense: if she had really been on their side, this vote wouldn't have come as a surprise.

In their shock, they didn't realize that Colibri was seated upright on the bed, staring at them. Food was beside her nightstand, implying she'd gotten up much, much earlier.

"She isn't answering me either," she said glumly.

"Smog," Calisto cursed, their breaths growing shallower. "What are we going to do?"

Center yourself, the voice of Sirius, their imagined mentor, cautioned. *You need to calm down.*

Calisto took a deep breath, holding it in, then releasing it slowly. They remembered how Sirius would be there for them during their missions. Once Calisto had pushed away an abusive mother who had been trying to stop them from taking her son. She had refused to let her herd intervene, and Calisto and Sirius had been sent in as an objective force to get the job done, but Calisto had forgotten that the mother had had a bad back. She fell to the ground when Calisto pushed her, and something in her broke, and she died on the spot.

Breathe, Sirius had advised at the time. *Just breathe. Focus on the mission.*

"We have what, an hour?" Calisto asked their wife as they returned to the present moment.

Colibri nodded. "I thought we would have more time."

"I'm going to the cafeteria to check in with our friends. Whip up votes. You go to the daycare to drop the kids off and do the same with the folks there."

She kissed Calisto on the forehead, doing her best to hold back a dramatic sigh. "I love you, you know that," she said.

"Yeah, same," Calisto echoed back, their mind only half there.

With Colibri, that made at least two votes.

Within a few minutes, both were gone, rushing down one of Mishagami's many narrow hallways. There was no time for strategy. There was barely time to get dressed and brush their teeth. Calisto did their best to dart to the cafeteria without seeming too desperate. They had to project strength, after all, confidence enough to overcome the will of a Chair.

Remember to breathe, Sirius reminded.

Calisto breathed in and out, sighed, and then selected their first table. It was filled with friendly acquaintances and even a few friends.

"How are you feeling?" one of the more amiable party members asked—a lanky man with black hair and clay skin.

"I'll hopefully feel better in an hour," Calisto smirked. "Can I count on you to make that happen?" There was no use dancing around the issue. Calisto didn't have enough time.

"Of course. I don't like that Roxane frackin' ambushed you. I think you can count on all of us." Everyone around the table nodded.

That made 10 votes.

Calisto managed to get the group to help them whip up more, and the lot of them each took a section of the room to ask people to vote on Calisto's behalf. It was not an easy task, as it was clear that Roxane's hardliners had been campaigning against them for days, if not weeks. People treated them like they were some stain to be avoided. Many averted their eyes whenever they walked toward them. One man snickered as Calisto made their pitch. He refused to acknowledge Calisto and instead gave his friends near him a look of disbelief or disgust that Calisto was even trying to approach him.

The hour passed, and Calisto barely received 29 more votes, most of which came from comrades they already knew. The entire crew constituted a feeble coalition of 107, a number that would only increase to 151 when Colibri returned from the daycare center, her eyes puffy and red.

She said nothing as she took her seat at the auditorium, her hand in theirs, whispering promises of revenge against Roxane in their ear.

FIVE

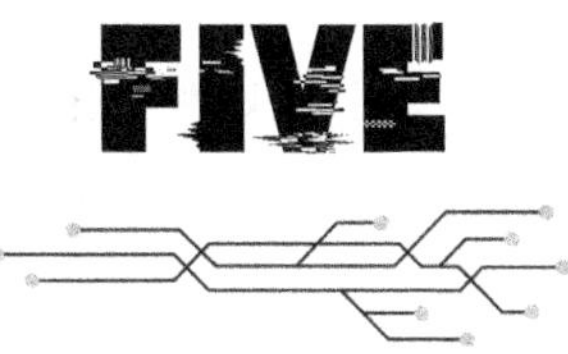

ROWAN

PRIVATE   COAR   THREAD/Communication/Haldan-Felipe/5-16-2101

-> *message chain:*
-> *Haldan Kramer: Can you delay the departure by just 5 minutes*
-> *Captain Felipe: No, Haldan Kramer. I swear to Gaia that if there's one thing I will not tolerate, it's tardiness. The Northeast Seven Shuttle is the Jewel of the Restoration. We can cram more people in this beauty and move more quickly than anything else in the fleet, and we will not mar that reputation. It's scheduled to leave the Cods precisely at noon today, and that's when we shall go. Be here, or risk taking the next one whenever it's scheduled. I can guarantee you it will not be on the Seven.*
-> *Haldan Kramer: By Gaia, you could have just said no.*
-> *Captain Felipe: Where would the fun in that be?*
-> *Haldan Kramer: You'll regret that.*

TIME: 11:52 AM
DAY: MONDAY 5-16-2101

She squeezed her son's hand tightly, not wanting to let go. Haldan was all packed for his voyage to the Bangalore Collective. His certificate of approval was in hand. The three of them were standing on McMillan Pier—a giant, pre-Fall construction made of treated wood and concrete. The ocean had risen significantly since the Fall, so the relatively nearby Neo-Boston Techno Collective had had to jack up the pillars and extend the pier past the flooded boardwalk ruins into the hills.

"Love you," Rowan said, placing a wet kiss on his cheek.

"Be sure to ping me when you land," her wife, Úna, instructed.

"Of course, moms. Love you too," he said matter-of-factly, squeezing Rowan's hand back before letting it go.

Rowan did her best to commit to memory every detail of his face before he turned away. His cute button nose. His long hair. His squat body. His smooth chestnut skin. He was so much like Úna in every way—stubborn, strong, beautiful—that she sometimes wondered what he had of hers. They'd both carried him, as womb transfers were common even in a small herd like Salem, but he didn't look like it. He'd had Rowan's eyes once, brown ovals like hazelnuts, but he'd biohacked them to be a deep purple, a fight she rather wished not to think about.

She felt so removed from him. Rowan had bounced from collective to collective, studying everything from nutritional science to her now-chosen profession, writing, while Haldan had waited over a year to get into this particular program for medical bioengineering. Even till the end, she'd still thought of him as a little boy, yet there he was, standing before her, fully grown and ready to leave.

Haldan went down the nano-alloy walkway to the ferry. He waved goodbye from the bow of the ship, and then he took his seat amongst the other 'collective-bound' headed up and down the East Coast. Rowan and Úna watched the boat depart as it hovered above the waters. Its propulsion created loud, turbulent waves that sent parts of the cliffside crashing into the water with a resounding thud. Within fifteen minutes, the ferry left, zooming away from them until not even the black dot of its outline remained. In less than an hour, Haldan would be 300 miles away in Maine, though to Rowan it would feel much farther.

Rowan and Úna initially said nothing on their way back to the herd. The wind was surprisingly cold for the height of summer, and Rowan couldn't help but think about how cold Haldan must have been on the deck of the ferry. She hadn't wanted Haldan to go. Herd Salem wouldn't make their way to Maine for some time, and it might be years before he returned to walk their path—if he decided to return at all. It wasn't typical, but some stayed at collectives their entire lives, and many more moved on to other herds.

"Sheesh, we'll see him again," Úna reassured Rowan.

She tried to touch Rowan's shoulder, but Rowan moved it just out of her reach. There was a silence between them. Rowan hated how perfect her wife seemed. Úna hadn't even expressed the tiniest hint of regret at Haldan going to study medical bioengineering in Bangalore. All she had done these past few days was work. Úna had thrown herself into her position as Head Shepherd, micro-managing their preparations to relocate to another campsite more intensely than usual.

She'd hardly let herself grieve, and Rowan felt like Úna was taking on the burden of losing their son alone.

"Okay, crazy, let's go to the overlook one last time," Úna suggested after a tense minute of silence.

Rowan said nothing, but she followed her wife all the same through the recent footpath that weaved through the scraggly scrub pines. They collected a few missed pieces of Fallen garbage along the way, always more trash to find, placing the dirt-caked refuse in green knapsacks they hung on their shoulders.

"Frack," Úna cursed, hitting the pad on her wrist.

"What?"

She pointed to a tall structure about thirty feet away with three spiny legs that elevated a bulbous container into the air: a nanoweave, one of those essential but annoying pieces of technology that allowed the Restoration to break down all the chemicals the Fallen had spewed into the world, the really nasty ones that natural mitigations like oysters and reeds took decades too long to handle.

"I forgot to route us around the weave," Úna said. "Gaia, it's going to mess with our comms for the next hour, at least."

"Another thing you forgot," Rowan jabbed.

Úna sighed heavily but, other than that, did not respond to Rowan's petulance. "Let's keep walking, my little grumpy bear," she said.

When they reached the end of the path, they settled on a flat rock with a direct view of the bay. Hundreds of years ago, this bay had been a sprawling landscape dotted with a variety of trees, bushes, and, most importantly, concrete, that substance Fallen humans seemed to love so much. Yet decades of extreme storms had rather violently whittled away at the stone until all that had remained was a sheer cliff. They sat there for half an hour, saying nothing, listening to the whistling of the wind.

In the distance, the barony was still chugging along. Several stacks of smoke emerged from it, tearing through the sky with dark, polluted ash. The Restoration didn't talk to corporate Baronies, as far as Rowan knew, and as such, they were exempt from its environmental mitigation efforts, though occasionally refugees fled from them. Reports of abuse and indentured servitude were common from survivors. They sounded like hell to Rowan.

"I wish that eyesore wasn't there," Úna remarked.

"Yeah," Rowan said simply. She was stubbornly willing herself not to engage— to be upset. Her son had left, and she didn't want to be happy about it.

"That corpo relic aside, this site is so beautiful," Úna continued, remarking on the expanse of blue sky and ocean before them. "We really cleaned this place up in no time."

"Yeah," Rowan repeated. "You weren't even weighed down by me being, what did you call me, crazy?"

"Only a little crazy. Anyway, we will see him again," Úna repeated, cutting straight to the heart of the matter, as if reading her thoughts. After three decades of marriage, if anyone could, it was probably her.

"You can't know that," Rowan said, after an icy pause. "He might never walk with us again, Úna. Neither of us returned to our herds after our first departure. When was the last time you walked with New London?"

"That doesn't mean we won't see him again. People do travel to other herds, you know," Úna chided lightly. "They visit their parents, too, even when said parents are being a lot."

"It's like you don't even care," Rowan shouted, trying to antagonize her wife into a fight.

"Hey, that's not fair," Úna huffed.

"It doesn't seem like you do." Rowan reiterated, digging deeper.

Úna took a deep breath. Rowan observed her Head Shepherd training starting to kick in. She was used to tempering people's dysregulation. She handled people every day and would need far more than Rowan's petulance to lose control. "I do care," Úna said firmly. "I just haven't wanted to admit it," she said, coming to the realization as she said it. "Sorry, I guess."

An apology. Nothing was worse when you wanted a fight. There was nothing left to do but take it. "Thank you," Rowan responded aggressively. "Perhaps it was unfair of me to say that you don't care. I'm just stressed and..." Her stomach growled. "Hungry," she continued.

Úna hugged Rowan and then kissed her on the forehead. "There, there, my sweet, magnificent, crazy little wife. Why don't we get you something to eat?"

They made their way back to camp, depositing the Fallen garbage in recycling carts positioned at the campground entrance. A hectic buzz of activity filled the air as people deconstructed their tents and rolled up their packs. That day, they would have continued their trek northward to another campsite. Haldan had waited until the last possible day to go to the collective so he could have more time with his family and herd. Salem had had a massive party for him and all the other collective-bound last night—though you wouldn't know it by how thoroughly everything had been packed away. The only remnants of last night's festivities were the gray ash in the center of massive fire pits, surrounded by rings of stone.

The two of them had already packed their belongings that morning, but as Head Shepherd, Úna had to check in with various people to ensure everyone was on task. There was always a last-minute dilemma that needed smoothing over, and they'd been on a tight schedule. Úna had told Rowan last night that the campsite Salem had negotiated for required that their herd claim it in less than three weeks, which wasn't much time. Rowan watched her wife in a panic as her muscular body bustled from tent to tent and cart to cart, ensuring nothing was left behind.

Rowan spent her time by the food cart, eating the breakfast leftovers as it was slowly being disassembled. She loudly slurped the broth of a mushroom-tofu soup. The mushrooms had been scavenged from the surrounding woodlands, and the handmade tofu had been processed in one of the herd's many fermenting tanks. She watched people pack up their large nanofiber tents and stuff them into small bags a fraction of their size. They lived their lives based on what they could carry. It amazed her sometimes how invisible their tech was. Even Rowan's suit could cool or heat her body, so it was always at the optimal temperature, though doing so was disrespectful to *Her*; cutting yourself off to Gaia was only meant to be done in emergencies.

Still, she had the option. Most of her electronics were integrated into it, and what wasn't could be compressed into miniature sizes. She wondered how her ancestors had lived in a world where things took up so much space. She had seen pictures. Thanks to *Her* benevolence, you could find fragments of pre-Fall buildings on the COAR, but she had trouble wrapping her head around staying in one place for her entire life. It sounded like it would get dull very quickly. She had gone up and down the Americas three times in her life, and every excursion had made her want to see more.

And yet, there was an odd pleasure in imagining a stationary life. She missed all the places she had visited—the swamps of the Floridian nub, the Catskills beaches. She remembered wading in the water, touching the cattails, picking up fallen ones, and turning them into stick figures for Haldan to play with. She'd never returned to these places because herds were always moving on to the next remediation site, cleaning up the messes of people hundreds of years dead, and now Haldan had left her to go to some place stationary. The one thing she wasn't able to give him.

"Uh oh, you must be thinking something big," Úna said. Rowan guessed she was taking a break from her shepherding duties to check in on her.

Rowan rolled her eyes. "Nothing much. Just about what it would be like to stay in one place." There was a hint of melancholy in her voice, as if she wanted to be transported back to that world of large houses and static routines, traversing the same landscape over and over again.

"Sounds like it could be fun," Úna remarked. There was an edge of something Rowan couldn't quite identify in her voice, a similar longing to Rowan's but not quite the same.

"How goes the herd?" Rowan asked, changing the subject.

"Good. Well, no, there are some problems. One of the 3D printer carts has broken down. We will need to send Chi and Ava to the High Rock Collective to get it repaired. And we're behind on our herd's biodiversity mitigation targets. But besides that. Fine."

Rowan smirked. She loved hearing her wife complain. "Always the worrier," she said.

"Comes with the position, Grumpy Bear. Besides, I thought you liked how attentive I could be." Úna moved behind Rowan and hugged her, placing a tender nibble on her neck.

"You're terrible," Rowan giggled, pushing her wife into her.

The two of them were being playful and energetic, part of their ritual to ease the tension after a big fight. Rowan was so happy, giggling at Úna's soft kisses.

She was distracted; it took her minutes to realize that there was a general murmur amongst the herdsfolk about something Rowan couldn't quite discern, something away from camp. Someone called out for people to follow them. Rowan did so with dozens of others walking hurriedly through the trees until they stood looking out over the cliff-side at the sea.

There, chugging along in the distance, was the Northeast Seven Shuttle. It had returned. She simply stared at the massive thing rippling through the water. The distortion from the nanoweave dissipated, and an old, unread message came in about her son. This was followed by another ping and another. All of them were from different people. All of them were of the same thing: a grainy video of a cramped hallway. Two men were fighting in it. At first, just with words, but then one of them shoved the other, and soon they were flailing arms at one another in that way men who can't fight resort to. It took her a moment to process that one of the men was her son Haldan, his ruffled suit the same verdant green color she remembered him wearing the morning she saw him off.

She wanted to call him. She made motions with her hands to ping his number, but this was interrupted by a call from a number that had attempted (and failed) to reach her all that afternoon: a hoarse voice that sounded solemn. A voice from the ferry. A person who claimed to be the captain was telling her something that made no sense.

"We found his body this afternoon. I'm sorry, ma'am, it's your son's."

He was telling her Haldan was dead. She didn't quite believe the news at first. She had dropped him off just that morning. She had seen him step onto the ferry, so excited to start his life, and now nothing. The first time, he'd left their herd, and someone on that boat had killed him, and all Rowan wanted to do was enact the same on whoever had killed her baby.

SIX

CALISTO

PRIVATE COAR DOWNLOAD/Digital Scan/Groundwork archives/Comrade Chair Roxane Chapman/5-10-2101

-> *Dear Dela*

-> *I am sending you this antiquated paper note rather than communicating on the COAR, because perhaps a change of medium will finally let the message sink in. I said no, and I meant it. Calisto Tremblay is not worth all this effort. Their recent frack-up makes any talk of membership a nonstarter. They almost killed the Peacekeeper Program single-handedly (and still might).*

-> *The Groundwork Party's power is our reputation, and Calisto's reputation might as well be in a mulch converter at this point. They lost the vote for a reason. If I have anything to do about it, their membership will remain revoked.*

TIME: 1:52 PM
DAY: MONDAY 5-16-2101

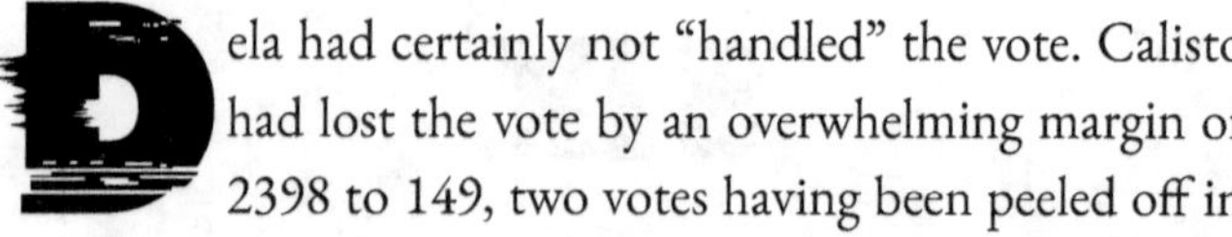

Dela had certainly not "handled" the vote. Calisto had lost the vote by an overwhelming margin of 2398 to 149, two votes having been peeled off in the minutes between the walk from the cafeteria to the auditorium. They weren't even sure Dela had voted for them.

They'd retreated to the warmth of their apartment, where they were sulking. Calisto didn't want to leave their bed. It wasn't because they were tired—all they'd done that day was sleep—but because they simply didn't want to face the world. They'd fracked things up too much.

It's not that terrible. The imagined voice of Sirius lectured.

When Sirius had been alive, he'd rarely been phased. He once talked a suspected barony slaver into putting her gun down long enough for Calisto to get a good shot at her (she didn't die, but her vocal cord was permanently frayed). Sirius never gave up during a difficult situation, or at least that's how Calisto remembered him.

There is always a way forward, he remembered saying to Calisto, as they maintained pressure on the suspected traffickers' wound. *We owe it to the Party to try.*

Yet Calisto didn't want to think about the perseverance of the human spirit. They wanted to continue arguing with Sirius, arguing with themself. "You call getting my party membership revoked a minor mistake," They admonished. "The CRS Delegation has barely allowed me to still work with them, and there might not be any more peacekeepers because of me. And now the GWP kicks me out?"

Sirius said nothing because he was really them, and Calisto didn't want to move on. They wanted to be petty. To not be so controlled. And getting back to work would mean putting back on the illusion of togetherness, which was a performance they didn't yet have the energy to resume.

Their wife, Colibri, opened the door, rolling her eyes as she saw Calisto sprawled out on the bed. She'd already gotten up, wearing an intricate nano-suit, faceted together with many ruffled pieces. She had programmed the outer layer to have a pulsating pattern of flocking hummingbirds, a little on the nose even for her. The flock of birds went down, almost to her mechanical leg braces: old ones that made a clanking noise with every step. The braces allowed her to move about the collective with ease, albeit noisily, which, of course, Colibri loved.

"Enough of this pouting," she chastised, whipping the covers off.

"Colibri," Calisto cawed in a poor Québécois accent. "Leave me to sulk, yes."

"No, I have no patience for it. Yes, what Roxane did was horrible, and you deserved better, but we lost, and there is only forward. Now make yourself useful and swap out my estrogen disk." She sat on the edge of the bed, turning so that Calisto could access a round, gray disk that interfaced directly with her skin, fitting perfectly into her suit,

Calisto frowned. "I still can't believe you haven't gotten used to this."

"I hate needles, even if it's only once a month, even if they're tiny. I hate them."

Calisto didn't prod further. Colibri handed them the small vial containing a clear liquid. They pressed a button on her suit, and out from the grey vial emerged an identical one, nearly empty. They replaced it with a new one. Colibri shuddered more from her fear of needles than from any pain, which had to be almost nonexistent.

"Thanks," she gulped.

"Thank Engels, I can do my T-disk on my own, or where would we be?"

"In the middle of menopause," she joked.

Calisto laughed, holding her in their arms, nipping her neck, and absentmindedly running their fingers through her brilliant black hair. They looked out at the Restored Lakes, glistening in the sunlight as they expanded to the hazy shore. It was hard to believe that water reformation had become such a redundant task that Mishagami was now more renowned for public health.

"You think those mudskippers that founded our Mishagami ever imagined this? That the lakes would not only return but become bigger than they'd had in generations?"

"I think they were too busy not dying of dehydration." Colibri laughed.

"Always the cynic," Calisto chided, and then, returning their attention to her suit, asked. "What's with the birds?"

"I like birds."

"No, really?" they responded sarcastically. "I thought you named yourself hummingbird because you wanted to eat them."

"You're smog," she said playfully, picking up a pillow and hitting them on the head with it. They offered weak resistance, preferring for her to fall into them. She positioned herself on top of them, and then they kissed.

"There, a smile," she smirked.

Calisto couldn't help but smile wider.

Pulling away, she said, "Cal, I've been talking to Dela."

Calisto sat up. "I told you not to. She betrayed me."

"I wouldn't say that, exactly."

"She told me she would handle the vote and then didn't." Calisto huffed.

"Well, she wants to tell you something. And the vote is over. There's no sense punishing yourself further like some fallen torture facility."

"You mean a prison?" Calisto smirked, placing their hands behind their back. "Besides, I thought you liked a little torture now and again."

Colibri twisted Calisto's nipple and then pulled away. She stood up. "It's fine if you don't want to hear what she has to say." She walked toward the door and opened it just ajar, the sound of children laughing and playing in the common area flooding into the room. She could be such a tease.

"By Marx, Coli," Calisto cursed, "you know, I want to know."

Colibri smiled. "She wants you on a case, Cal. Some murder that happened on a boat. And it's an important one, too. The collective waitlists for the entire East Coast have been messed up because of it. She said, and I quote, 'a quick wrap-up could mean major favors.'"

Calisto sighed performatively, "Fine."

She beamed. "Good, because Dela's already on the line."

"What?"

"Enjoy!" Colibri said, darting out the door as she turned on a nearby projector that cast a blue light onto the wall in their room, buzzing alive with the petite, soft brown face of Dela Feinberger-Wu.

"Hello," she greeted.

Calisto said nothing.

Dela sighed. "Are you still mad at me?"

"What do you think?"

"I told you I would handle it, and I still mean it, Cal. It's just taking me a tad longer than expected. Chapman isn't the easiest opponent."

Calisto rolled their eyes. "Please, you love this. I wouldn't be surprised if you had some scheme going."

Dela smiled but admitted nothing. "I assume Colibri told you about the case."

"Barely, and I don't want it."

"Just think about this, Cal."

"I have," Calisto replied petulantly.

Dela ignored them. "Smog, just listen to me. Removing you from the Party was the first step in Roxane's plan to remove you from the CRS Delegation."

This news didn't make sense in Calisto's brain. "But the Party defended me. I got an award."

"Roxane defended the *Peacekeeper* Program. She wants you gone. Make the whole incident about one bad apple, you."

"Frack. So I'm done for then."

"No, you certainly aren't." Dela smiled. "That's where this case comes in. Still don't want to hear about it?"

"It looks like I don't have much of a choice."

"You don't," she said coldly and then, taking their silence for consent, proceeded with the details of the case. "So the breakdown, it's a mess, Cal. This murder is connected to the largest shuttle in the federated fleet. Others have been put into circulation, but they're straining to keep up. It's putting a wrench in collective transfers all over the coast. I need someone I trust on this thing, and if you solve it, well, Chapman doesn't run everything."

"Yet," Calisto added.

Dela didn't disagree. "So, do I have a yes?"

"You want a frack up like me?"

Her lips pursed. "Chapman thinks that, not me. People make mistakes, Cal. You know, not everyone has to like you."

"Fine, whatever."

"Good, I already sent you the files. And get dressed. By Marx, it's the afternoon. Act like it."

The call ended: the projection of Dela's face blinking out of existence. They weren't sure they could trust her. They appeared to be a game piece in her chess match against Roxane, so desperate that Dela probably thought Calisto would do whatever she wanted, and she was probably right.

Colibri knocked loudly the moment Calisto switched off the call. She'd clearly listened in, most likely. "Can I come in?"

"You know you can."

Colibri darted in, giddy and excited, but said nothing.

"So where's this herd in the middle of nowhere?" Calisto continued.

She beamed. "Salem. They're currently on the Cods Archipelago."

"The Cods what?"

Colibri walked back to Calisto on the bed, smiling. "An island chain. I searched for images of it on the COAR. It looks stunning. Me and the kids might have to visit. After you solve this case, that is."

Calisto rolled their eyes. "You just want a vacation?"

Colibri twisted Calisto's nipples again. "Yes. And, that's ma'am to you."

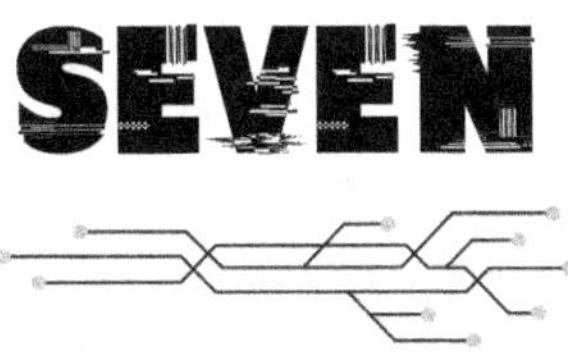

SEVEN

ROWAN

PUBLIC COAR DOWNLOAD/Article/You Can Create A Religion Out of That/Author Tulip Bellwether/2-17-2099

-> The Gaiaverse sprung up organically on the road, and I am not an academic or nothing. But smog, I think it had to do with the Internet: that's what they called the Common Archives (COAR) before it was collectivized, and private markets reigned. The first herds started moving from place to place because the environment wasn't stable enough to support any one group for long.

-> And the Internet got real patchy in that time, I hear. The Fallen were practically raised on that thing from birth, and so when they stumbled into a 'plugged-in' area, the messages sort of became sacred. Those with devices started reading out updates like doctrine, and before you knew it, people were talking about Gaia this and Gaia that. How She exists not only within plants and stuff but also inside the Internet.

TIME: 11:45 AM
DAY: TUESDAY 5-17-2101

Yesterday had been a blur, trying to process what exactly had even happened. Salem's Community Repair Specialist (CRS), Strummer, had asked her to go over details of the morning and night before her son's apparent death—smog, it hurt to say. She relived her last moments with him, still raw and unprocessed: what he had said, what he had been wearing, all jumbled up in her brain. Strummer had taken it all down and written a quick report that she had published to the COAR, but apparently that was not enough. A peacekeeper, a CRS from outside the herd, had to hear her too, for some reason—the CRS Delegation was insisting, and she didn't feel it in her power to say no.

That morning, shepherds directed her to a spare tent that had been inflated to house the newly arrived peacekeeper of the CRS Delegation. Their name was Calisto Tremblay, and they were unlike anyone Rowan had met in a long time. She had been rooted here, moving up and down the coast, for decades. It was rare for someone so different to arrive. Salem was a place sooner to attract a hermit than a resident of a collective, and those who did dropped that aesthetic long before arriving. Calisto hadn't received the memo. Everything about them was strange. They spoke a language Rowan didn't quite understand. French, her pad told her, mixed in with a dialect called Québécois.

Worse, the peacekeeper's suit had sacrilegious tech modules all over it, colored white and a stunning blood red, like a gem-encrusted demon. She spotted an infrared module on the peacekeeper, a scent-calibration one, and a half a dozen others. She had to stop herself from openly shuddering with disgust. Adherents of the faith were not barred from using tech, but trash; there had to be a balance. We weren't supposed to disconnect ourselves from the glory of nature any more than technology—it was all *Her*, after all.

The peacekeeper seemed unbothered by Rowan's discomfort, or at least they didn't say anything about it. After what seemed like the most calculating of small talk, they had asked her to remember the day of the murder. Rowan had deflected. She had already given Strummer her account. Who was this exo demanding Rowan remember this? That she remember anything at all?

But they persisted. "I'm afraid I need you to tell me, legally, I mean."

"I thought the Chamber's directives were non-binding?" Rowan said indignantly.

"I believe your herd ratified the CRS Delegation's most recent directive," Calisto lectured. "Last spring, if I'm not mistaken. I take it Salem doesn't use consensus?"

Rowan shook her head. "I voted against it," She scoffed, doing everything in her power not to delve into a long-winded rant about how she'd done so on principle. Rowan hated the peacekeepers and their laws or 'directives' and how they'd started to prop up everywhere in the Restoration. She almost hated them more than this exo's suit, but bit her tongue and swallowed the lecture. Rowan did her best not to sigh performatively and nearly succeeded.

"Fine," she conceded. "I'll tell you."

Rowan had expected the account of her time with Haldan before he was—before he went on the ferry—to come out haltingly, like you see in films where the bereaved parent is too shellshocked to talk. However, her words poured out like a poorly-compressed food waste processor, which was annoying. Of all the days to be compliant! She told the peacekeeper everything, and they nodded throughout her account with what Rowan was sure was a false smile.

"Does that story satisfy you?" Rowan said, her voice cracking as she came to a close.

The peacekeeper thanked Rowan for her account and attempted to say some smog about pain and loss. Rowan didn't pay attention and continued to stare hatefully at Calisto, wanting to punch the smug peacekeeper squarely in the jaw.

"I don't intend to offend," the patronizing exo said, seeing Rowan grimace uncomfortably, their sacrilegious modules pulsating all over their body. They continued: "This must be hard."

Rowan rolled her eyes. "Of course it is; what kind of statement is that?"

"Apologies. I have some clarifying questions if you don't mind," they said, and then, seeming to decide it was better to plow forward than give Rowan a chance to protest, said: "Did your son ever genetically modify himself?"

Rowan swallowed hard. "Yes," she replied.

She paused. It was not a pleasant subject. Gaia was very clear on this matter. Technology shouldn't cut humans off from their primary senses, and biotech did precisely that with its intensive alterations. She and Úna had forbidden Haldan from ever getting them, not that their permission amounted to anything but words, but he had disagreed, getting them anyway. It had been quite the scandal, and the herd had voted that Úna and Rowan had attempted to exercise unnatural authority on their child, and Haldan had stopped living with them for a while.

"He expanded the light spectrum in his eyes, made them purple. I know there were probably many more. It was the reason he went to Bangalore," Rowan continued. "We're less tolerant here of major violations to the body." She slowly eyed Calisto's suit up and down in a way that made her judgment quite apparent. "He disagreed with my interpretation of the Gaiaverse, thought it was too strict."

"It doesn't sound like you were happy with his reason for leaving?" Calisto prodded.

"No, I wanted him to stay. I must sound terrible, and maybe I am, but that's how I feel."

"And did he get any modifications recently?"

"I'm not sure I would be the right person to ask. He would have confided in Peter, Anderson, and his other the-ater troupe friends, not me."

"Anderson, I've heard of that name."

Rowan had to stop herself from loudly groaning. They didn't know Salem's representative?

The peacekeeper continued: "That's the guy trying to pass an amendment to stop something the Restoration al-ready doesn't do, right? Or something like that."

She sighed. "Stopping the ownership of land. It's a sym-bolic gesture. Part of his feud with Groundwork Party. We select our Chamber representatives by sortition. I'm not sure he would have won a straight vote; too cantankerous, but I'm sure you've done your research enough to know that?"

The peacekeeper looked like they were going to say some-thing, but then pursed their lips. "When was the last time you saw Representative Anderson Leek?"

"Sunday Night. I know people saw him on the ferry the next day, arguing with my baby, my son. People are saying he did it; is that true?"

"Too soon to say. You'll be sure to tell me if you or anyone sees your Representative?"

Rowan nodded.

The peacekeeper smiled approvingly. "So, to recap. You claim to have dropped Haldan off yesterday, Monday, at the Northeast Seven Shuttle."

"I did drop him off."

"Very good, so this body that you claim matches Haldan's description..."

"I don't claim anything," Rowan interrupted, "It's him. I identified his body this morning myself."

"Please, Mrs. Kramer. I'm not talking like this to discredit your version of events. It's merely how I couch my words to remove bias."

Rowan said nothing. She didn't think what the exo was saying was true, but she let them continue anyway.

"Now," they continued, "his DNA is...irregular. It's been tampered with on a genetic level that goes beyond a simple Cas9 tweak. Some of them are quite recent; it's possible even up to death."

"You mean, they experimented on him before they... they killed him."

Rowan didn't know what to think about this information. She had read stories on the COAR about biohacking. Rowan had even penned one or two short stories on the matter, but that was fiction. From every post she had read, the reality of the technology would have made it quite obvious that the body had been tampered with. Why would anyone do that and expect to get away with a crime?

"Maybe even after, too. It's too early to say why a perpetrator would do so, but these experiments have made our analysis extremely difficult. Testimony, including yours, says that he was alive Monday afternoon, but necrosis in some parts of the body set in on Sunday night around 11 PM, which would have made walking to the Northeast Seven Shuttle, like you said, pretty impossible. I can't see how someone with these results could have moved anywhere."

"That can't be right. I told you, I saw him board."

"I'm inclined to agree. Methods to pretend to be someone else have defects when going for long walks during the day. If it were a holomask, you would have seen artifacts in the projection, small shimmers when exposed to too much direct sunlight, and you haven't mentioned such things." Calisto pulled out a holomask, laying the silky gray fabric on the table. "You work with these, correct? For your play?"

Rowan nodded, running her hand along its surprisingly coarse surface. They were useful tools that allowed people to slide into roles on stage more easily, but, as the exo said, she had seen these images degrade when hit with too much light. At lower UV concentrations, the holoimage would skip with static, but at higher ones, the light would break down the guise completely and reveal the person's true skin underneath. That hadn't happened on her walk with him yesterday, and it had been very bright.

"It had been his face. I wasn't looking at him all the time, but enough, I think."

"Try to remember." The peacekeeper said gently.

"I..." She thought back to that day, one that she seemed like she was never going to escape. She saw Haldan. He was often obscured by Úna, the two of them chatting away, oblivious to the future ahead of him, but she had seen him. The sun touched his self-assured smile as he made a joke that Rowan couldn't quite remember. He had to have been real.

EIGHT

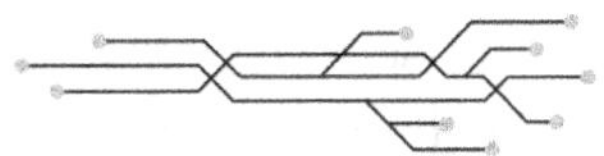

CALISTO

PUBLIC COAR DOWNLOAD/Book/The Restoration Is A Paradox/Author Hosa Liu/3-8-2094

-> How does anyone get anywhere on time? That's the question the surviving nation-states in Europe, Africa, and Asia constantly ask the Restoration 'officials' they confuse with Heads of State. How does a 'disorganized' assortment of herds, collectives, cooperatives, associations, and councils keep the trains and ferries running on time without central organization or the threat of money?

The answer a Restoration proponent will give you is through collective organization. People decide how they want the trains and ferries to run through the decision-making of their choice, and when someone chooses not to help with that labor anymore, a new person (or set of people) steps up. It's an answer that works well enough most of the time, but just like in the most capitalist nation-states on Earth, sometimes the trains simply don't run on time.

TIME: 1:07 PM
DAY: TUESDAY 5-17-2101

Calisto watched their balance as they stepped onto the boat. They grabbed hold of its oak composite railing to prevent themselves from falling directly on their ass. They had gear for this, auto-processing modules that allowed their body to cut through the air like a knife, but someone had told them their modules made her uncomfortable. So they had removed several of them hastily on the way here, and one just so happened to have been their auto-processing module: the exact fracking thing that would have helped in this situation. Their hand scraped the railing as they jostled upright. If it hadn't been so sturdy, that would have drawn blood.

Polluted Gaiaverse. They were supposed to love technology. Their blasted God resided within the COAR. But these small herdsfolk were radicals. Anything that dulled your senses was 'blasphemy,' apparently. And yet Calisto couldn't help but notice all of them were wearing nanosuits—hypocrites.

Easy, the imagined voice of their mentor, Siris, cautioned inside their mind. *You need to be more objective than this. You can't have an adversarial relationship with the community you are repairing.*

Calisto sighed. Sirius was, had been a better person than them. He had been the kind of peacekeeper who brought Mishigami chocolates wherever he went, handing them out to people, especially tearful children who needed a pick-me-up.

However, Calisto was having trouble being that benevolent. They were thankful to be away from that herd, if only for a moment, staring out onto the murky waters of the Atlantic. They had wanted to be here earlier, but they very well couldn't have justified not interviewing the parents first: that would have been a bad look. But Dela had made it quite clear where their priorities should be. They were there to mitigate the damage of this frackin' mess. Murder on a transport, and one as massive as the Seven that normally sent collective-bound all over the North, was a logistical nightmare that could freeze up slots across the Restoration. None of which could be resolved if this investigation were drawn on forever.

Which brought them to this boat, standing in the cramped hallway where the fight had taken place. And in front of them, where the body had been discovered hours later, was a small utility closet on the second level. It was a short, damp thing that could not fit two people sprawled out, let alone one, making it hard to picture a body having been there. Strummer had already created a 3D scan of the body before it had been moved back to Salem for burial rites. Calisto consulted the image on their wrist, gazing at the slumped-over, desiccated body of Haldan Kramer on their screen and picturing how it had sat here, discarded.

Various virtual tags, accessed via Augmented Reality, were pinned around the crime scene. Salem's CRS Strummer had placed these to mark points of interest: blood spatter on the wall where the body had thudded to the floor, already dead; a trail of blood indicating where it had been dragged from; a marker for where the body had landed on the scuffed wooden floor, a dried puddle of blood surrounding it. The murderer had to have killed Haldan somewhere else and then dragged him here to be found later.

"So you're the smog that's grounded my ship," said a voice from behind them. "Someone said you had just boarded."

Calisto turned around to see a squat femme. His eyes were dark, but there was a slight purple tinge to them, no doubt the result of flashy cosmetic contacts. They wore a wide-brimmed straw hat. And so it didn't fly everywhere in the wind; it was tied down with a thick black strap, mostly held up by his messy black hair. The hat had a tall crown and a downturned brim, and it looked like it came out of a Fallen New England catalog of fashionable, upper-caste people. The man was speaking Spanglish, and Calisto adjusted the language settings on their suit, which worked well enough. The translator bot pumped a crude real-time translation into their ear, but they had to keep referencing the screen on their wrist for context, which was annoying.

"Captain Felipe, I presume? I haven't seen you much off the Seven."

"Yup," Captain Felipe scowled, spitting over the railing as they approached. "You make a habit of not asking permission before entering someone's property?"

Captain Felipe's bitter reaction was typical. The Party's line was that herds only called for a peacekeeper when there was a problem. When herd relations had broken down, they contacted the Delegation for an 'outsider's' perspective, but that was not entirely true, especially in this case. The CRS Delegation had gotten permission from the Transportation Council to ground Felipe's ship. The Delegation had then negotiated with the various herds and collectives the Sevens passengers came from to remain in the Cods for the investigation or face a community-wide review. A process that had occurred so quickly that many passengers had reached their destination, only to have been informed by their herds and collectives to turn around and anchor in a place all but a few from Herd Salem were familiar with. It was a level of coordination and authority unseen in generations, and although every democratic process had been technically followed, no one seemed happy about it.

"Apologies for the inconvenience," Calisto said.

"I don't want your apologies," he said, slamming his foot against the metal deck. "I want to leave," and then, after a pause, shouted, "Now."

Calisto maintained a neutral face, but they were happy Felipe was talking. At least angry words revealed something interesting, though Sirius would chide that even silence hid something. Let's see, he was frustrated. He clearly distrusted authority and didn't like it when issues were danced around.

"I am sorr-..." Calisto paused, erasing sorry from their vocabulary. "I told you, you cannot leave until we learn what happened to Haldan on this ship. The Chamber did not give my Delegation a writ of this magnitude so lightly."

"I'm telling you, no one saw him enter that closet."

"Well, that's a problem because his parents saw him board this ship, and multiple passengers claim that someone looking like him fought with Representative Anderson Leek that afternoon. So, yes, a murder may have happened on your ship, Captain."

"No one has seen Anderson since then. For all I know, he abandoned ship and is halfway to La Fédération Française."

"The Seven is a big place to hide. If you and your passengers would simply give up your suit's geolocation data, then we could solve this in an instant. Most suits have a default setting that allows them to passively interface with other systems they encounter. We could filter out all the suits that didn't interface with his at the time of travel, and then bam, most of you go home. "

"And why should any of us do that? You ground us here, and then you want to take away our privacy, too?" Calisto tried to butt in, but he was not stopping. "The nerve of your Groundwork Party forcing your authority on us."

"Captain, I'm part of the Community Repair Specialist Delegation, specifically its Peacekeeper Program. I'm simply a CRS who does repairs outside my community. I don't represent the Groundwork Party..."

"Trashin' lie," Felipe cursed. "I remember not too long ago when there was no CRS Delegation. And then the Groundwork Party comes up in the Chamber, and we suddenly have a Delegation and peacekeepers, where before there used to just be herds minding their own frackin' business."

"Captain, I assure you that someone in the Transport Council requested our presence."

"No doubt after being prodded by Groundwork to request the CRS Delegation to send one of their blasted peacekeepers. I know how you all talk, with half-truths and canned replies. Well, my ancestors didn't fight a war against Corpo Trash so I could go and live in another police state."

"Look, I feel as though we have gotten off on the wrong foot. It's a simple request. The data we pull would only be for a limited period. We wouldn't even be able to access current geolocation data."

"No," he barked.

"And you speak for everyone on the ship."

"I do. Although you're more than welcome to ask yourself. Maybe you can put all us, difficult people, on a list."

Calisto swallowed. They actually had started sorting some difficult passengers into a list that morning, an internal one they hadn't intended to share with anyone, but that distinction was best not shared with Captain Felipe.

"Well, that's that, then, I suppose," Calisto said as politely as they could muster. "Thank you for your time. I will be seeing you around."

"Be sure to see yourself out," they said, waving them off with a half-hearted goodbye.

As they descended onto the loamy ground of the Cods, having found their bearings now and finding it much easier to descend the railing, they were not sure if they were more welcome on land or at sea. Had everyone around here lost their polluted mind? Calisto permitted themselves a forlorn sigh—this case might take longer than they thought.

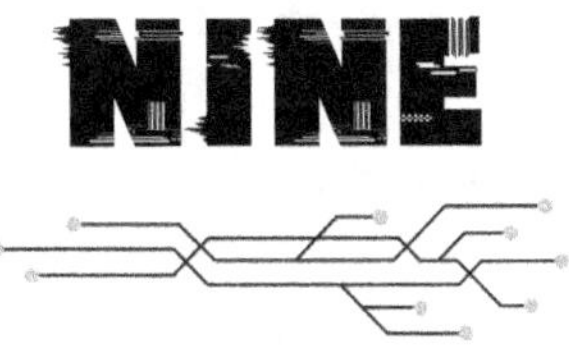

NINE

ROWAN

PUBLIC COAR DOWNLOAD/Article/They Party To The Grave Here In Salem/Author Tulip Bellwether/1-5-2099

-> I haven't traveled much, but in my not-so-humble opinion, no one quite does funerals like Gaiaverse adherents. They leave the body out for three days on top of a mound of sticks and earth. There are no chemicals pumped posthumously through its veins. The body starts to decay, and then, after the end of the third day, it is lowered into the ground in an unmarked grave.

-> You would think that such a sight would be incredibly depressing, but both the laying of the body and the lowering of it into the earth are preceded by a massive balls-to-the-wall celebration where we all get incredibly drunk.

TIME: 1:22 PM
DAY: TUESDAY 5-17-2101

Rowan was already drunk. She had missed the early half of the laying-in ceremony because of that frackin' exo and their questions. Not having the decency to understand that in Salem, saying I *could* interview during a certain time was not the same as saying I *want* to or *should*. She had attempted to make up for the lost time by pounding several shots of an alcohol that tasted a lot like vodka but was not fermented with potato or any other tuber, for that matter. It did its job, though, and in no time, she was wobbling amongst the throng of partygoers celebrating the life of her dead son.

People cheered as she walked up to the body, holding a fallen twig she had picked up from the ground. Before Haldan's corpse was a mound of sticks, so many sticks, and the clumps of dirt that held them together. Each one had been hand-selected by a partygoer and placed on this pile.

"We remember him," She shouted to the crowd before placing her stick onto the pile.

"Let *Her* watch over him," the crowd responded, in between drunken bouts and chaotic whoos and whistles.

They had opted for a green shroud to cover his body, at least for tonight. That peacekeeper had not been exaggerating when they said someone had experimented on Haldan. Red gashes were running up and down his body, especially along his face. She really hoped that these had all happened post-death because the thought of someone causing her son to flail and scream in pain as some sick smog cut him open was too much to contemplate.

She took another swig, pushing the image down.

"Easy there, Grumpy Bear. That's like your sixth drink. We don't want things to get too crazy," her wife cautioned, apparently having been monitoring her nearby, unnoticed. She hated how observant Úna could be at times.

"But you like it when I'm drunk, my Úni with the Booty. More head that way." Rowan joked.

Úna blushed. "Just drink some water, okay. I don't want you to embarrass me."

Rowan considered rejecting the metal flask Úna offered her, but thought better of it. She took a swig and hated how refreshing it was to have the cool water move down into her stomach.

"Thanks."

"How was the interview?" Úna inquired.

"Lonnnnnggggg," Rowan slurred. "She wanted to see if our son was real."

Úna grimaced at this, perplexed. "I don't follow."

Rowan tried to assemble the thought in her head, but it was not coming out as coherently as she wanted it to. "If the person we walked to the floating box thing that sits on water..."

"Boat?" Úna filled in.

"Yeah, boat. If that person on the Seven was our baby or some fraud," she blurted out. "Something about the time of death not matching up...with something. I don't really want to talk about it."

"But we dropped him off," Úna said, ignoring her request. Rowan felt just numb enough not to respond with a cutting remark. A part of her got why her wife was being so insistent. The search for an answer was almost enough to forget he had died, and that was the kind of distraction that she thought she needed right now.

"And he looked normal, right?" Rowan asked, The part of her that needed to know winning out.

"What are you asking?"

"That there wasn't, I don't know, something out of place with the way he looked."

Úna shook her head, "Now you really are sounding crazy. No, he looked normal."

Rowan frowned. She wished Úna were lying, a conspiracy she could unravel and put all her energy into solving, like one of the protagonists in her stories, but no, he was just dead. Rowan took another swig of water. "Needs more alcohol," she smirked, dumping the water on the ground.

Rowan went away to fill her flask from a container sitting on a tree stump. She let it fill up so high that it started leaking out over her hands and onto the ground. She licked the residue and took another shot.

When she got back to Úna, there was a throng of people who had haphazardly picked up instruments: hand drums, pan flutes, synthetic keyboards, and the like, playing them as a form of cathartic entertainment. It somehow didn't sound terrible, or maybe Rowan was just drunk. She let the beat of the music take her, swaying from side to side in that way she did when she pretended to know how to dance. It felt good to just be here, not thinking.

"Smog," she cursed aloud. Now she was thinking again, thinking about her baby lying on the ground, dead. She thought about how, as people's feet jumped up and down on the Earth, they caused her son's body to vibrate ever so slightly, almost like he was breathing in and out from a deep sleep.

She thought about how easy everything would be if he just woke up right now and claimed that it was all an elaborate prank—one of her baby's little jokes meant to make some grand point about their herd's dogmatism. A joke so clever she wouldn't even hate him for the hell of these last few days.

Instead, the crowd moved closer and closer to his body until its many hands lifted it up and gently placed it on the mound of sticks, where it would sit for the next three days.

TEN

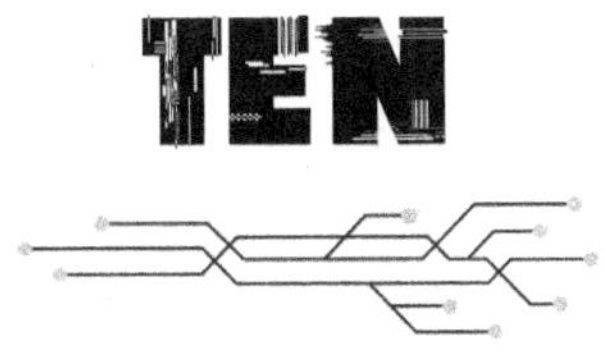

CALISTO

```
PRIVATE COAR THREAD/Communication/Haldan-Ander-
son/5-15-2101
```

-> message chain:
-> Haldan Kramer: Are you cumming tonight, sexy?
-> Haldan Kramer: **Sends Picture**.
-> Anderson Leek: Dog panting emoji. Yes.
-> Haldan Kramer: Good slut. I have a cross you're going to be tied to the entire night. Understood, slut?
-> Anderson Leek: Yes, sir.

```
TIME: 2:00 PM
DAY: TUESDAY 5-17-2101
```

alisto found themselves getting terribly lost on their way back to camp. Mishagami had hallways and helpful signs that told them exactly where to go. There were bells that rang during meal and prayer times. Soft lights that guided your path when it was dark, and most people were in their apartments resting from a long, hard day of work.

Yet this was all woods. Some footpaths wound through the short scrub pines, but they lacked a centralized design. There was no bird's-eye planning by committee. The paths were merely formed by convenience and habit, worn into the earth as people tread on them over and over again, and Calisto, barely having walked them before, could not pick up the thread that led back to Salem.

Thankfully, they weren't alone in the woods, and soon enough, they bumped into a lanky, awkward-looking enby with mellow-brown skin. Calisto had seen them at camp, one of the Assistant Shepherds to Úna. They seemed to have been looking for them.

"There you are," they shouted energetically, "Úna's looking for you. The laying-in ceremony is wrapping up, and she wanted you to check the body now that it's less crowded. Also, hi, I'm Sam."

"Calisto."

Sam nodded and started walking back toward camp, with the implication that Calisto should follow. Calisto did, listening as Sam chattered about this and that inane detail. They still couldn't get over how people in Salem talked. Sam was speaking an archaic dialect of pre-Fall English: not the more common Spanglish variety, but 100% English with New England characteristics. It was like walking into a time capsule: one of those oddities you bump into whenever you come to a smaller herd like this one. Calisto once again adjusted the language settings on their suit, but Sam did not seem comfortable using a translator bot, so Calisto had their voice box on their neck turned on as well, trying to patiently give it time to translate.

"So you're the peacekeeper they sent?" Sam continued. "The Delegation," they added, with perhaps a hint of judgment. "We've never had one of you before."

Calisto buried the insult. *Don't snap, Cal.* Sirius lectured.

Sirius had held the perspective that Groundwork's specific brand of Christian Dialectical Materialism made them uniquely qualified for the peacekeeper role. Their understanding of history made them as objective as it was possible to be, enabling them to see how history unfolded in real time.

We cannot afford to get down to their level. We must sometimes carry them so we can be there to listen to what drops.

"I am," Calisto's bot said. "Murder is an incident the Restoration thinks people from outside a herd should assist with. But don't worry. I will be sharing responsibilities with Head Shepherd Úna and your herd's CRS, Strummer. This isn't a takeover."

Sam nodded at this. "And you are here to catch the trash who did this?" They said, whacking at a branch in the path's way as they did.

Calisto's bot replied: "I'm here to gather a record of what happened. That's all for now."

"By Gaia, you definitely sound like our CRS," Sam huffed.

"Are you referring to Strummer?" inquired Calisto. An insider's impression of Salem's CRS—now that was something Calisto wanted to hear. There was only so much that reports could get you, after all.

"I just saw her. She's trying to be calm like you," continued Sam, "The Fallen-loving smog. I hate her for it sometimes. And I don't like the Delegation and exos like you being in our business like this. Why are you even here? We don't need an outside police force telling us what to do."

Calisto opened their mouth but pressed down hard on their lips a second later and said nothing. They were used to being called an exo. The Restoration was meant to be open to all, but in-group behavior hadn't gone away. A part of them wanted to tell this defensive trash that trauma didn't give them an excuse to dump on someone trying to help, but they could hear Sirius mocking them for this impulse already and thought better of it. More productive to let Sam sit on what they'd just said.

"Sorry," Sam said a few seconds of silence later. "I don't know why I'm acting like this."

"You've just experienced a loss," Calisto's bot said as neutrally as it could. "You have the right to feel unsettled by it. The right to be hurt about things left unsaid."

Sam grew quiet. "We dated, you know, Haldan and me," Sam said almost in a whisper. "It ended several years ago, before his latest polycule, or whatever you want to call it, but I don't know. I always thought...." They didn't complete their sentence, gasping for air in that way people do when the pain becomes too much.

Calisto swallowed quietly. This was perfect. These were the moments you trained for when being nice and comforting gave you genuine information and not just a spit in the face. Calisto could hear Sirius's smugness inside their head.

See, Cal? See what happens when we let the Party's principles guide us, when we name the material forces of our world plainly. See how much you can learn through the sheer act of listening to history turn?

"I didn't know Haldan was in a polycule?" Calisto said with an upswing in their voice, indicating false surprise. This was a lie, but questions like this worked best when it didn't seem like they had read a brief on everyone before arriving.

"Yes, Peter and he were close. Also, Tulip, once upon a time. Oh, and Anderson, whenever he was in town."

"Representative Anderson Leek," Calisto clarified. "Salem's representative to the Chamber?"

Calisto was trying to keep their voice calm, but Anderson was their highest priority at the moment, well, right before resuming the Shuttle's schedule, that is. No one had seen Anderson since his fight with Haldan, which made him *thee* primary suspect.

Sam nodded, teary-eyed. "Yes, they were all theater kids growing up. Well, not Tulip, she came after, but anyway, I saw Haldan and Anderson the night before." Sam paused. It was clear that the word murder was not something they wanted to say. "Before the thing. They were doing a scene together, a kink thing where Haldan tied Anderson up and started hitting him...consensually. I may have been watching for a bit," Sam said, blushing.

Their expression then turned angry again. "I can't believe Andi killed him. If you ask me, we shouldn't have representatives like that at all. Representatives are authoritarians in the making. If anyone should be on your suspect list, it's him."

"I will keep that in mind." Calisto nodded.

Sam stopped talking for a bit after that, trudging silently forward. And then they stopped moving altogether, staring at a patch of yellowed and dying grasses, presumably where some kind of gathering had taken place. Calisto placed a consolatory hand on Sam's frozen shoulder, but they shook it off.

"Is there a problem?" Calisto asked.

"This is where I saw him last," they said, the 'him' unnecessary to explain. It looked like any other clearing in the woods, with tall grasses and short, stubby tree saplings racing upward toward the sky. The only distinguishing features were some discarded pieces of pleasure equipment: a red fiber dildo, ready to decompose given enough time; several used condoms; a pair of lost handcuffs. "That's where Anderson and Haldan played," Sam said, pointing to a medium-sized tree trunk where several holes had been drilled.

"Anderson was tied to the trunk?" Calisto confirmed.

Sam nodded. They stood there for a moment, saying nothing. "Let's go," Sam said at last.

Calisto chose not to pry further, marching silently forward.

They made it back to the center of camp, where Haldan's body now sat like a scar. Head Shepherd Úna was looming over it, gesturing at them to come over. Úna seemed drunk and smelled like it, too. She gave Sam a tender hug, her large, muscular arms enveloping them like a blanket over a child, and then, once it was over, patted them on the shoulder.

"Sam," they slurred. "Amazing, I asked you to get the cop, and you got the cop."

"You're welcome?" Sam asked uneasily.

"You're dismissed, Shepherd Azule," Úna said loudly.

Sam did not need to be told twice, darting past the tent's threshold into the distance.

"So," Úna slurred, gesturing in Calisto's direction with gun fingers and making 'pew pew' sounds. "You're here."

"I am."

Úna was far drunker than Calisto first thought. Her cheeks were red and puffy from drinking, and Calisto could tell immediately that Úna was using it to mask her grief. She was in that period where you believe that if you just keep moving fast enough, you don't have to deal with your pain.

Boy, is this one going to be a tough cookie, they heard Sirius joke.

"Go easy on them," Úna said, gesturing in the direction Sam had run off to. "They're a new Shepherd. A little weak, you know?"

"Merely having a conversation," Calisto's bot said matter-of-factly. "How are you holding up, Úna? You know, you don't have to be the one supervising this case. The herd would understand if...."

"No," Úna interrupted, "we're not doing that. I want you to find the Fallen piece of trash that did this, not psychoanalyze me. And turn that bot off; I have the same tech as you."

Psychoanalyze, Calisto had to stop themselves from grimacing at the outdated term. Corrections did not work on people processing grief or, in Úna's case, suppressing it. "I shall respect your boundaries," they said, making a show of turning off their bot. "I was told you wanted to see me?"

Úna paused, confused, before peering at the translation on her wrist. "Ah. I called you here because you haven't examined the body yet." She said, gesturing to the dead body lying beneath her."

"Oh, Strummer sent me a bioscan already of your son's, the victim's body. I didn't think..." Calisto paused. They could tell that the word son had hurt Úna there.

Say nothing about it, Sirius advised.

Úna paused for a moment, looking like she was about to express herself, but she said nothing.

"Very well," Calisto continued.

Calisto tossed a small sphere into the air. It was a droid that floated there as if gravity did not affect it. A bright blue, shimmering aura pulsed around it.

"Sirius," Calisto ordered, "Begin Standard Victim Analysis." The droid said nothing, but its blue light started scanning the body.

"You named your droid after a star system. An amateur astronomer, are you, cop?" Úna chided.

Calisto smirked. "After a friend, actually. He passed away not too long ago. Does the name bother you? I can change it for the duration of my mission."

"No," Úna said coldly, clearly bothered by the reference to death.

"Besides, I do love space," Calisto continued. There was silence at this remark. Calisto pressed on, whipping the green shroud off of Haldan's body and tossing it onto the ground. "Strummer indicated many cuts on the body, precise ones like he had been operated on. I am not intimately familiar with Gaiaverse traditions. Will I be violating your burial rites if I touch the body?"

Úna, still uncomfortable, said, "No. As long as part of him is touching the sticks, he'll be...fine. You're not going to cut into him, are you?" She said this as if trying to pose an indifferent question, like giving orders as Head Shepherd on any normal day, but her voice was cracking, and her eyes were now indeed watery.

"We hardly need to cut into things nowadays. I'll gently scan him, examine his skin, and that will be that. Most of our analysis comes from his suit's internal sensors."

"That's good," Úna gulped.

Calisto started to undress Haldan, cutting his clothes off with a pair of tiny, precision scissors that emerged from their suit. They started explaining what they had read in the report, more interested in satisfying Úna's micromanaging impulse than actually examining the body. "The report indicated two cuts, unlike the others. One was an injection point on the neck, here," they said, referring to a small bruise at the base of the neck. "We detected a modified version of Vecuronium bromide, a fast-acting paralyzing agent that weakened his vocal cords, making it more difficult for him to speak. He could have been screaming, and well, you get the idea."

Úna grimaced at this fact, but Calisto didn't stop. The Party's internal directives were very clear about how peacekeepers should treat those who disrupted their authority. This was what Úna had said she wanted, and Calisto wanted to make it clear to her what such micromanaging would lead to. They continued: "The other is a long cut along the length of his face," Calisto said, tracing a line running along their cheeks and jawline. "These cuts were so precise that Strummer wasn't able to detect them without more complex instruments, but they had to have been agonizing, even with the paralyzing agent. He would've eventually passed out from the pain."

Úna was now unable to look at the body directly, which made Calisto start to reel in the pressure: there was only so far you could push someone. "Will Mrs. Strummer be joining us? I pinged her, and she hasn't gotten back to me, and I could really use her perspective on this."

"Strummer's a little overwhelmed at the moment," Úna replied. "Most of the herd's therapists are, well, they were at a conference. Terrible timing. She and the junior Community Repair Specialists are handling backup until the therapists return later today."

"No matter. I'll coordinate with her later."

Úna bopped her head drunkenly.

Calisto finished removing the last remnants of Haldan's suit. They looked over at his dirt-stained body. It still didn't get any easier to see someone so young dead. His tawny skin had still not yet given way to the decay of death. Haldan's expression was one of terror, as if he'd struggled to the last moment. Some person had poked and cut at his body until he no longer could resist. His stiff, muscular hands had been constrained, as there were marks along his wrists that hinted at some level of bondage.

Calisto said unthinkingly. "He was restrained, and inelegantly so. Whoever the killer or killers were, they didn't care to make the body look like anything less than a murder."

"The trash," Úna said angrily.

The droid beeped a satisfying ding. "Scan is done," Calisto read the information; nothing on it surprised them. "Strummer's scan was not mistaken. He was killed the night before heading to the Seven. It matches up with the decay I am seeing here."

"But we saw him. We saw him that night. He came inside our tent and slept with us. I don't know how that could've been anything but our son."

"Did he seem off to you? Like someone wearing a holographic projection. It would be easy to tell. Maybe not at night, but definitely the following day. Artifacts can often give it away."

"No, he. He was acting like himself." Úna smiled bitterly.

"Of course," Calisto said calmly as they snapped pictures with a camera built into their suit. "The best liars always do."

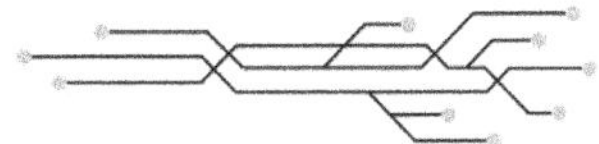

ROWAN

PUBLIC COAR DOWNLOAD/Interview/DW/Interviewee Representative Anderson Leek/05-01-2101

-> The following transcript has been translated from German to English and edited for clarity.

-> *REPORTER: President Anderson, can you answer a question for our viewers?*
-> *ANDERSON: Representative, please. I'm not a President. I was chosen by lot among the Chamber [The Restoration's Main Legislative Body] to represent the Restoration at this Executive [air quotes] Summit. We don't have an authoritarian to rule us, like Germany.*
-> *REPORTER: I see. [Nervous laughter] Since the Greater American Civil War, there are a lot of things our viewers still don't understand about your country. Particularly, how things happen without laws; there are tall tales about roving gangs of lawless thugs. In brief, could you explain this?*
-> *ANDERSON: I'm afraid that is a much more complicated topic than a few sentences can do justice. [Laughter] First, we're not a country.*

The Restoration does make agreements at a federated level through a body known as the Chamber, and directives are passed, but they cannot be permanent and are not universally binding, as we consider that a hierarchy. All directives are approved at the herd or collective level and are constantly reassessed, lest they become a tyranny unto themselves. At least, that's the idea: it doesn't always go to plan.

TIME: 7:05 PM
DAY: TUESDAY 5-17-2101

Rowan didn't know who this person thought they were, forcing everyone to come to this paternalistic 'herd meeting.' It was Úna's duty to facilitate herd discussions, not some outsider who knew nothing of Salem's ways or culture. Calisto even sounded like a silly name. The COAR said it was related to some ancient myth about a woman who had transformed herself into a bear. And here they were, thrashing about, metaphorically speaking, all over Salem's traditions as if a bear had come raging through camp.

The herd was seated on a circle of logs on the outskirts of camp. People had voted to hold the meeting here out of necessity more than anything else. While an auditorium was under construction, it had not yet been finished. The alternative they normally resorted to was in the center of camp, but Haldan had been laid to rest there that morning, and having a meeting there so close to his laying-in ceremony would not be right. There were days left of mourning before they lowered his body into the Earth and uploaded his files to the COAR in memoriam, a fact that Rowan still had trouble processing. How could they be expected to do anything when her son was dead?

Everyone seemed understandably antsy about the meeting and was gossiping to pass the time.

"I heard the murderer is from a collective," a man nearby whispered.

"Well, that makes sense. A collective probably did this," conspiratorially rejoined a familiar voice, Tulip, the storyteller who had played the jester in Rowan's most recent play. She wore her long hair down as it met the creamy skin of her shoulders. Tulip had set her suit to a vibrant pink, dramatically taking center stage even now. "How do we know they aren't in cahoots?" She theorized.

"Maybe someone from his polycule did it?" A person in Tulip's group postulated. "He was quite the heartbreaker."

"Weren't you in that polycule?" The man asked.

"And didn't he break your heart?" said another.

"Scandalous," gasped the first one.

"What nonsense are you talking about? I broke up with him. No one messes with Tulip," she said flamboyantly.

Rowan rolled her eyes, retreating from the conversation and letting her mind wander to something other than this narcissist.

"If they don't let us go tonight, I think we should riot," loudly whispered a person over to Rowan's right. He was someone from the shuttle, though Rowan was not sure who. He had worn his black hair out so that it effortlessly ran down past his shoulders. The man was short but feminine, with blush running along the side of his thick beard. He was wearing a novelty yacht captain's hat back when such things existed, no doubt an inside joke between him and his partner.

"Please cool it, Captain. I'd prefer not to spend my next three months in a rehabilitation center," counseled a man holding his hand.

"Am I running too hot, buttercup?" he said, squeezing the man's hand. It was Peter, and Rowan felt her stomach drop, disappointed at how quickly he seemed to be moving on.

"Like the sun." Peter joked.

"Just a tiny riot, then," bantered a man Rowan was pretty sure was Captain Felipe, head of the Northeast Seven Shuttle.

Rowan wanted to hurt all of them — petty people focused on their petulant wants rather than the fact that a real person had been murdered. She turned her attention away from them to avoid getting into a fight. She saw that Calisto was on a log near the center of the circle beside Úna and CRS Strummer, taking it all in, casually sitting there like it was just any other day. Like Rowan's son hadn't been murdered. Like they were one of us. They wore a more muted suit today. Everything was a shade of green, and more of their modules had been removed. Their suit's aesthetic lines had all but disappeared, leaving only a pattern of forest-green stripes and splotches of their rich ochre skin to break up the monotony.

Úna cleared her throat. "Quiet all. Thank you. Thank you. Quiet."

Some people quieted down, but the murmuring amongst the herd did not cease. "We want to know if you caught the Fallen Trash who killed Haldan?" shouted someone in the sea of voices. This question was followed by some 'yays' and claps.

"And when can we leave?" yelled Captain Felipe.

"We'll get to that, Captain, but I need ya'll to respect these proceedings," Úna commanded. Not afraid to use shame when it was necessary. "Everyone's going to get a chance to talk, but you need to let us talk first, you understand?"

Felipe did not respond, and Úna took this silence as assent. "Now, the CRS Delegation has sent us over a smart one to assist Strummer in this investigation. CRS Strummer, Peacekeeper Calisto, do you mind explaining what you know so far?"

Strummer gave Calisto a nod, who nodded in return and then proceeded to stand up to speak. The peacekeeper's words were harsh and strange, and then when they finished speaking, the box on their suit boomed over in a translated New England dialect that didn't sound like this person at all. "Thank you, Head Shepherd Úna. And I wanted to thank everyone for being so understanding during this tragedy. It cannot be easy to have a stranger come into your herd during such a difficult time. The facts I can share are as follows. Haldan left for the Bangalore Collective on the Northeast Seven Shuttle on Monday morning. Not long after getting into a fight with Salem's Chamber Representative, Anderson Leek, on the Seven, his deceased body was allegedly found in one of the shuttle's closets. We've been unable to locate Anderson since then, and any help in locating him would be much appreciated. Now, Strummer, would you mind going over the analysis of the body?"

"Of course." Strummer was a stout, muscular woman in her mid-40s. She tapped her suit's right shoulder, which began projecting an image of a body: Haldan's body. It was not a picture but a scientific-looking model of his skin and bones, with the words 'multiple stab wounds' and 'operation suspected' typed out in small, unfeeling letters. Yet before Strummer could get started explaining what this meant in earnest, she was interrupted.

"We already know he was butchered. We want to know why." Someone familiar shouted. This comment came from Tulip. The storyteller, who had been friends with Haldan and had once been a partner too.

"Now, what did I just say?" chastised Úna. "I will put you under community review if you don't shut it."

"I'll put you under review, fascist," Tulip threatened, technically correct as anyone could put anyone else under community review.

Calisto spoke words, and then their box said, "It's okay, I am happy to answer this question." That condescending witch then looked directly into Tulip's eyes, and their box said, "Unfortunately, we don't yet have a good handle on motive. I know that's not the answer you were looking for, but we feel if people were more cooperative in surrendering their geolocation data..."

Several in the crowd booed at this appeal. Rowan couldn't help but smile.

"That's not how things used to go before these peacekeepers," someone shouted.

"Sorry you can't personally oversee the investigation," Úna scoffed sarcastically. It was clear that she was not on her game. Úna was gruff, but when interacting in a professional capacity, she was usually not quite this rude. Rowan wished she could take her away from these silly questions and expectations, but at the same time, a part of Rowan hated that they were expected to surrender so much information to this would-be cop.

"Strummer, would you like to continue?" Calisto's box politely cut in.

Strummer continued her presentation of the body. She started to talk about the stab wounds, and then she dropped a detail that didn't make sense. She continued: "According to, now, multiple analyses of the body, the time of death directly contradicts testimonies that we've gathered about him being dropped off at the Northeast Seven Shuttle. We cannot say if the victim was indeed killed Monday morning or even Sunday night."

Rowan found Strummer's words no longer fitting inside her. She knew she had slept next to her son that night. She had then dropped Haldan off the next morning. It had been his voice, his face. He had even made a joke about a family trip they had made to the Cascadia Archipelago. A small anecdote about when he had refused to eat potatoes for an entire year until one day, while at a food stop, he had broken his fast after the waiter, his first crush, had suggested the mashed potatoes. It was all he had wanted to eat after that.

"I sure know how to make up my mind," he had joked.

Úna had laughed, but Rowan had not. It had been a tense walk they had made to the dock as he prepared to leave their herd behind. The way his hair had been messy from his night of goodbyes from his polycule. The confident smile on his lips. His mind was set on his future in Bangalore and away from her.

"And there is another update," Úna added, Rowan pulling herself back from dissociation. "And I figured I'd sift through the smog now since I doubt y'all react well later. Since the m...," she paused, the next word difficult for her to get out. "Murder," she continued. "Because we still aren't sure if the murder happened on the Northeast Seven Shuttle or not, it will be docked here indefinitely until we can get to the bottom of the time and place of death. We will continue to be hosting the Seven's passengers over the next few days, so please, please be respectful."

"We don't want those exos," someone shouted. There were murmurs of agreement.

"I'm not sure I like ya'll very much either," Captain Felipe quipped.

Úna looked like she was going to burst into flames. "We will not be having that. None of it," she shouted. "We don't go discriminating against outsiders like the Fallen before us. We're better than this, Salem. Aren't we?" Úna's voice was hoarse and raw.

Shame seeped into the crowd for upsetting a mother who had just lost her son. A few mumbled apologies were made, too quiet to make their way to Úna's ears, but mostly there was silence.

After moments of tense quiet, Calisto began to thank Úna. "I know you'll have questions, but we will be working toward providing you with updates on a regular basis."

They started talking about how they would be dispersing updates on the case in the future, but Rowan did not want any of it. All of it was trashin' nonsense. She knew her son had been alive that morning. She stood up. At first, to storm off, but as all eyes looked at her, she decided to speak instead.

"I know what I saw with my own eyes," her voice cracked. "He was alive that night. I saw him. I spoke to him about things only he would know. Days you've had to learn the truth, and you've learned nothing. Well, I don't want to wait around while you let the person responsible make their escape."

"Grumpy bear," Úna said gingerly, not to the crowd, but to her. It was like they were speaking from across a river: distant and separated. She didn't understand. If only Úna could see things like Rowan could at this moment: the network of life was so clear. Rowan felt a chill go up her spine. It was Gaia comforting her, as she did in every moment. She lowered the heat barrier on her suit so the wind could prick at her cheeks. For someone who spent much of her life healing Gaia, she realized how much she closed herself off to her.

"I can stop this," Rowan stated confidently to the crowd of people starting to stand around her. "I'm going to catch the person who did this," Rowan clarified, as she forged a plan in the heat of the moment that was more emotion than strategy. She turned to the crowd. "We need to do a thorough search of the camp, but I need your help. We need to form a search party now before this person leaves, if they haven't already," she yelled. "I'm serious, I need all of you to get your frackin' asses up now."

Feet clambered toward her. She waved toward the center of camp, and a crowd of people followed her. She made it to Haldan's body in a blur. Standing over it, she observed the bundle of sticks her herd had so carefully prepared over the last few days, each member finding a fallen stick from a place that spoke to them to prop up his lifeless body lying there, stiff as the wood beneath him.

In the end, he had stayed with her after all, and yet, in his typical way, he had done it in the most unsatisfying fashion. Simply another disappointment in a pile of trash stacked so high that it might soon topple and bury her alive. And a part of her didn't want to stop it. What was the point of any of this if she couldn't even say goodbye to Haldan?

She picked up a stick from the pile and held it in her hand, turning it from side to side like you would when you wanted to start a fire. She got on her knees and prayed to Gaia. Her herd was gathering around her, wordlessly praying with her. The night was cold, and she moved them toward the direction of the wind. Gaia would be her guide.

TWELVE

CALISTO

PUBLIC COAR DOWNLOAD/Article/The New Workers Collective/Author Garykillsfascists/5-17-2101

-> *Calisto Tremblay just can't seem to catch a break. After being the person to almost kill the Cop (I mean Peacekeeper) program, they get assigned to a high-profile murder case, which was probably a last-ditch attempt at redemption for the recently exiled Groundwork Party Member.*

-> *Yet they've hardly been there a day, and things are already going off the rails.*

TIME: 7:55 PM
DAY: TUESDAY 5-17-2101

Calisto received a ping from Colibri, a flirty one asking how their nipples were doing. They had to ignore it: there was too much going on. Calisto had to stop themselves from fixating on the thought that everything was going to shit.

The herdsfolk in Salem were unhappy, which was standard for a murder investigation, but in their over forty-seven closed cases, they had never experienced anything this intense. Calisto had asked the shepherds to shut down the search party, and people were incensed. A swarm of herdsfolk surrounded Calisto, all scared and upset. Dozens of eyes peered into them like predators appraising their prey. Everyone was shouting and yelling, seemingly angry at *their* existence.

"We want answers," demanded a storyteller called Tulip. "Why can't we engage in the search?" Tulip had changed her suit's colors to a pulsating black, and she was screaming almost to the point where they couldn't speak over her.

Calisto tried to ignore her and stay on course, shouting over the crowd. They upped the volume on their box, and it boomed: "Please. We'll have an update shortly. But we need you to sit still. This search party could be providing the murderer with the perfect cover to leave. The exact opposite of your intentions here, and the privacy of your fellow herdsfolk is being violated in the process. People are searching each other's spaces without permission, and it's dangerous."

"You would say that as an exo." Someone mumbled that Calisto couldn't quite see amongst the crowd.

Calisto swallowed hard. This whole situation made them feel uncomfortable. Most people didn't understand the CRS Delegation or the Peacekeeper program under it, believing it was this unscrupulous entity that could arrest people at will. And yes, it was an independent organization, in the sense that it wasn't attached to a herd or collective, but it reported directly to the Chamber, and its powers were limited. They couldn't even arrest someone without a polluted Chamber vote. Standing here, hundreds of miles away from their home, they were scared. It's not like they had a gun. Their suit wasn't spec'd for weapons. They were technically an adviser banned from using force by the CRS Delegation under threat of revoked membership: a precautionary measure in response to recent events.

Úna stepped in to give Calisto some breathing room. "Walk away," she advised before turning her attention toward Tulip and the others who hated them. It was all Calisto could do. They left the crowd to their angry questions. Strummer and Úna would have to take care of things until this polluted herd calmed down.

They walked back to their tent, exhausted. Calisto lay down on the ground, huddled in the fetal position. They had been doing this grounding exercise since childhood, sinking into the earth when the pressures of the world became too much.

Colibri pinged them again, and Calisto answered, flicking their wrist in a way that activated the line. They did not turn on visuals, not having the energy to face her, even if it was only a 3D model of her face, not the real thing.

"Colibri," they panted. "I..."

She interrupted them. "So when can we head over there for our vacation, wretch. I've been making a new whip for the occasion."

"I don't know, Colibri. There are some things more important than your fun. Can you just leave me alone?" They gasped and then hung up before she could reply.

They slumped further, their face touching the cool earth. They could feel an insect crawling on their arm, a small obsidian thing they did not know the name of. A module would have provided them with a query for its name and description just by looking at it. Another would have prevented Calisto from feeling it altogether. But instead, they were rolling amidst the dirt, uncomfortable and disconnected.

"I'm frackin' up everything," they said to no one in particular.

It's okay for you not to have the answer, the voice of their mentor, Sirius, reassured them.

Once Calisto had been chasing a suspect through a staging collective. Maybe it was the Asbury Park one? It was an active site, and people from the collective were coiling large spools of nanowires to ship off to herds across the region. The suspect was getting away, and Calisto fired their gun at a spool being lifted into the air by a cable. Their aim was perfect, and it snapped, the spool dropping onto both the suspect and the worker who had been lifting it up. The suspect broke his hip. The worker didn't make it.

At the time, Sirius had said that 'mistakes happen.' That being at the forefront of history had inevitable complications.

We can't be expected to be perfect, he had comforted.

It had made them feel better, and yet somehow the same logic did not assuage the guilt they felt now. If anything, everything felt worse.

"It's never been this bad," Calisto cried. "Besides a polluted Representative, I can't even locate; I have no leads, and no one is talking to me."

Calisto was going to have to start using hard power—Restorate writs and sanctions, new authorities the Groundwork Party had recently managed to give the CRS Delegation's Peacekeepers— to get some people to fall into line, and that reality alarmed them because it would only inflame community tensions: the exact opposite of their intended purpose here.

We are not there yet, Sirius said softly.

"But they aren't listening to me," Calisto told him, or at least the idealized version of Sirius inside their own mind. The man who always seemed to be two steps ahead. The person who had made them see their first murderer was not a meticulously planned serial killer but a negligent technician too ashamed to admit they weren't good at their job. Calisto could certainly relate at this moment.

Things aren't what they seem. It's not about you. Listen to what their actions are telling you, he continued. *This community is scared. Someone they loved died. It's not an easy trauma to recover from.*

"Well, they are being mean."

Hurt people do that. They imagined Sirius saying with a smirk.

There was a cough as someone cleared their throat. Calisto peered up to see Úna peeking her head through a flap in the tent.

"Come in, I guess," Calisto's box said, exhausted, sweeping their legs forward as they raised themselves into the air.

Úna did not need to be told twice. She barged in and said. "I had something I needed to," but then paused, accidentally kicking a half-packed bag of compressed tools on the floor: equipment someone had left here accidentally, and Calisto had not yet had time to pick up. Compression sacks were now everywhere, all in various stages of unwinding, like the translucent shedded skin of a milk snake, yet perfectly intact.

"Shit," Úna said as she knocked another device, a tiny nanoweave, an arm's length away.

Calisto said nothing, focusing on the item bouncing on the floor. They had seen larger weaves at other herds. There was even one or two at this camp. Giant pincers that eerily hung over the land like discarded bones, breaking down the hazardous plastics and noxious gases across the wastelands with some type of nanotechnology Calisto did not entirely understand. They normally interfered with signals, but these small devices were new and better at filtering out interference. Designs that had come out of the Neo-Boston collective, maybe? They didn't know for sure. Marx, they missed their modules. They could already have had this information.

Úna guiltily picked up one of the many nanoweaves she had kicked across the floor and started squeezing it back into its designated bag. Calisto watched as it started to pop back into a small disk, a fraction of its former size.

"Ignore it," Calisto commanded as Úna instinctually let go, and the device spurted out onto the floor. "I'm sorry to be trash, but what do you want?" They continued bluntly. Calisto did not feel as polished as they usually were, but it couldn't be helped. This case was tough, and their patience had been pushed to its limit.

"My herd is being a lot. I wanted to check in on you and see what you need."

"I *need* your wife to stop this," Calisto's box began, and then they shut it off since they knew Úna despised it. "She has to stop this," Calisto continued.

Úna looked at the translation on her wrist, though one was sparsely needed. "I know, she's been a bit crazy recently," She responded guiltily, not trying to deny anything. "But it gives them something to do."

Calisto was unsure if she was talking about the herd or her wife.

"Well, it's preventing me from performing my role. I'm all for herd participation, but this isn't restorative justice. It's a mob, and I can't talk to a mob."

Úna said nothing, so Calisto continued. "First, I can't track where people were during the murder, and now this search party nonsense."

This comment seemed to catch Úna by surprise. "Trash. I didn't know you hadn't gotten that information yet. Can't you just pull people's locations up on our suits?"

Calisto sighed, frustrated that even Úna appeared to have not listened to them at the meeting. "Are you able to do that, Úna, with members of your herd?"

"Well, no, but..."

"We aren't the Fallen police state that once occupied this land. Most suit data is encrypted and not backed up. I would need the Chamber to pass a separate override vote for *everyone* in this camp who doesn't cooperate, and I sense that would be a lot of people. That vote would take the CRS Delegation months to arrange. Not to mention the time it would take to crack the security of each suit, and they do have more important stuff to do than appeal to your herd's leaf-thin sensitivities." Calisto lectured bitterly.

"By Gaia, I get it. I know tonight was trash, but ease off my clit, okay? My wife is already on my case, and you're the one who is supposed to make my role easier, not worse."

"Sorry, you didn't deserve that," was all Calisto could think to say.

"Apology accepted. It honestly makes me feel better," Úna smiled. "To know I'm not the only one messing things up."

This is good, Sirius affirmed. *You're more human to her now, flawed. See how even mistakes can lead to victories.*

Calisto breathed, hoping that this was true. Cases could explode if you alienated the Head Shepherd too much. Calisto once spent a month too long on a case just because the Head Shepherd of Herd Los Angeles would never invite them to meetings. The killer turned out to be the lead coordinator: something quite obvious once Calisto got access to the Fallen-loving calendar.

You were very unripe then. They could hear Sirius chide.

"So what do we do now?" Úna asked.

It seemed like she truly didn't know. Calisto grabbed her hand, holding it gently. They expected Úna to push it away, but she didn't. Calisto then said, "I think you'll know what I'm going to say."

"That might be tough. Moments like this. It's better to let people cool off."

"Please, Úna. There is so much about this case we don't understand. Who knows what evidence could be tampered with in these moments? Doesn't your son deserve justice?"

Úna sighed. It was a fresh wound Calisto was picking at, but they didn't care. This needed to get done. Úna tapped on the comms on her suit's wrist. "Shepherd Nova, I need you to tell people to call off the search. Send a ping now. Anyone who isn't back in 20 minutes will be placed under review. And I mean anyone."

"Understood, Úna," Nova affirmed.

"Thank you." Calisto smiled.

"Can't promise it'll work for everyone. People are already really nervous about the Shuttle Passengers walking around. By Gaia, my next election is going to be a trash heap for me. Any other wedges you need me to drive between myself and the herd?"

Another person ducked their head inside. It was Shepherd Sam. They were panting and looked like they had been running. Streaks of dirt ran across their face.

"Now what?" Úna groaned.

"Come in," Calisto welcomed.

Sam sheepishly entered but said nothing for a few seconds and then joked to Calisto, "I'm starting to see you more than my actual therapist," chuckling to try to diffuse the tension for themselves.

Calisto did not laugh.

"By the network, spit it out, Sam," Úna barked.

"Right, sorry. There has been a development." They paused, everyone looking at them expectantly, and then said, "Right, you want me to tell you."

"That would be good," Úna muttered, her rage barely constrained.

"Well, it was weird, right, because I had only just sat down after the whole emergency broadcast situation, and when Peter came rushing in, he was on community watch with me, you see, and I thought it had to do with that. But apparently, no, he comes in gasping for air and tells me that a search party has been assembled. We didn't know who had organized it, so I ran to get Úna, and.... "

Calisto held out their hand. "What is the 'emergency broadcast situation' you just mentioned?"

Sam made a perplexed look. "Right, that's what I came to tell you. There has been so much going on that I haven't had an opportunity to tell anyone. When the meeting started, we kept getting pings from Representative Anderson's suit. Area pings, what you do when your suit is in range of a camp, and you want people to expect you."

"Wait, Anderson, Representative Anderson. Like the person who may have been the murderer? Where the frack is he?"

"We're not sure. That's what was so weird about it. I sent Peter to fetch him. An area ping is more often than not a request for assistance, but he wasn't at the pinned location. We sent him a message, and nothing, but the pings kept coming, each time from a different location. It's like something is scrambling it. So I sent Peter around camp to try to triangulate the signal, but we weren't able to find him."

"So when did the pings stop?"

Sam's face grimaced. "That's the thing. They haven't stopped."

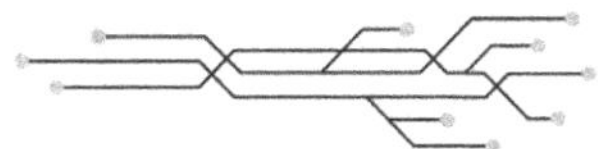

ROWAN

```
PRIVATE   COAR   THREAD   HERD   SALEM/Communica-
tion/34-A/Rowan-Sam/5-18-2101
-> message chain:
-> Sam Azule: Hey, Row. I hate to be the bearer
of bad news, but I am requesting that you be put
under review for harm. A lot of people are upset
about the search party, and I figured it would
be best if the request for review came from me
rather than less objective parties. I didn't
want to post it only in public areas and have
it come out of nowhere, so yeah, please don't
hate me.
-> Sam Azule: Hey, I am posting the review now
in the public feed.
-> Rowan Kramer: ok


TIME: 7:48 AM
DAY: WEDNESDAY 5-18-2101
```

owan was under review. Her wife had used a lackey to place her under polluted review for 'interfering with a community repair.' It was nonsense. Didn't Úna understand that she was trying to help? That she was working under Gaia's instruction. Even now, she could hear the wind calling to her, its gentle caress telling her that there was more work to be done.

The two of them had not slept on the same mat last night. Rowan would not give Úna the satisfaction of settling their difference through closeness. She had set up an alternative mat on the opposite side of the tent, their less comfortable one, assembling a de facto wall out of half-packed bags so she could block out the sight of her traitorous wife.

She dreamed of Haldan, her hand slipping from his grip as he made his way toward the boat. He fell from the ramp, not over it, but through. His feet sank through the metal ramp, sinking into the ocean. She reached out to grab him, but it was too late. She watched as his purple eyes drifted into the bay, like beads of sea glass making their way home.

When the morning broke, and Rowan, who had slept like trash, was tossed awake to the chirping of loud birds and the glorious wind, she found herself being viewed by an already awake Úna.

"You sleep okay?" Úna asked calmly. She knew what her wife was trying to do. She wanted them to hash things out, but Rowan didn't feel like providing that closure. Why was it always on her to forgive? A part of her wanted to file her own reviews of every shepherd involved in this case.

"No," she responded swiftly. She wouldn't be the one to prompt this conversation. Rowan would will herself to be angry if it were the last thing she did.

"Please, can't we talk about this? You're acting unhinged."

Rowan wanted to scream, but she held her tongue. She would not let Úna become the victim here. "You're the one who put me under review. Save it. Sam's your shepherd. This came from you. I can lose my position in the Writers' Cooperative over this. It took me years to find something I liked, and you jeopardized it without even thinking about me."

Úna started fidgeting with a vibrant green leaf that had made its way inside their tent. "You might not receive a sanction. It's just a review. And even if you did, it would start a repair process. The goal isn't punishment, you know that."

"But I could still lose my spot if the Writers' Cooperative votes on it. All because you went after me for going against you. For your handling of this shitshow. If Anderson's suit is sending out a ping, he could still be alive. The murderer is out there, and it's like you don't care."

"How did you hear about that?"

"I hear things," Rowan said, obscuring the fact that she had overheard this information from Úna on a call and wasn't, in fact, getting it from somewhere else, like she was implying. She then deflected: "Besides, you're just mad at me because I tried to find him, the one thing that dear exo cannot. Hence the review."

Úna sighed. "By Gaia, first of all, you couldn't have even known about the area ping until after the meeting."

"You don't..."

"Secondly," Úna interrupted. "This isn't about you, Rowan. Stop acting crazy. A notice for review was sent to everyone who didn't come back when I asked. You can't get special treatment. I have to do my role. "

"And I have to do mine. " Rowan quipped, standing up as she said this.

"Where are you going?"

"To find our son's killer," Rowan huffed. "I saw our son that morning, Úna. We saw him. We walked him to the ferry the night after he was supposedly killed, and I don't care what that outsider, that exo, says in their frackin' report. I know what I saw, and he was alive. This peacekeeper doesn't know what they're talking about," Rowan said, choking on her words.

Úna's open mouth tried and failed to form a reply and settled into silence.

Rowan exited the tent in a flurry of steps. If she stayed there any longer, she wasn't sure how much more she could constrain herself.

Rowan made her way outside of camp, meandering up a path toward the cliffs. She had been lying when she claimed to be going somewhere in particular. She didn't have a plan. The pursuit last night had given her so much purpose, but now she was at a loss over what to do. Rowan didn't know how to solve a murder, even if it was for someone she had written about a thousand times over. Even if the victim was someone she held very dearly in her heart.

A lot of people in the herd were aimlessly wandering about the woods. Salem had done its role here. The woods here had been cleared mostly of pollution and debris, and while some people were picking up the few remaining pieces of trash out of habit, most were enjoying the break-in routine with games and other fun. People were lying about on the ground, picnicking, and gossiping. Some were moving down the twisting trails to the sea. It felt strange that this moment was a joyous occasion for some when all Rowan wanted to do was break down.

She realized at some point that she was looking for Tulip. She had at least been asking the tough questions last night of that exo Calisto. Rowan hadn't seen her at camp, though she had not been consciously looking for her. She considered doubling back, but as luck would have it, Rowan found Tulip and her acting troupe huddled in a circle, engaged in a warm-up acting exercise.

"Zip," she saw one of the storytellers say.

Rowan waved awkwardly at them. "Hey, Tulip," she said.

"Hey, Row...and Fallen trash," she cursed, having missed her turn in the game. "Okay, I'm out," she ducked out of the circle with the other storytellers who had lost the game. She was wearing a more muted gray today, which contrasted nicely against the dark brown of the gnarled scrub pines behind her and the green of their leaves.

Rowan used the time to approach her. "I thought the question you asked last night was very insightful," Rowan said genuinely.

Tulip smiled. "I'm just not satisfied with what they're doing. It was brave of you to organize a search. A bunch of us participated in it, though we're now under review."

"Same," Rowan said.

Tulip leaned back against the tree behind her, looking almost like a bulge of metal the tree had grown around, and said: "That weirdly makes me respect Úna more, though that probably isn't what you want to hear right now."

Rowan grimaced. Why was everyone against her? "It's fine," she said. "I'm sure I'll get over it eventually. So, what're you thinking of doing now?"

Tulip looked confused. "Like today? The troupe was going to practice some scenes. We're going to put on a comedy soon. We've been practicing it for a while. It's about a giant, and it's quite humorous. Figured some levity might do people some good."

"No. I mean, I'm positive that it will be great, but I meant with the murder."

Tulip frowned. "Oh, I was going to keep a low profile until after my review. I don't want to lose my spot in the Troupe."

"Makes sense." *Coward*, Rowan thought bitterly. *Everyone was a Fallen coward*. "Well, I have to go."

"Rowan." Tulip was silent for a second and then said, "Please be careful. I don't know what you are going through, but I've spiraled before. I'm here if you need...." Tulip struggled to find the words.

This piece of trash was really trying to lecture her? Tulip, the woman who everyone thought was overly dramatic and self-involved? Why was everyone trying to help her in every way except the one that mattered: finding her son's murderer?

"Thank you, but I'm good." Rowan rebuked.

Rowan didn't need her. She didn't need anyone. She stormed off for the second time that day. Was no one interested in solving this case? A part of her felt like she was going crazy. Tears streamed down her cheeks. The salty water hit her lips. She was looking over the ocean now. Rowan had walked so far up the trail that she had unconsciously gone to where she and Úna had sat when Haldan had first left. Back when they thought the farthest he was going to was Maine. It was too much. A heavy weight hung over her chest. The air in her lungs began to contract, and it was difficult to breathe. She felt like she was choking, but there wasn't anything lodged in her throat but pain and disappointment. She gasped.

"Hey," said a familiar voice. "Are you okay?"

Rowan turned to see Tulip. She looked like she had run here and was breathing heavily.

"I..." Rowan choked, unable to say more.

"You might be having a panic attack," said Tulip. She appeared concerned, but her voice was trying to compensate with practiced calmness. "Look around," she instructed. "Point out five things for me."

Rowan didn't know how she could do anything. She had lost her boy. The sweet, inquisitive know-it-all was gone. It was all too much. "Haldan."

"Don't think about that now. What do you see? It can be anything."

"Tree." She could see a large pine that had grown into the side of the cliff, its roots keeping the erosion of the cliff at bay.

"Okay, good. What else?"

"Stone." The cliff that dropped down. It's cut, exposing layer upon layer of rock going back thousands of years.

"Good, keep going."

"Bay...Birds." Seagulls flying over the water, diving to grab fish.

"One more."

"Dirt." The earth. The loose sandy soil her feet sank into, proving that even now, she was connected to Gaia, to everything.

Rowan felt slightly better. She breathed in deeply, the world easing into place. "Thank you, Tulip. How did you find me?"

Tulip frowned. "I followed you. When I saw you were headed toward the cliff, I just wanted to make sure you were okay."

Tulip thought she was going to jump? Rowan wanted to scoff, but she tried to consider it from Tulip's perspective. Rowan could, from a certain point of view, be perceived as erratic. She had lost her son. She was disobeying the orders of the Restoration's peacekeeper. She was fighting with everyone. She hadn't come up here to jump, but she could see a world where she did. She shivered.

"Thank you."

"Don't take this the wrong way..."

"How could I?" Rowan quipped, unthinkingly latching onto the punchline.

Tulip smiled. "I'm glad you're in a joking mood. Are you seeing someone?" She asked. "A therapist, I mean, for what happened to your son?"

"No, I know the repair will probably require me to, but Úna and I have never been therapy people."

"Well, it beats jumping off a cliff," Tulip joked.

Rowan let out a deep chortle, spit flying from her mouth, and nodded.

FOURTEEN

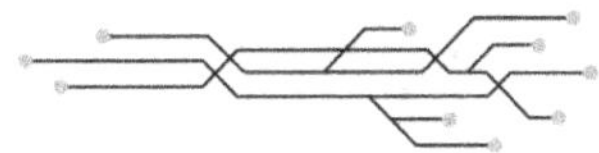

CALISTO

```
PRIVATE  COAR  DOWNLOAD/Memo/Peacekeeper  Direc-
tive A152-7/Author Dela Feinberger-Wu/4-11-2101
```

-> *What you have to understand is that the Community Repair Specialist (CRS) Delegation is relatively new. A coordinating body less than a decade old, and the Peacekeeper Program underneath it is even newer. Herds and collectives used to decide how to settle their own affairs at the community level, and they still largely do.*

-> *While expanding, our authority is limited to an advisory role, and we should under no circumstances imply otherwise. The last thing we need is to be compared to Fallen police officers.*

```
TIME: 11:35 AM
DAY: WEDNESDAY 5-18-2101
```

The seagulls were in full force that morning, terrorizing the line with their ugly gawks. They swooped and dove at the passengers and herdsfolk alike, people who were waiting for Calisto to interview them. The disgruntled attendees batted fruitlessly at the birds, their anger and frustration growing as they baked in the late-morning sun.

Many of the passengers from the Seven were wearing their usual oversized hats, protesting having to be out here in the sun, something Calisto had very little sympathy for. Calisto had had enough of the tedious back and forth with these obstinate suspects. It was their own polluted fault if these extremists failed to adjust their UV and temperature settings.

Calisto had set up a table, a small, sleek, compressible thing, on top of the sands at the entrance to McMillian Pier. They sat on a mat behind it. This was the spot where they had decided to do a second round of speed interviews. These were mandatory, something Úna had signed off on, and Herd Salem and the passengers of the Seven shuttle had voted for under the promise that it would get results: a promise Calisto wasn't sure they would be able to keep.

The interviews were staggered, but even with this precaution, there was still this frackin' line in progress, as thirty or so feet away, ten or more suspects waited and waited. Shepherds were there to assist with quality-of-life concerns, ferrying water and food to the disgruntled participants as they complained about how 'unfair' it was for them to be there. No one was taking this seriously. The Northeast Seven Shuttle passengers—the difficult ones who had uprooted their lives and stayed in Herd Salem longer than necessary for the principle of the matter—had been no help. Most interviews were simply a request for the interviewee's geolocation suit data, something many were hesitant to provide.

"Is this permanent?' a nervous passenger asked over their feed.

"No, just for that timeframe," Calisto's box assured them. "You can send it as a compressed file. No access needed."

The passenger nodded. Progress had been slow, but people were bending. Only about half had so far refused to comply that morning, which was much better than when this whole ordeal had started, but still, it was tedious. If Calisto wasn't able to get results today, every person who refused to provide information would have their stay at Salem extended even longer for a more formal background check. And no one would be happy with that outcome.

"I didn't see him, so I don't know why you are asking me," a collective-bound from Herd Catawba had complained that morning, treating Calisto like they were no better than the Fallen colonizers who had raped and destroyed this land. A hundred years of cleaning up their mess and tensions were still not great; they might never be completely healed.

"Would you be able to verify that with your suit's geolocation data?"

"No, I refuse on principle."

Calisto had to stifle a groan. These interviews had been like pulling teeth from a horse in mid-gallop. They looked out at the various trails leading away from the table. One of these tracks seeping into the sandy soil might be the killer. They followed the spontaneous tapestry of small and large footprints with their eyes. Some were shallow. Others were deep impressions left by sprinting or marching. It was pure chaos. There was no making sense of any of it.

"You'll have to stay longer, then."

"Catawba is voting to leave the Restoration, cop, so I don't think I will."

"What?"

"You heard me."

Herds sometimes threatened to leave the Restoration. Few had. It was almost always a bluff. "Good luck with that. Next," Calisto called out to the line.

Striding up came a tall, scrawny Salem resident named Peter. He had braids that went down to his neck. Peter's file said he was a soil decontamination expert who also took on community watch shifts. Apparently, Herd Salem had members shadow official Shepherd roles in an attempt to be more transparent. This herd was very critical of authority, which had been a polluted pain in their rear.

"Hello, Peter."

"Peacekeeper," he said simply.

"I wanted to affirm the details you told me yesterday. When was the last time you saw Haldan?"

"The morning he headed out to the Shuttle. I wanted to say goodbye."

Calisto nodded.

"And the night before. When did you see him?"

"Umm," Peter blushed a deep red.

"It's okay, there is nothing to be embarrassed about."

"Of course. We were being intimate. Well, us and a lot of people."

"Would you mind confirming that with your geodata?"

In an instant, Peter's expression turned sour. "Why should I give you anything?" he said, not quite shouting but verging on it.

Calisto held a neutral expression: "You're not required to do anything; just note that my investigation will have to be more thorough if I don't get the necessary information. If you change your mind, know that the data gathered is limited and not meant to be intrusive."

"Why should I be afraid if I have nothing to hide, right?" Peter said indignantly. "Sounds like Fallen fascism to me. It's the reason why," and Peter was speaking louder now, more to the crowd than Calisto, "I'll be advancing a resolution in Salem to debate the merits of withdrawing from the Restoration."

"Another one. Well, we don't want that," they said, trying not to roll their eyes. They had been told that Salem debated Restoration membership quite frequently as a regular point of order, but seeing it used so casually as a threat like this made them very uncomfortable. "Very well, Peter, you're free to go. Just know that I might have other questions coming."

He stood up in a huff. His braids of hair shook violently against his creamy neck as he did so. His skin was weathered, marked by faint scars along his forearms—perhaps remnants of past fights or accidents?

"Fine, whatever," Peter scoffed. "It's Anderson you should be talking to anyway."

"Representative Anderson?" Calisto inquired.

Peter nodded. "He went into the woods the night before the murder. They fought at one point. Not like on the Seven, but verbally. Said some awful stuff."

"You know what about?"

"Politics. Anderson is trying to pass an amendment in the Chamber to stop people from owning land, and Haldan opposed it. Thought it was a redundant, petty jab at Groundwork. I had to separate the two of them, and then they made up minutes later and engaged in, well, other activities. That was sort of their way. I never thought it would ever be more than words."

"Interesting, so this wasn't the first time they fought."

Peter shook his head.

"Thank you, that was helpful. You can go. Calisto dismissed. They called out to the crowd: "Okay, we're taking a five-minute break."

Calisto relaxed their posture, their spine giving way as they sank into the mat. A morning of interviews and no new leads except for another direction pointing toward Anderson. A ping had been sent out to herds across the Restoration asking to report Anderson's location if they saw him. They had to find this smog and soon. No one had been able to track him down, even with his suit pinging from some unidentified location every hour on the hour. He was their only real lead, and he had vanished after that fight on the Seven. The CRS delegation was drafting a subpoena, a first for the peacekeepers, to search Anderson's office in the capital. Well, Dela was the real one writing it, but she was sitting on it, hoping that another day would stop her from having to cause a public scandal by raiding a Chamber official's office.

"Sirius, what's the verdict on query X-7A?" Calisto stated, hoping that they would get a different result from when the morning began.

The droid sent the results to their wrists with the message: "Unchanged. No new participants interfaced with suit ID #00023674, AKA Haldan Kramer, after his public encounter with Anderson Leek on the Northeast Seven Shuttle."

Hours of work and nothing learned, after all.

"Okay," Calisto sighed, turning to the crowd and shouting, "Line back up. We are starting the interviews again!"

The remaining people started mumbling curses and profanities about their time being wasted, and Calisto couldn't blame them. They didn't want to be here either.

FIFTEEN

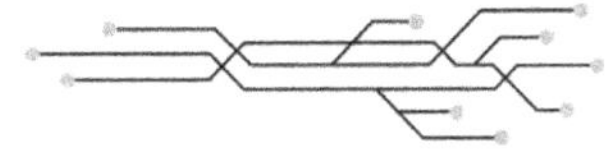

ROWAN

PUBLIC COAR DOWNLOAD/Interview/DW/Interviewee Representative Anderson Leek/05-01-2101

-> **The following transcript has been translated from German to English and edited for clarity.**

-> *REPORTER: So, Representative Anderson, I wasn't expecting you to be this forthright about your government's flaws.*
-> *ANDERSON: Why not? I can't stand the Groundwork Party and their cop-lite program [flips off a nearby German police officer], and I hope to reverse it the first chance I get. I can say whatever I want. I don't have to defend an administration, or a cabinet, or whatever politicians in Germany do these days. I'm selected for a single term, and that's it.*
-> *REPORTER: Term limits are across the Restoration, then?*
-> *ANDERSON: You're still not getting it. There is no 'across the Restoration.' Each community decides its own, well, almost everything. Even our Restoration-wide directives have to be agreed upon by every herd and collective out*

*there, and they agree to them in their own ways.
Someone does something bad, and there isn't a
standardized law some tyrant judge can throw
at them. We do repairs, not incarceration, and
more often than not, the outcome is an apology
and therapy. Makes it really easy to shit-talk
your representatives when you think they're
frackin' up. At least, that was the standard
before Groundwork. That smog.*

TIME: 3:03 PM
DAY: WEDNESDAY 5-18-2101

still don't understand why it has to be you," Rowan growled at Strummer.

Rowan was sitting against a tree on top of the cliffside she had bumped into Tulip a day earlier. Strummer had asked her to pick a location she liked, and this was as good as any. She liked the ocean: the way the sun glistened across the blue water, like a murky mirror, always shifting.

Strummer was sitting on a plush mat across from her, staring observantly like a would-be attacker waiting to strike. She had her hair tied into a neat, orderly bun, and she was wearing brown glasses with a smooth wooden frame. She was the type of person who seemed to love using pastes to accentuate her skin, brightening her eyebrows with a blue powder that made her skin pop.

"It doesn't have to be," Strummer responded. "I have the training, but I can book you something at the Neo-Boston Collective. They have more capacity for therapists than we do at the moment."

Rowan ignored the comment and carried on. "It's ridiculous that other people were able to book time over me. My repair mandates I see you, and I'm the polluted mother of the...Haldan," she said, refusing to say the word deceased at the last minute. The name of her son came out like something trapped in her throat.

"Does that frustrate you?" Strummer asked with all the paternalism of your typical CRS bureaucrat.

"Of course it frackin' frustrates me."

Strummer paused. "May I be direct with you?" she asked, still annoyingly polite.

"Go on," Rowan said, bracing herself for an attack.

Strummer breathed in shallowly. "From my observations, you externalize your emotions onto others through anger. I'd like to use this time not to focus on others, but on you, on how you are feeling."

Rowan stared blankly at the CRS. "And how should I be feeling?" She condescended.

"I want you to tell me. If you are comfortable, I would like to talk about your son's death. The herd is putting his body into the ground tomorrow. How are you preparing for that?"

The honesty was like fire searing her skin. As a girl, she had burned herself when she was stressed. Nothing too serious, simply taking a small lighter and marking it somewhere underneath her clothing. She had been a sad child, everyone had said so, even her parents. She was the kind of person no one had wanted to be around, but then she had learned how to twist that sadness into a biting wit. She had learned how to be entertaining enough for people to want to keep her around. Anger had propelled her through everything, but it was doing shit to help her now. This pain was not like the immediate relief that came with fire, but one that lingered. A pain she was reminded of, whenever bad posture or tight clothing accidentally pinched her raw flesh. Not the relief, but the aftereffect that lingered for weeks and months afterward. Talking about Haldan, even thinking about talking about him, was like a reminder of a burn, a reminder of something shameful.

She swallowed and then shrugged off the thought. She would die before talking about something that personal. Besides, it was irrelevant. All of this was irrelevant. "I don't want to talk about that," Rowan continued. "I don't have time to talk about that."

Strummer nodded. Her skinny fingers clacked on a portable keyboard she had brought to make notes. "I will respect that. What would you like to talk about then? You scheduled this time for a reason," Strummer adjusted her posture, staring directly into Rowan's eyes.

"I was forced to come here. My wife Úna put me up for review, and now I might lose my place in the Writers' Cooperative if I don't get your A-okay, doc."

Rowan felt impetuous even mentioning it. Surely, the possibility of no longer being in a Writers' Cooperative was small, insignificant even, and yet it still bothered her. She had sacrificed so much for this community. Given them so much joy and contemplative sadness with her plays. Her poems. And now, because she had one bad night, because she had done what she had thought was right, they might discard her.

"I take it you haven't reviewed the results yet," Strummer asked. Rowan bet she had voted against her. "Rational" people like Strummer always did.

Rowan turned away, not looking at her. "No, I haven't looked at them."

Strummer, still typing, nodded. "I was surprised you opted for an entirely virtual review on the COAR. I would have thought you'd want to make your case in person."

"Closer to *Her* that way," Rowan said, reconnecting her gaze with Strummer. The woman's bony jaw readjusting, straightening, appraising Rowan like a snack.

"I see. Would you like to review the results together? No pun intended."

Rowan didn't laugh at the flat humor. "No, I don't need to learn how a bunch of my friends and family have decided to betray me the day before we put my son into the ground."

Strummer's face twitched. Rowan swore she had suppressed a frown. "Do you think you're externalizing again here?"

"Don't ask it as a question. Just say what you are thinking." Rowan commented bitterly.

"Understood," Strummer responded. Her voice was flat, stiff. "You're externalizing your anger again. When you seem more angry with yourself."

Rowan stood up, no longer wanting to sit still and feel like she was sinking into the scratchy grass beneath them. She had disabled even more settings on her suit to be closer to *Her*, and the ground irked her, almost a burning sensation against her skin. Everything did. They were outside, but even so, the air around her felt stale and hot.

"Take a deep breath." Strummer lectured.

Rowan, standing behind Strummer, shook her head. "Don't tell..." But Rowan didn't finish that statement, realizing that she was doing exactly what Strummer had just lectured about. That smog. Did she have to be right, too? She paused and then, thinking, asked: "What could I possibly be angry about?"

"You tell me?"

"I told you to be direct."

"I'm asking for context because I cannot read your mind. You best know how you feel."

Rowan was pacing around Strummer, going around and around her mat. "It's so hot. Why is it so hot out here?"

"We could go inside. My tent can trap cool air."

All of them could, but Rowan didn't say that. She found herself biting her words.

"No, I don't want to go inside," Rowan asked as she continued pacing. "I don't like how... It's so much. I have to keep being normal, like everything is fine. Like it's unacceptable not to lose my polluted mind when my son has died. Like it's so easy to put him in the ground and move on. Like this party we are throwing erases all that...," She paused, not knowing exactly what she wanted right now from Strummer. A medal? Recognition?

"Is that the first time you've had to acknowledge his death?" She asked plainly.

"No, I had to recount everything to you, and that peacekeeper."

"Is it possible..." Then Strummer caught herself and said, "I suspect that some of your resentment with the investigation might be tied to that. It's not an easy thing to have to relive the loss of a loved one so shortly after their passing."

"No, I don't care about some frackin' peacekeeper. I care about how I'm going to lose my position in the Writers' Co-operative."

"You didn't lose your position." This time, Rowan was almost certain Strummer had suppressed a smirk.

"What?" Rowan gasped.

"I already read the results." Strummer said, "And you were only given two weeks' probation. Your position is fine."

"Why would you just...just tell me like that?" Rowan was not as angry as confused. She had asked Strummer not to do something. Wasn't that supposed to be how therapy worked? They listened to you complain and then, in exchange, provided a nugget of wisdom that led you to some over-hyped epiphany.

"I'm adjusting to being more direct with you. Besides, I don't think we would have made progress until you knew."

Rowan sighed. "I hate that it makes me feel better."

"You don't have to suffer all the time, you know. Mourning is not linear."

"Make it more cryptic, and we can start a moody band."

"Or a religion," Strummer added, an edge of humor in her voice.

Rowan laughed. Sacrilegious humor always made her chuckle.

The rest of the session felt less contentious. It consisted of small, banal details concerning what Strummer called 'the work, which meant recognizing thoughts and adjusting them. Rowan was starting to realize that therapy was not all epiphanies and revelations but a lot of general maintenance. It was only as the session was coming to a close that something unexpected and entirely unrelated happened. A young man from the acting troupe ran up to the cliff in their direction, only to ignore them entirely once he arrived.

"I am in the middle of a session," Strummer said, the first time a sense of annoyance was in her voice.

He waved her off, panting. "I knew I wasn't seeing things," he said more to himself than to either Strummer or Rowan.

The man pointed to the water. Rowan looked out over the bay. She had been so lost in her conversation with Strummer that she had not seen it. He was pointing at the Eastern Shore Trading Combine: the dome-like corpo barony that existed off the shore of the Cods. Unlike every other day that Salem had been there, there was not a stack of smoke to be seen.

SIXTEEN

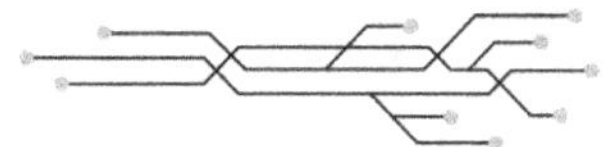

CALISTO

PUBLIC COAR DOWNLOAD/Book/The Restoration Is A Paradox/Author Hosa Liu/3-8-2094

-> *The Restoration considers itself post-capitalist. There are many different economies across the Americas. Some collectives and herds share everything through a central administrative body, particularly ones like Mishigami, which are ruled in all but name by the Christian-Marxist Groundwork Party. Others, like herd Michigan, are a type of gift-giving economy in which people continuously give away their surplus to community members.*

-> *It's not true, though, that capitalism has stopped existing in the Americas. The Second American Civil War, sometimes referred to as the Greater American War, the War of Liberation, or simply the Revolution, ended when the People's Federated Army and the Corporate States of America fought each other to a standstill. Over time, these corporate entities have stagnated into neo-feudal entities, which we call the*

*baronies, where capitalism very much continues
to exist.*

TIME: 10:12 AM
DAY: THURSDAY 5-19-2101

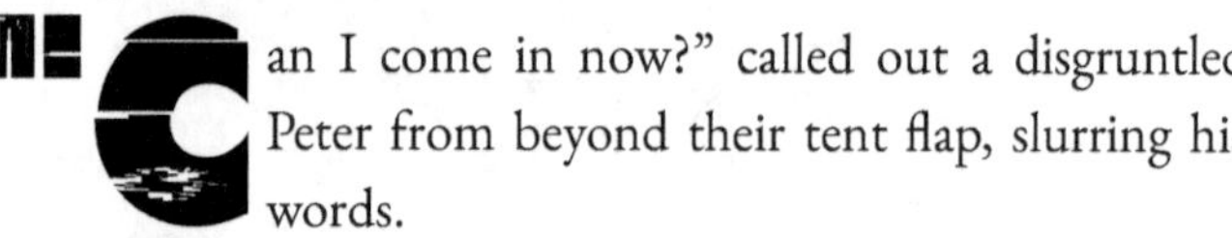an I come in now?" called out a disgruntled Peter from beyond their tent flap, slurring his words.

"Not yet," Calisto shouted back.

Concerned herdspeople, drunk off the wine from Haldan Kramer's upcoming backslash ceremony, had been stumbling in all morning with liquid courage to demand Calisto tell them how long the *Seven* passengers would remain in camp, and Calisto was tired of it. "Go away, Peter, I'm busy."

Calisto couldn't deal with Peter's petulance right now when they were behind on administrative work. They were typing a report meant for their supervisor, Dela, using an attachment of small metal levers that plugged directly into their suit—each wire corresponding to a letter in the French alphabet.

"Hello," they typed and then paused as they struggled with what to write next.

They were seated on a small foldable chair they had pulled out of their pack. It was mainly a couple of metal bars and a nanomat, but it was sorely needed when preparing to spend an hour filing a report like this: one that was delivering more bad news. The remaining passengers for the Northeast Seven Shuttle—the ones who had refused to forfeit their geolocation data, making everyone's lives more difficult—were going to have to stay for a little bit longer if they didn't want to face review from their herds and collectives back home.

"Haldan Kramer's suit," Calisto continued to write, "whether worn by him or not, was on the Northeast Seven Shuttle past boarding. I have cleared the passengers who have provided their data or have been eliminated as suspects through third-party interviews. Many have already left. I further request that a writ of privacy invalidation be filed with the Chamber to promptly obtain this data for those who have not complied. These non-compliant passengers should not be released until we have this data or we have an identifiable suspect in custody."

Reading the bureaucratic garble made their minds glaze over, but they knew Dela would have an entirely more charged reaction. A third of the passengers had opted out of sharing their data, and they were digging in. This was not as bad as the two hundred they'd started with, but it was still holding up dozens of slots in collectives across the Restoration.

There was also the matter of Representative Anderson, who hadn't been located, despite a rather public search of his office in the capital. A search for him, a proper manhunt by peacekeepers across the country, would have to be called in soon. The search should have already been declared, in Calisto's opinion, but Dela was dragging her feet on it. They pictured Dela sitting on her office mat, projecting this memo on the wall, cursing violently as the bad news trickled in. Maybe she would have a drink, sipping some of that Cattail moonshine she liked to make from foraged leaves, sighing as she pulled up their writ demanding Representative Anderson be found and then taken in for questioning. Maybe she would do nothing and ignore it for a couple more days.

"Furthermore," typed Calisto, their fingers tired and sweaty, "as herd Salem is quite insular, we risk further community harm by keeping these passengers here without proper mediation. I recommend that a request for more cultural exchanges with Salem be emphasized as soon as possible and that more facilitators be sent."

Calisto was being diplomatic. These people were xenophobic: not at the same level as the Fallen had been, but it was worrisome. How could these people exist in the same Restoration? The same polity built on decolonization and environmental restoration. It was in the polluted name. Maybe Haldan had called one of these people an exo.

That was sure to get him killed, they thought bitterly.

"I must insist I come in," said Peter, barging in without waiting for a response. His stubby nostrils flared. Some of his braids had been completely undone while dancing around Haldan's grave this morning, maintenance he had probably neglected over the last few days. Calisto remembered that Peter and Haldan were...had been lovers. Peter still appeared to be mourning, projecting his grief as anger...onto them.

Don't take it personally, Sirius advised.

Calisto had to stop themself from groaning at the voice inside their head.

Peter was with two unlikely figures. One was Captain Felipe, whom Peter must now be fucking because the sexual tension between them was thick. Felipe was fabulous and grouchy as ever, covering his rich terracotta skin with the widest black-and-white checkered sun hat Calisto had ever seen. They were also with Salem's Head Shepherd Úna, who hung in the back, observing.

"We demand you send these exos away," Peter said.

"Hey, watch it, your nice ass is only going to get you so far," Felipe warned, also appearing to be completely drunk from the party, and then turned to Calisto. "But he has a point. I don't want to be here either."

Calisto mustered the most bureaucratic smile they could. "I am not deciding anything. Every decision gets cleared by Salem's CRS, Úna over there, who this herd voted for, and for more major decisions, often the CRS Delegation. And the facts of the case are...."

"We've heard about all that," Peter cut in. "And last we heard is that Anderson did it; ergo, his sexy booty," he said, pointing at Felipe, "should be allowed to leave."

"And we don't have the capacity to take in more people," Úna interjected for the first time, far more sober than the other two. "My herd isn't supposed to be settling in at its current location. The local environment can't support our numbers in the long term. The El Paso Forest Sprouters have a much smaller population than ours, and now with these people coming in. It will undo our mitigation efforts."

"Careful," Felipe cautioned again. "These people can pack a wallop."

"What's this?" asked Peter, referring to the assortment of sticks, rocks, and shells Calisto had lying on a wooden board that they'd been using as visual aids to help them work out the case. Haldan was a shiny black rock they'd pulled from the shore, the shuttle was a curved wooden stick, and someone, whom Calisto was representing as an old, gray oyster shell, was the murderer. There were several oyster shells because Calisto still wasn't sure how many murderers there were, and Peter was, funnily enough, holding up an oyster shell in that way drunken people do when they decide rummaging through your shit is the most entertaining thing in the world.

"Please put that down," Calisto instructed.

"It's important then," said Felipe triumphantly, picking up a shell as well.

"Gentlemen and Úna, I will say this again: I'm not hoarding information."

"Did you see it?" asked Shepherd Sam, with flushed red cheeks, barging into the temporary tent Calisto had made home without asking for permission and then, not waiting for a reply, said, "Is it related to the case? It can't be a polluted coincidence, right?"

"Does no one ask for permission before violating my personal space?" Calisto bemoaned.

Sam mumbled an apology and continued. "Have you been paying attention to your feed at all?"

"I've been busy," Calisto said exasperatedly, motioning toward the trio in front of them.

"Well, stop whatever you're doing, the barony, the one off of our shores had...is having a Civil War, and corpos are landing on the beach."

That caused everyone to shut up. Calisto did stop what they were doing, relieved to be leaving this trio of grumpy people behind them, and followed Sam as they motioned toward the shore. It was a crisp day for the summer. The ocean breeze was strong and chaotic. It was hard to imagine anyone would swim miles across the bay on a day like this. They arrived at the site to find Tulip and her troupe providing blankets and food to the countless men and women huddling for warmth on the beach.

"By Gaia," Sam cursed as they looked at the mass of refugees. "We have to find Rowan."

Calisto didn't understand why, but they scanned the crowd. There were so many refugees. They spotted Rowan in the thick of the action, holding onto a tablet with an application of some sort, answering questions as one refugee looked at it.

Rowan was the one using her box for a change. "No, you aren't required to sign it. Membership in the Restoration is automatic," her box answered to a question Calisto had not heard but assumed was about citizenship.

The corpo Rowan was talking to, a short male-presenting person wearing an all-white one-piece, handed her a gray metal rectangle with a circular hole in the center. Rowan frowned, shaking her head no.

"We don't take money here."

The corpo looked confused, extending the money until she acquiesced.

When Calisto arrived, Rowan handed the tablet to one of the troupe members and walked over to them. "I'm so glad you are here. I have no idea what I'm doing. They just started showing up in droves."

Calisto looked up and down the white sands of the beach. There were over a hundred people here, all in the same white one-piece. "This is, wow, has to be...."

"107," Rowan clarified. "And more keep coming. I don't know the details, but it seems some sort of polluted civil war is happening in the Eastic."

"I was told... Eastic?"

"That's their name for the corpo barony, the Eastern Shore Trading Combine. Here I have someone you need to talk to."

Rowan took them over to a woman who appeared to be helping the other Eastic residents get adjusted, translating various needs the refugees had with Salem's residents. Her hair was buzzed short, and her fawn skin looked still wet from her swim in the sea. She had the same all-white one-piece as everyone else. Calisto hadn't had a chance to truly look at it. It wasn't like the techno variety Restoration residents typically wore. It was made of simple cloth and embedded in glossy orange lettering that read: Property of the Eastern Shore Trading Combine.

"Three-Seven," Rowan said gently. "I have someone you should meet."

The number already told Calisto that everything they'd heard about the baronies was probably true, or at least enough of it, anyway. Trash, they knew that the baronies hadn't stopped the practices of the Fallen, but they didn't know how much worse things had become. The contracts of the Fallen had always been coercive, but this? Had it always been like this for their ancestors?

Three-Seven looked uneasily at Calisto, as if she wanted to will herself to disappear and sink through the sand into the Earth. Rowan tried to calm her. Rowan was holding a small screen, a stand-in HUD that was used during emergencies when suits broke down, or in the case of this situation, they had no suits to begin with. "Their name is Calisto, and their job is to solve problems. Go ahead," encouraged Rowan's box. "It's okay. You can tell them what happened."

"I...It's bad in there. Chaos. And I saw how it started with my own eyes, my lord."

"Three-Seven, I said we aren't lords." Rowan's box corrected.

"Of course, my apologies, my Rowan."

Calisto felt an immense pang of guilt, but they didn't show it.

Empathy is what they need the most, the voice of Sirius lectured. *They don't know any better.*

Calisto turned on their box as well. "It's okay. You were saying." Calisto's box continued.

"It started, I don't even remember when. I must have been in those vents for days. I was on Beta Shift for S.O.D., that's Sanitation Optimization and Development."

"Cleaning," Rowan added for context.

"Right, yes, cleaning. I am sorry, my, my," she stuttered.

"It's okay," Calisto's box affirmed.

Three-Seven continued: "Well, I come into the conference room, that's a meeting place for the lords. I go there to clean. There was a meeting, but the royals don't pay attention much when I'm there. But I still hear things. And Lord Manager Benison, who's in charge of Security and Development, gets into a fight with Her Majesty, CEO Jane Smith. They're arguing, and then Benison shoots Her Majesty in the head. May her soul rest with the ancestors."

"You said this happened days ago? Why are we just noticing it now?"

"Someone locked it down. We crawled through the vents to get out. It took a while, and many stumbled into..." she paused. "Security measures. If only Her Majesty were still alive, she'd protect us," Three-Seven wailed.

Calisto held out a hand to touch her on the shoulder, which Three-Seven turned into a hug. Calisto had interacted with people who had empathy for their abusers before. Domestic violence had not gone away with the Fallen, but usually, it was a system or group that was operating at the fringes of society. This was an entire society enslaving people, and seeing the reality of it stung in a way that they couldn't fully process. Was slavery happening *this* close to the Restoration?

This sadness is your strength, Sirius told them sweetly. *We see this barbarity for the historically obsolete behavior that it is.*

Calisto held them tight and whispered, "I know this is difficult. Do you know what the fight was about?'

Tear-stricken, Three-Seven continued: "I'm, I am afraid I only got snippets. The Eastic, the royals thought it was going to expand soon. And the Lord Manager wasn't happy with the holdings Her Majesty, rest *Her* name, would give him. And now His Lord Manager has started a war over it. It's treason, it is. He started executing all the property of the queens, and so, I ran. Because I am a coward."

Calisto was angry, and they could not help themselves. They didn't know who this Lord Manager Benison was, but trash them. "You're not a coward, Three-Seven. You were smart and brave. You saw your chance, and you took it, and there's nothing you should regret about it."

"But my children."

"Even with that, you did nothing wrong," Calisto said as affirmingly as they could.

Calisto couldn't be there anymore, or they were going to howl. The last trafficking case they had dealt with had been the one where Sirius had...it had been the last case he'd ever served. It was too much. They needed a moment to process all of this before jumping in again.

They continued: "Now one of these fine people is going to help you with your assistance application, and then you won't have to worry about this ever again."

"I'm afraid I have to go back. My, my Calisto. My children. They're still there."

Calisto tried to maintain an unfeeling smile. The Party had always been clear that peacekeepers' emotions shouldn't get in the way of cases. They were meant to be an objective hand for Marx's blessed history, and here Calisto was, letting their feelings taint the Party's will, *His* will.

Calisto swallowed hard and continued: "The Restoration won't stop you, but consider talking to someone here before you do. Strummer," Calisto's box said, calling to Salem's CRS. Strummer, who had just arrived, holding a pad with an application in her hands, took over.

"Rowan, a moment," Calisto said. The two of them walked further down the beach. The cold breeze was picking up as the sun started to set. The green flies buzzed around them as they traipsed along the shore. "Thank you so much for this. You've done a great job."

"Thanks. It's a lot, isn't it?" Rowan said insightfully. She looked like the weight of what was happening in the Eastic had already hit her. "The trash over there," she said, pointing to the dome in the distance. "Gaia is not with them."

"How did you get them to cooperate so quickly?" Calisto deflected, wanting to talk about anything else.

"It was Tulip. She's a former corpo, not from the Eastic but some barony up near the Anchorage Collective. She opened up about her experiences, and it made it easier for the refugees to trust us."

"I didn't know she was a former corpo."

"I didn't either. She doesn't like to talk about it very much, apparently."

"Understandable," Calisto thought of how Three-Seven had described herself as property and had to stop themselves from shuddering. "Well, thank you all the same."

"You're welcome," Rowan responded.

They realized they had been avoiding confirming an important detail with their most difficult lead, and now was as good a time as any to do so. "I have something I've been meaning to ask, but it's about Haldan, and it doesn't need to be answered right now."

"Ask," Rowan said.

Calisto went forward. "That day you saw him off to the Seven, I mean, are you sure it was him?"

Rowan shook her head. "I don't know. A part of me does. I wish I could say that some intuition told me the person that day wasn't my son, it would certainly make everything easier, but he looked like him. Talked like him. If it wasn't him," Rowan paused, her voice cracking.

"Take your time."

Rowan took a deep breath. "It's like…if it wasn't him, did I even know him? What kind of mother does that make me?"

"One that trusts her son," Calisto said softly.

They both stopped talking, looking out at the Eastic in the distance. It was strange for a war to be so close and yet feel so far. People in the Restoration often thought of themselves as living in a world without strife, but it wasn't true. Conflict was ever ready to burst from just below the surface, and not always from whom you suspected.

SEVENTEEN

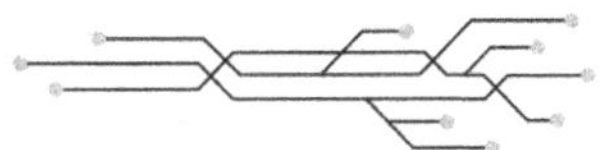

ROWAN

PRIVATE COAR DOWNLOAD/Journal Entry/Frackin' Gaiaverse Backslash Ceremonies/Author Haldan Kramer/6-27-2098

-> Our funerals are mostly awesome. What's not to love about a three-day party? But backslash ceremonies are so boring. Everyone goes from gleefully frolicking about and swapping funny stories to bawling their eyes out.
-> And the worst part is that the party ends.

TIME: 4:00 PM
DAY: THURSDAY 5-19-2101

Rowan walked alongside Úna and several of her shepherds carrying Haldan's corpse through the trees. The body was concealed by a brilliant green shroud, like a leaf drifting on the wind. They were meant to begin the backslash ceremony earlier, but the refugees had interrupted the flow of the day, so they were doing so now, the sun high in the sky.

Rowan had been thankful not to have to think about the ceremony for a few hours, clinging to the relief duties of that morning as a distraction. She hadn't suspected the details surrounding this to be so hard. Rowan was angry at her son, and it was for the silliest of reasons. She was angry that he had gotten himself killed. He was supposed to have gone to Bangalore, realized that he hated it there, and came back to live with her and Úna. She hated herself for selfishly wanting that even now, for this all to be one big elaborate joke, and for Haldan to whip the shroud covering his desiccated body and say: "I can't believe you all fell for that." And then she would hug him, and slap him, and not talk to him for a day before finally forgiving his stupidity.

Haldan didn't move, however. The procession placed him on the ground right before a freshly dug hole. They unwrapped the shroud, tossing the ropes away from the hole's edge, letting his sienna-toned body, badly cut and bruised, be visible to all those close enough to see. There were some repressed gasps as those who had not seen his decaying flesh for the last three days were finally able to.

Rowan moved forward. She had volunteered to be the administrator for the backslash ceremony. Anyone could be a conduit for Gaia. There were no 'official administrator positions,' at least not in Salem, but there hadn't been any takers besides her. She suspected that everyone had assumed either she or Úna would do it, so she stepped in front of his body and turned to the crowd of mostly drunk onlookers. It took everything in her not to wail right there. She peered around, straining her vision to see if anyone else was coming, but the crowd sprawled out far past her sightline. Except for a contingent left at the beach to help the refugees, it looked like most everyone from both Herd Salem and the Seven was here.

Near the front of the line, she could see Úna and Three-Seven—the latter of whom hadn't known what a backslash ceremony was until this morning (non-premium members were apparently recycled with little ceremony when they died). She smiled at the corpo, moved by how willing she was to be there for a stranger she hardly knew.

"Let us begin," Rowan said grimly. "Gaia: the person who wrote the programming of life, whose essence permeates and surrounds us all. We are gathered here in grief because another person has left us, and it brings us pain. We have lost a package of matter and energy that blessed us with its spontaneity and uniqueness and will never be seen again."

Rowan paused for effect, something she had seen other administrators do in the past. She looked at the faces standing around her. People were crying now; the sound of sniffles made when someone tried to push back tears rippled through the crowd. Úna could hardly lift her head to meet the drained face of her son. His body picked at by the bugs and other creatures that had been able to nibble on him for the last three days. That is why they placed him in the center of camp, so they could prevent larger animals from dragging his corpse away and, in the process, stop his 'transfer' or 'back up' into the earth.

Rowan swallowed and continued: "For three days, we gathered up sticks and laid this soul on a bed of your body, your essence, so that we may remember that we are always connected to you. That even when people leave, they are not really gone."

She felt a solitary tear drip down her cheek. He shouldn't be dead. Some trash had ripped him from his place on the Earth and carried him off well before his time. If Gaia let her, she would trade that killer's life for his. She imagined punching the mysterious killer in the face until they bled red, cried, and asked her to stop. She imagined the life leaving this imaginary figure forever. She then took a deep breath, let that anger go, and continued saying the rites.

"We commit him to you," she croaked. "So he may become a source of new life. His body was never ours. This was merely an illusion: us confusing the complexity of the form for independence. Though painful, these moments remind us that we are always a part of you. That we never stop being separated from your whole and that death is itself a reminder of this truth."

There was some comfort in these words: a screed from a hacker prophet who had been one of the first to channel Gaia, back when Gaiaverse was nothing more than a string of messages posted on a decaying Fallen information system. The Corporate States had taken everything from the refugees that had dotted the flooded coasts of America, but they had archaic communication devices called phones, and through these machines, they had been able to listen and plug into the Gaiaverse and see life for what it was. A connection to *Her*, to life, and to death.

Rowan finished the stanza. "Haldan Kramer has plugged into the Gaiaverse. He never left, and there he shall always remain."

She signaled to one of the shepherds to lower his body into the hole. They rolled up his corpse back into the green shroud, a biodegradable knapsack that would allow Gaia to take him apart more slowly. The shepherds lowered him as softly as they could before they let him go, his corpse hitting the earthen floor of the hole with a tiny thud. He was covered with loose rocks, then dirt, and then they were done. He was underground now, so he could transform into forms of life that would hopefully last a little longer this time around.

"Go now in *Her* light," she told the crowd.

Her completed sermon was like a magical spell cast on the crowd to disperse. Some stayed behind to offer their condolences, but the rest started filing out across the forest, committed to finding a semi-private corner so they could tell their compatriots their favorite stories of Haldan, or their worst: resentment tended to stay with people long after death. Úna went with the crowd, the duties of a Head Shepherd never done, but not before squeezing Rowan's hand and giving her a soft kiss on the cheek.

"Find me after, grumpy bear," she suggested, knowing better than to press her wife to go somewhere she didn't want to follow.

She left, and Rowan stood beside the mound of recently packed-down dirt, with Three-Seven, and weirdly enough, Calisto too, who was wearing all red, which they had claimed was meant to be respectful during times of mourning. Three-Seven had claimed that the Eastic didn't have funeral rites for enslaved people, a description she was growing accustomed to using. She had still tried, however, changing her suit from its default steel grey to an off-white. Baby steps, Rowan reminded herself.

"You spoke elegantly," Calisto affirmed.

"Yes. I must say I find it strange to spend energy on some-one who can no longer labor. We wouldn't do that in the Eas-tic." Three-Seven's box said.

"No," Rowan breathed in heavily, doing her best not to chew out this poor, traumatized woman. "You wouldn't. That would require respect those Fallen...," she paused, "...those people didn't afford you."

Three-Seven nodded thoughtfully. "Why three days?" Three-Seven's box asked, not offended by the characteriza-tion. Three-Seven did not read Rowan's comment as any-thing more than an honest assessment. She was probably used to worse. "Why do Gaiaverse adherents wait three days to lower the body?"

"It's meant to be a reminder that this form is ephemeral and that we will all return to the Gaiaverse in the end. It goes back to the early days on the road when we had to get used to death. So many died, and it was a way to show that the cor-pos couldn't break us. That we would lay down our dead on our own terms. I'm not sure every herd keeps the tradition, probably not."

Rowan had only recently realized, rather naively, that the world was a lot bigger than her small, little herd. Gaiaverse was one of the dominant religions in the Restoration, but there was far greater diversity than in the Fallen States of Old. There were probably many herds where this tradition was considered strange, even among Gaiaverse herds that weren't quite as...extreme.

"I'm glad Haldan was returned to the Goddess proper-ly," Calisto said gently.

"A part of me hates it," she whispered. "He never left *Her*. That's what I am supposed to take from all of this, but it doesn't make it hurt less...."

"I lost someone not too long ago," Calisto told her somberly, looking away. "Even after I paid my respects, it still hurts."

"I think my children are dead," Three-Seven interjected, her voice raw. "I saw Lord Manager Benison's guards execute the children in the development center during the coup. My kids were there. I just didn't want to believe it."

Rowan put a hand on Three-Seven's shoulder. "I am so sorry for what those people did to you. It's not okay."

"I appreciate that, Rowan, really I do. Except it wasn't just them, was it?" Her box said, her sadness morphing into a streak of anger. "Because you're all here too, aren't you? And you're watching it happen."

Rowan's defensiveness was immediately triggered. Who was this woman to lecture her on the day of her son's frackin' funeral? She was prepared to say exactly that, but first she breathed. She let Gaia's cold, crisp air fill her lungs, and then she thought better of it.

"We are, aren't we?" Rowan conceded. "The Restoration might be too comfortable in watching."

She held Three-Seven as the woman wept, and in comforting another, Rowan felt a little less alone.

EIGHTEEN

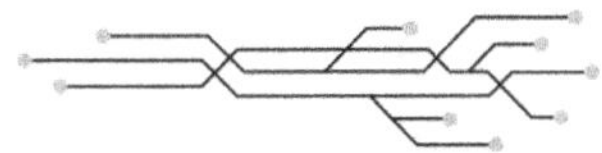

CALISTO

PRIVATE COAR/Message Thread/05267/Roxane-Smith-Úna/5-19-2101

-> message chain:

-> Roxane Chapman: I wanted to inquire if you had received my note about the events near Herd Salem.

-> Smith Taylor: Yes. I utterly agree with you that the recent events at the Eastern Shore Trading Combine represent an escalation that must be dealt with. For too long, we have handled our borders too leniently.

-> Roxane Chapman: Are you sending them?

-> Smith Taylor: I want to, but it's not up to just me. I am looping in Salem's Head Shepherd. Úna, one of our peacekeepers, has requested that we send additional members of the Delegation. Will you permit this?

-> Úna Kramer: Gaia, it's just one thing after the other with you all. You're asking my entire herd to hate me. You realize that?

-> Roxane Chapman: You filed a complaint about the Eastern Shore Trading Combine's refugees, correct? You want them out of your herd. We could work on that.

-> Úna Kramer: Fine, your peacekeepers are au-
thorized to come, but only for a week.

TIME: 11:45 AM
DAY: FRIDAY 5-20-2101

t normally would be an idyllic day. The sun was hot, but not too hot. The humidity was nonexistent, and the wind was cool and refreshing. However, you couldn't hear anything long enough to enjoy an otherwise enjoyable day. The singing birds and chirping squirrels were drowned out by a bitter argument as Calisto positioned themselves between two screaming people on the verge of throwing more than mere words.

One was a peacekeeper who had come in on the CRS Delegation's orders to monitor the refugee situation. A tall, pale, lanky man who couldn't be more than twenty-three years old, who carried himself with a sense of unshakeable righteousness. A party member who more than likely had received unofficial orders from Dela, and maybe even Roxane, and was too young to realize those orders were anything but right.

The other was a herd member Calisto had only encountered in passing. She was large, boisterous, and old enough to no longer want to suffer the foolishness of young men telling her what to do. She was dangerously tired, like she was about to start swinging at any moment.

"I would like an apology," the young peacekeeper demanded. "You bumped into me on purpose, I know you did.

"And I would like you and your other cops to leave," she quipped.

"We aren't cops," the young man corrected. "And I am...

"You say tomato, I say fascism," she interrupted.

"Ma'am, I am authorized to be here, and I don't appreciate...."

The woman stepped forward, pressing up against Calisto. Her hot, angry breath flew in their face as she shouted at the peacekeeper to frack himself.

The young peacekeeper also moved forward, pressing up against Calisto's back, repeating: "I am authorized to be here," as if it were some magical incantation that would compel the woman to back down. Calisto imagined that in the circles this man ran in, such a statement would be expected to go unquestioned. The Delegation had asked the Chamber to ask Úna to allow them there, so why would anyone resist if the chain of command had been followed? It was logic that Calisto wouldn't have questioned too long ago either.

Calisto turned their back to the herdswoman and faced the peacekeeper. "I need you to step back," they commanded of the man who was theoretically trained to avoid the very argument taking place here.

"I am authorized to be here," he repeated.

"De-escalate, comrade, step back."

And yet, he stood his ground. His eyes looked past Calisto toward the woman defying him.

More Salemers came over to see what the commotion was about, and soon they were not facing off against a single person but a crowd pulsating with anger and confusion. Many voices joined together, making it difficult to tell where one began and another ended.

"Why are you giving her a hard time?" asked one of many.

"Here come the cops," they mocked as more peacekeepers stepped in, joining in a line of men and women pretending to be stoic and unmoving, jostling around at the various people pushing up against them. The two abstract forces of the people and the state, or at least an aspiring one, clashed against one another in a way that had not been seen in the Restoration for some time. This was not what Groundwork said would happen with this program, but it was probably what it wanted.

Doubts, I see, said the facsimile of Sirius. *Good*.

Except that couldn't be Sirius because Sirius had died believing that the party was just, that they were fighting for the correct, inevitable interpretation of history. It was Calisto who was having doubts. Something had shifted.

It took them a second to realize that someone was screaming—not a simple chant or curse at the peacekeepers, either, but a shout so primal and raw that they could hear the strain it was causing. It was a righteous voice they were familiar with, and yet as they turned to face it, the source still surprised them.

Rowan. She looked as angry as ever but also so incredibly tired. "My son is dead," she screamed. "We buried him yesterday, and you do this," she said, pointing to the peacekeepers. "We're hurting, and you come here and cut at our pain like it's nothing. He's dead," she said more softly. Her voice was too hoarse and overextended to hold this tenor.

The energy that the peacekeepers had—the resolve that they were on a mission of absolute certainty—dissipated in an instant. They were not so hardened by the emergent aspirations of the Party to discard this woman's pain.

Though, give them a few years, joked Sirius darkly.

Calisto couldn't help but shudder.

"Step back, comrades," Calisto repeated.

The young peacekeeper stepped back first, removing his hands from his comrades. He was in the center, as his fellow peacekeepers had gathered around him. This divided the line in two, forcing it to then break apart so quickly that Calisto could not keep track of which men and women retreated when.

The crowd applauded as the peacekeepers retreated. There was a rush of woos and whistles about this small victory, which was much bigger than it seemed.

"Thank you," Calisto told Rowan. "That could have been a lot worse."

"You think," she retorted, her voice not so raspy as to lose its edge. "Keep them in line," she said, referring to where the peacekeepers had fled. "Or better yet, send them away."

"I will try," Calisto assured her, not sure if such a thing was even possible.

NINETEEN

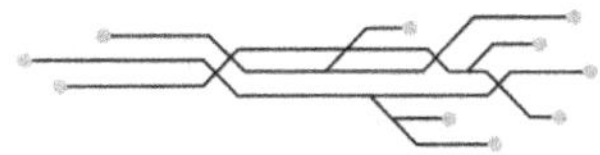

ROWAN

PUBLIC COAR DOWNLOAD/Journal/Why the frack is everyone so xenophobic?/Author Tulip Bellwether/3-2-2099

-> *I've loved my time in Salem. The solitude of nature is what I have needed after a lifetime cramped in an oil refinery barony near Anchorage, stuck in the same few hallways and platforms my entire life. But something I've been frustrated with is how, and I guess there is no other way to say it, xenophobic this herd is, and really much of the Restoration. They think of themselves as so 'tolerant,' and they are to some extent. The baronies and capitalist nation-states of the world are not places I would want to live. But still, many in the Restoration…they treat the people who come from those places with such disdain, and it bothers me to no end.*

```
TIME: 1:17 PM
DAY: FRIDAY 5-20-2101
```

owan was threading two old pieces of nanofabric together. The magnetic stitching was always a pain to navigate. Her wand, an old black rod with a grip that was starting to wear down after years of use, had a bit of give as she clumped the threads together. There was a feel to it that required practice to get right.

"Damn," Three-Seven cursed, frustrated as the pieces mushed together into ugly lumps.

Rowan was not familiar with the curse word, but there were a lot of things about Three-Seven's old way of life that she didn't understand. The two of them were parked under a temporary canvas, repurposing old suits into reusable tents. The refugees were spending their time in Herd Salem as they got their bearings, and that meant they all needed more tents.

People had come in from all over the Restoration to help, flooding into their community with unthinking resolve and good intentions. In the distance, Buddhist monks were making cornbread. An entire sect of Spiritual Atheists was chatting heatedly amongst themselves, reconfiguring the fabric's data settings before it could be reused and passed over to Rowan and Three-Seven. Even a hermit had come in from the unmitigated wilds, quietly cutting whatever rolls of fabric were given to xem in predefined cuts of cloth.

The CRS Delegation had sent even more peacekeepers, wary of the refugees and the barony they represented, but doing nothing about it. They wore fatigue patterns programmed for these woods, so if you unfocused your eyes, you might lose sight of them. They had been instructed to come and stand and do nothing else, idly standing in the center of camp where Haldan had sat only a day ago. Rowan knew their suits were spec'd with weapons, and while that was hardly uncommon in a herd, she didn't like the idea of a bunch of armed cops occupying her community. But like everyone else, she said nothing about it, continuing her stitching silently.

Tulip approached them. "Here you go," she said as she dropped off a basket of reset fabric, picking up the new ones Rowan and Three-Seven had stitched. She had unofficially assigned herself the role of coordinator, ferrying various stages of the tents from one part of assembly to the other. "I'll bring these over to...to recalibration," she said.

"Thank you, Lady Tulip," said Three-Seven.

Tulip frowned but held her tongue. Rowan thanked her as well and then resumed her work before Tulip had even left her sightline. She found she had been spending a lot of time with these two lately, especially with Three-Seven, who had been one of the first corpo refugees to ask to help with the tent project. "I need something to keep my mind off things," she had reasoned. "Besides, I miss cleaning."

Three-Seven looked calmer today, now that she had not come directly out of the ocean. She was wearing a used Restoration suit, though she hadn't figured out how most of its settings worked. It was at its default silver-steel color, with no shapes or patterns whatsoever. She had had to mess with her translation settings, since most people in the Eastic did not speak English, and she had managed to make her box's voice too high-pitched.

"Can I ask you a question?" Three-Seven's box squeakily asked as the two of them tried to even out the lump in their tent.

"Anything."

"Does your wife, this lord Úna, no, that's not it. You called her a what?" Three-Seven asked.

"A Head Shepherd."

"Yes, this Head Shepherd Úna. She wants to stop taking us from the Eastic, in. Does she have the authority to do that?"

Rowan pursed her lips. This had been an argument with her wife recently. Úna had made the case that resources were tight and that, for the sake of the herd, they should probably relocate the refugees elsewhere, merging her request with Peter's resolution to leave the Restoration. A resolution to leave was not as dramatic as it sounded. Salem threatened to leave the Restoration all the time as a matter of routine procedure, and yet something about this logic seemed off—almost Fallen-like. Why pressure the Restoration to use force to remove refugees? Other herds were even now sending their surpluses to Salem to help them; what did it matter if a few hundred people stayed for a while—it wasn't anyone's land.

She started to construct an argument in her head, and then realizing that she was perhaps crafting an answer too complex for what Three-Seven was asking for, said: "No, not technically. We don't own the land. Can't stop you from being here. I'm sure the Chamber is voting on a condemnation as we speak," responded Rowan, not stopping her work as she answered.

She pursed her lips, not sure if this was true. The peacekeepers, when they talked amongst themselves, sounded like they were backing Úna's relocation plan, and she wasn't sure how many in her herd would resist such an effort. People in Salem were already so upset by the outsiders from the Northeast Seven Shuttle's brief stay here, and the moment most of them had been cleared to leave, now corpos and peacekeepers had arrived. Gaia could be cruel sometimes. A part of her felt that most in Salem would accept whatever would return things to normal.

"No, you want to make sure not to press down too hard," she said, correcting Three-Seven's technique.

"You're good at this. I thought you were a writer?" Three-Seven asked, confused. "But you know how to repair things too."

"I am a writer, but most people here are not one thing. We take on shifts for whatever is needed. I'm guessing the Eastic Barony was not like that?"

Three-Seven shook her head. "I've been in Sanitation Optimization and Development for over 14 years. Her Majesty CEO's assistant assigned me to do that when she purchased my contract."

"That's not, it's not," Rowan stumbled over her words, trying not to sound paternalistic. Every time Three-Seven talked about the eastic, it sounded like a nightmare. "It's not how we do things here," she continued.

Three-Seven nodded thoughtfully. She looked out at the forest surrounding them as if this were some profound revelation. "Then why do you call yourself a writer if you do other things, I mean?"

Rowan hadn't really thought about it much before. "I enjoy it the most, I suppose. It's also more prestigious. The Writers' Cooperative doesn't accept everyone. They cap membership, and I was on a waitlist for years. I could still write, mind you. We don't deny people the labor they want to do, but my hours are not counted as much in trades with others. It's not like we do one-to-one trades like in your barony, your Eastic, but people here tend to value the plays and vids written by Co-op members more; they are made into more community events, and you get more for it. Does that make sense?"

"I'm not sure. You don't have money, but you have, like, standing? Like, instead of your salary paying for things, your ranking does? So how can a Lord Manager get more than a SOD worker?"

"Sort of. People can't be denied basic resources. Most herds have collective rations, and that makes debt servitude harder to do." Rowan had to stop themselves from shuddering. She continued. "But for luxury items, good food, dances, yeah. I'm not an academic; I write fiction, but Hosa Liu, xem is an economist. Xem called the Restoration 'an anarchistic, quasi, prestige-based economy, except for when it wasn't.' I can send you a link to one of xe's books in the archives."

"I'd like that." Three-Seven sounded excited, as if reading a textbook was the most exciting thing in her life at the moment. "You'll have to show me how to access the archives. My settings are still a mess," she laughed, referring to her suit.

There was a clearing of a throat. Rowan turned to see Calisto. They looked less haggard than they had been in days. "Rowan," they said, a warmness in their voice, "I am so sorry to interrupt, but could I talk to you for a moment?"

Trash, what did this person want? The sight of them still made her angry. Rowan couldn't help being resentful of the person who had failed so far to bring her justice. She didn't trust them, and a part of her wasn't sure if Calisto's 'nice act' was genuine or a front. Was she still in trouble for the search party? She had tried to ignore the murder investigation for the past day, throwing herself into the relief effort, but that didn't mean she hadn't contributed to derailing it.

Whatever it was, Rowan didn't want to have this confrontation in front of a traumatized refugee. She looked over to Three-Seven, who was still looking off into the distance, processing some unspoken thought. "Hey, Three-Seven, I'll be right back."

"Of course, if there is one thing I know how to do, it's get lost in my work."

Rowan didn't know what to say to that, so she said nothing. She walked with Calisto off past the tree line, away from the prying ears of those in camp. It was a nice day. The warm rays of the sun kissed her face. She had spent the last hour hunched over a table, and giving her legs and back a good stretch like this was pleasant.

"So what's this about?" Rowan asked bluntly. There was a moment of silence, and Rowan realized that she might be coming off as annoyed. "Sorry, I didn't mean it like that. I just meant, am I in trouble?"

"Oh, frack, sorry, I should have been clearer."

Rowan peered into Calisto's eyes. She was normally trash at analyzing their expressions, everything they said falling behind an impassive wall of objectivity, but right now, their words were not stiff or measured as they had been over the last few days.

Rowan did her best to smile. "It's fine. I mean, we're good."

Calisto let out a sigh of relief. They removed something from the pouch they carried, a wispy white one attached to their suit. It was food. The smell of salt and burnt crisps wafted through the air. "Nuts," Calisto asked, offering a handful. "I skipped breakfast."

Rowan shook her head.

Calisto swallowed a handful, chewed, and then said: "I've been impressed with how you've been organizing the relief effort."

"Is that why you came over? It was nothing."

Calisto frowned. "It's not nothing. I don't mean to be rude, but your herd is not the best with outsiders. With this vote to leave the Restoration, if the refugees aren't relocated. What you are doing here says a lot. It says a lot about you."

"Thank you?" Rowan said, still confused by what was happening here. This was more awkward than doing waste-to-mulch conversion. Was Calisto complimenting her for handing out a few blankets? She knew her herd could be touchy, but they were ultimately good stock. Surely, this was not the reason why they came over here?

"Though you're right that I have an ulterior motive."

There it was, Rowan thought triumphantly.

Calisto continued: "I wanted to ask for your help...with this case, I mean."

Rowan had to stop themselves from laughing. What was this exo even on about? Why would a peacekeeper want them to do anything? "What? But you were nervous about looping me in before."

Calisto paused, probably not wanting to offend Rowan: the coward.

"I was nervous because we weren't communicating, not because of getting you involved. Peacekeepers can loop community members into investigations. It's even encouraged.

Doesn't Strummer draw on community members during repairs?"

"Yeah, but she's not, you know."

"Not a peacekeeper, you mean."

Rowan was silent.

"It's okay. I understand. We aren't always the most understood Restorate organization. The Delegation was made for community repair specialists across the Restoration to just communicate with each other, and technically, any member can volunteer to be a peacekeeper. The rules aren't supposed to be any different. It's just some of us do work within a herd or collective, and some of us, peacekeepers, move between them."

"Nice speech and all, but you peacekeepers are different. We didn't even start calling Strummer a CRS until the Delegation formed. It was just a thing she did. And other CRS aren't required by law. I mean, sorry, directive." Rowan corrected, placing the word directive in air quotes.

"Technically, you're right. Listen, can we debate the finer merits of the peacekeeper program later?"

"You're only saying that because I'm winning."

"You're going to be very good at this."

Rowan smiled. Maybe this exo wasn't so bad after all.

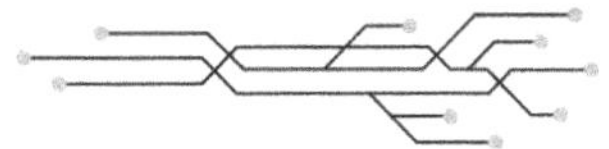

CALISTO

PRIVATE COAR DOWNLOAD/Article/How to keep your polycule in line/Author Haldan Kramer/9-7-2100

-> *Listen, with polyamory, everyone talks so Goddess much about communication this and communication that, but that's smog. Some people don't have time to check in every day, especially when years together mean that you know, for the most part, what your partner wants and thinks. You don't need to ask for permission for every little thing. Sometimes, you know what's best. That's why...*

TIME: 5:47 PM
DAY: FRIDAY 5-20-2101

Calisto and Rowan. It felt strange, the two of them attempting to work together. It made sense. Rowan was close to the events at hand, an ideal person to loop into the repair, but still, weird. The two of them met over by one of the more permanent food carts that Salem was leaving here for El Paso, the Forest Sprouters slotted to come next. The cart was built into the Earth's foundation and had a clay stove and a stasis chamber to store all sorts of proteins and carbs. A person was manning it, serving an assortment of soups that filled the area with the smell of meat, making their stomach crave the rich broths and salts.

They sat down on one of the small tree logs surrounding it, which had been filed down to serve as a weatherproof table. Sam was there, too, slurping on a bowl of soup and happily chatting with them. This conversation was not meant to be intimidating; it was just background and harmless questions.

Rowan started by mentioning that morning's Gaiaverse service. Strummer had apparently volunteered to lead it and delivered a passionate, albeit on-the-nose, sermon about grief.

"What's that she said about how grief can manifest as irritability?" Sam said in between slurps. "I felt really called out."

Rowan set down her spoon, laughing. "I thought she was talking about me."

"I guess we've all been affected by his death," and then their gaze drifting to Calisto, said, "Most of us, anyway."

Calisto swallowed a sigh from leaving their lips, deciding that this was yet another one of those frustrating microaggressions they had to let go.

"You told me you used to date Haldan?" Rowan continued, squeezing Calisto's hand ever so discreetly. "I remember you being around him all the time several years ago, and then you just weren't. What happened there?"

Sam seemed visibly uneasy. "Oh, yeah, it was, well, I have a lot of fond memories from that relationship."

Calisto cut in, deciding to use their tension with Sam to heighten their anxiety. "Why did it end?"

Sam looked at Rowan, a shameful look that Calisto knew read something along the lines of 'Please don't make me trash an ex in front of his mother.'

Calisto continued: "It's fine, you can speak freely. This is about the repair."

"I know he was sometimes an ass," Rowan affirmed.

This made Sam lighten a bit, though not entirely. "Well, sorry, Rowan, but he wasn't just oblivious; he was cruel sometimes. And he and Peter were always teaming up against me."

"I'm sorry," said Rowan, touching Sam's hand. "I didn't know. Not to that extent."

Sam accepted it, continuing. "Once, they both tried to convince me that I had agreed to mind them during a concert festival when I knew I hadn't. I am talking active, unapologetic gaslighting. It was small, but I spent an entire four days herding their high asses around, doing labor I didn't agree to, and it bothered me. It wasn't the first time it had happened, but it was the straw that broke everything. Our relationship didn't survive that weekend."

Calisto could sense Sam holding back even now, and this was good because it meant that a truth was still buried. "Would you say he was abusive?" Calisto asked gently.

"It's not; well, there were good moments too," said a flustered Sam, irritated eyes on the cusp of tears, answering Calisto's question in all but words. "And he didn't deserve to die over it."

"Were you the only one he treated poorly?"

"Well, there's Tulip. We were technically together. We didn't connect much when both of us dated Haldan. It was always the Haldan and Peter show, but I saw how they treated her."

"I heard they pushed her out of the polycule?" Calisto asked.

"Haldan, specifically. He convinced us to vote her out. Said she lied and was sleeping with other people. We were exclusive with each other, and at the time, by Gaia, I was so enamored with him."

Calisto was piecing together that Haldan was not the best person. "So that's why the relationship ended, because of the lying?"

Sam frowned. "No, not just that. I didn't like his politics either."

"Can you elaborate?" Calisto asked.

"It was the way that he talked about collectives sometimes. He thinks, thought that we, the Restoration, I mean, relied too heavily on what he called 'the commons.' He thought people should be more self-reliant, and I don't know, it felt so retro to me."

When they met up with Peter later, during a planned stroll in the woods, he was much blunter. "Yeah, his politics were weird," Peter said. "I love him, loved. I really did, but he had this habit of talking about how the Restoration had gone too far."

Peter was walking frantically as he said this, not paying attention to the various vines and bushes along the footpath that could snag a person if they weren't careful, and indeed, they had to stop walking as the prickles of a wild holly plant nicked an opening in his suit along his ankles.

Not one to let another's misfortune stop her, Rowan asked: "Others implied that you and he bullied partners together."

Bent over, pulling a tiny prickle from his skin, Peter sighed, and more than that, he looked ashamed. "We did. It's true. I am not proud of it. I probably wouldn't have stopped if he were," there was a pause. "If he were still alive. That sounds terrible, but it's true. I felt so strong with him."

"Have you checked in with a herd therapist? A CRS? Community therapy? Anyone about this?" Rowan asked. There was a forcefulness in her voice: an anger.

"No, I...I wanted to ignore it."

"Don't," Rowan said. "This is how people get killed." She swallowed hard on the word killed. "Go to Strummer and ask to do repair work with you and Sam, or I will." She then stormed off, leaving Peter to stew on her words.

Calisto looked at him. He looked very sad: a bully bullied by a man no one could even blame anymore because he was dead. Marx's hammer, life could be cruel. Who else had Haldan pissed off?

TWENTY-ONE

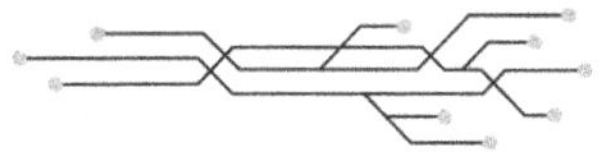

ROWAN

PUBLIC COAR DOWNLOAD/Article/The New Workers Collective/Author Garykillsfascists/5-21-2101

-> We all knew the militarization of the peace-keepers was inevitable. Let people pretend to be cops long enough, and eventually, they will start thinking they're an army. Reports have come in that peacekeepers mobilized in Salem, not to focus on a repair but to keep an eye on all of its new corpo refugees. We are on the precipice of a police state, mark my words.

TIME: 2:23 PM
DAY: SATURDAY 5-21-2101

Rowan was glaring at Úna, who was fidgeting with a new attachment she had fitted on the right arm of her suit. It was a weapon, a stun gun that could materialize into a small turret that lobbed a pellet that could briefly stun someone with ease. Her partner was playing with a gun, causing the jet-black, double-ended turret to form and reform like a child playing with a toy.

She was trying to concentrate, examining old drawings and COAR messages Haldan had sent her, to try to make sense of what Sam and Peter had said. Had he always been this cruel? And why hadn't she noticed? There had to be an answer buried beneath these terabytes of data, but every time she skimmed through painful mementos on her wrist, she became distracted by the clicking of Úna's arm as the gun spread into being like water and then clicked out of existence into a small, spherical half dome.

"Careful where you're pointing that thing," Rowan hissed.

Úna, who had been leaning on a comfortable bean bag chair as she fiddled with this weapon, made a face—a 'please don't overreact right now' face.

"It's not even armed." She added.

Semantics, her partner was really trying to argue her way around this? Had she learned nothing about their relationship in the past 15 years? "I don't care," Rowan huffed, "It's bad enough peacekeepers are running around with those *things*. You don't have to bring them inside our tent."

Úna tilted her head, analyzing Rowan like an insect in a jar, examining, prodding. "I need to learn how to work this thing. Only a couple of guys in Salem have these specs, and I don't want the peacekeepers to be the only people here who are holding this much firepower."

"Fine, frack the peacekeepers," Rowan said, and then added, not really giving up the argument. "All of this trouble because a few people show up. They're just refugees."

Úna shrugged. "I don't know, I just don't like it, and I don't like that we have cops roaming around either. There are too many non-Salemers around these days."

"Well, it feels xenophobic." Rowan cut.

"Maybe," Úna conceded.

"You know, it's really annoying when you just agree with me like that. Takes the momentum out of the fight."

Úna merely shrugged.

"I love you," Rowan said, moving over to Úna to give her a big wet kiss.

"I love you too, Grumpy Bear."

Rowan waved her wife off and left their tent. The herd was a bustle of activity. Tents were firmly rooted. Carts were serving up food. They had spent so many weeks packing their lives into boxes and bags, and now they had sprawled out again, acting as though they would live here forever. She even saw some soil-mitigation experts messing with seed guns, doing the work that a Forest Sprouter like herd El Paso should be doing. Boredom bred disruption, she supposed.

She met Calisto deep in the woods, away from any foot-paths, in a clearing with no noticeable landmarks or vistas. In a region surrounded by beauty, it was a boring sight, but the work they were doing required as few prying eyes as possible, so boring was good.

Calisto saw Rowan coming and waved. They had fitted their suit to have a camouflage pattern, something Rowan shifted to the moment she saw it.

"Rowan," they stated simply.

"Calisto, how's life? You have kids, right?" Frack, this small talk was awkward. Just because Rowan no longer hated this person's guts didn't mean they knew each other that well.

"I do. Two. A boy and an enby. They miss me. My wife, Colibri, is upset that I haven't solved this case yet so that she can come here on vacation. She might be packing her bags as we speak, for all I know."

"Oh," Rowan said guiltily. She hadn't conceptualized Calisto as their own person with a life that the difficulties of this case might have disrupted.

"It's alright. She will manage. We have nothing to lose but our chains."

Rowan smiled uneasily. She truthfully hadn't spent a lot of time with Christian Marxists. Salem was very insular when it came to religion, or at least, she hadn't heard many people talk about anything other than Gaiaverse. She was beginning to realize that maybe that wasn't the same thing.

"Apologies if this is rude, but I hadn't heard you talk about your religion that much?"

Calisto looked taken aback. "Oh, did I say something?"

"You talked about chains."

"My scripture is slipping. I hadn't realized. I try to tamp down on that stuff when I'm on a case, but it slips sometimes. Habits and all."

Rowan nodded thoughtfully. What were her habits, she wondered? She needed to think on that. "Don't apologize," she continued. "People shouldn't have to, for thinking differently."

Calisto stared at her with a wide-eyed expression.

"What?" Rowan said.

"You realize that not that long ago, you were reading into me for dressing in a way that you didn't like."

"Sorry," Rowan said sheepishly.

"Am I having an effect on you, Rowan Kramer?"

"Shut it," Rowan blushed. "Let's do the thing we came here to do," she said, referring to the tent bundle she had in her hands.

"Let's," Calisto said simply.

Rowan walked to the center of the clearing. She set the bundle, a wispy mesh that was perfectly still and could be confused for an ordinary piece of refuse, down on the dirt. From a distance, it became lost amongst the weeds and tall grasses, but Rowan could see it there, waiting. She pulled on a clear red string on its side and stepped away. Over about thirty seconds, the tent expanded to the size of a multi-person hover vehicle.

"It never gets old to see that happen," Calisto said.

Rowan considered disagreeing; as for someone in a herd, it was as routine as flicking your wrist, but she bit her tongue and reconsidered.

We are trying not to externalize, remember, she reminded herself.

Instead, she added to the thought. "It is amazing how advanced we've become in such a short period. Talking to Three-Seven has made me appreciate that more. I suppose that's a thing I've stopped noting until recently."

"Habits are a polluted pain," Calisto joked. "You ready?" they asked, opening the flap of the tent, *his* tent. Haldan had left it behind to be reused since he would've had housing provided in the Bangalore Collective. In all the craziness, she hadn't had the chance to wipe the data living within its fibers or sort through the small box of static knick-knacks he hadn't brought with him.

"I thought I would be more ready for this," Rowan breathed heavily. He was dead. He was really gone. "With his body buried, I thought, I don't know that it would be easier. Gaia, I hate this."

Calisto turned to her. "Does touch bother you?" Rowan shook her head, and Calisto placed a reassuring hand on her shoulder. "This reaction is normal. With all the hecticness of this case, you haven't had time to grieve much."

"I know that intellectually, but every time I start to think about it. It hurts so much, and..." Rowan gasped a deep, painful breath, her eyes watery.

"Take a breath. We can pause this if you need time."

Rowan took a deep breath, held it in, exhaled, and repeated the process: "No, I don't need that. I want to do this."

Calisto nodded empathetically and pulled out a box with a nanowire interface protruding from it. Rowan watched as Calisto plugged the interface into the tent. The data for the tent was encrypted, but Rowan knew the access codes (an old sign of trust from her late son), and with a few clicks of their wrist, Calisto used them to override the tent's security.

"I'm sending you access now," they said, and then added. "Friend."

Rowan didn't respond to this addition, but she didn't dispute it either, and instead, she focused on the old files flooding her wrist feed. Haldan had had so much of his life in these fibers. Pictures of when their herd had passed through the Florida Nub and encountered an endangered congregation of American alligators, their grey scales half-emerged in the murky waters. Pictures of the Cheyenne Wastelands, their suits filtered with hundreds of ugly patches meant to filter out the radiation. Purple and green crystals budded outward like trees from a failed Corpo Remediation Plan, so that the background was like an alien forest. She sorted through smiles and frowns. Pictures and entertainment videos from streamers. Even some Salem Writers' Cooperative content written by Rowan that made her want to smile and cry all at the same time. He had loved her.

He also had been a frackin' heartbreaker. She came across an old nonencrypted diary feed. It felt like an invasion of trust to read through it. When he was younger, their rule had always been that Úna and her would never look at this unless there were a very good reason. She guessed being murdered qualified. His most recent entries depicted how he had maliciously planned to manipulate his way into Bangalore.

"Listen to this from a couple of years ago," Rowan called out to Calisto, who was also wordlessly immersed in their feed. "I need to get into Bangalore. This herd is causing me to lose my mind. Everything is so inefficient, so chaotic. They are all so content to be small. I hate it, but I've been on the waitlist for a year, and waiting any longer feels like torture. I have a friend who might be able to tamper with the rankings waitlist."

"That's definitely manipulative behavior. Sorry, that must be rough to hear," said Calisto.

"I didn't think he was this bad." She wanted to punch something. "Why didn't we catch this? Why is this psych work being done now?" Rowan wasn't sure if she meant it for this case or in life. She guessed she meant both.

"I should've done it," Calisto affirmed. "Truthfully, my supervisor had asked me to end this case quickly. Haldan had a psych profile that Strummer sent me. It seemed adequate at the time. Clearly, I was wrong. Too many things were rushed in this case for convenience's sake."

Rowan hadn't realized that she had been pacing around Calisto like a shark in the water.

"Do you want me to, to give you space?" asked Calisto uneasily.

"No, I'll unpack this in polluted therapy later."

Calisto nodded, always nodding, because they frackin' cared. "Are you prepared to learn more information?" They asked gingerly.

"Yes." Rowan barked out.

Calisto, who had returned their eyes to their feed, moved back to the case. "When I look through your son's media, I see a lot of Fallen titles. Your son loved films about business. He even read pro-resource extraction scholars such as Ayn Rand and Adam Smith."

Rowan had moved to hover over Calisto's shoulder, looking at the information they had curated. "Smog, his most read text was Wealth of Nations?"

"I think it's clear that he had pro-corpo sympathies. He had even pinged the bio information of every barony within the Restoration and a few outside of it."

Rowan couldn't help but think that she had never understood her son at all. Had he always been an abusive, narcissistic libertarian? Had she and Úna really raised this stranger? This person who could manipulate this system like he was moving chess pieces across a board?

"Let's look at his keepsakes," prompted Calisto after several seconds of Rowan being too wrapped up in her thoughts. She pinged Strummer to ask for a therapy session soon, and then nodded.

Calisto lifted the lid of the static metal box. It came off readily. They placed it on the tent floor and started examining the items inside the box. Rowan picked up a piece she remembered giving to Haldan: an old writer's pad she gave him back when he loved writing, back when he wanted to follow in her footsteps. A stage that had lasted less than a month. He had to have been no older than seven? Eight?

"That looks...like a history vid," said Calisto. They lifted a clear sphere with a bronze metal base from the box. Inside the sphere was a diorama of a Fallen building inside, what they used to call a skyscraper.

"It's called a snow globe. I never understood why he'd printed it. It used to be where he kept his 'super secret diary,'" Rowan laughed, placing super secret in air quotes.

Calisto perked up when they heard this. "How did it work?"

Rowan grabbed the snow globe and twisted the base until part of it fell off with a click. Underneath was an entry pad for a code, flashing with eight dashes. "It's not networked. Analogue. He designed it after going through a cryptography phase. And if you type in the right passcode, the data port unlocks."

"Can we brute force it open? There are only eight inputs?"

Rowan shrugged. She was not sure. "I remember him building a program to wipe the data if there were enough wrong entries, but he was 11 when he built it and deleted his diary several times because he forgot the password." Rowan laughed, briefly forgetting that her son was dead. She frowned. "It's a kids' toy. Surely you don't think there's anything on it?"

"You never know," Calisto said hopefully. "Do you remember the code?"

Rowan shook her head. "He never told me. We tried not to pry into that sort of stuff."

Calisto consulted their wrist. "Could be a date. Try 09-03-1776. It's when the *Wealth of Nations* was published, according to the archives."

Rowan typed it in, but nothing. They tried several entries. His birthday. Peter's birthday. Úna's birthday. Her birthday, and she felt like trash when that one didn't work. After the Fifth attempt, it flashed a warning that it had only four more attempts left before deletion.

"We have to be careful," Calisto warned, not many chances left.

"I have a suspicion," Rowan said darkly, not wanting to be right, but I don't want to type it in, could you, could you do it?"

Calisto nodded as she handed them the snow globe. Gaia, let her be wrong. He had been so happy when he got to the Cods. She assumed he was happy to be going to Bangalore, but there was something about the way he had looked out that night over the water.

"Let me just get the date right," she said, scanning the bio of a particular barony. "Type 02-11-2030. It's when the Eastic was founded."

There was a click as the port container opened. The information shouldn't have been a surprise, given the realization that opened the diary. Haldan had apparently been quite the believer. As they read his diary, there was a grandiose way he depicted his history and beliefs. "There is a burden in knowing that you are a Great Man trapped in a society that is soft," began one ancient entry written six years ago. "The Restoration is a sick, weak place that confines Great Men to small things. We must build something better, something natural."

"Listen to this," Calisto, who had ported a version over to their suit, said. "Tulip is no longer useful. I'm going to convince Sam to vote her out of the polycule. Peter will back me on it." Calisto looked up from the feed. "Sounds like Sam wasn't lying."

"No, they weren't," Rowan said weakly.

She had nothing to punch. By Gaia, why was there nothing in this tent except for a small box and an even smaller snow globe she couldn't touch because of this frackin' investigation? She considered throwing it, imagining chucking it against the ground as it shattered, the pathetic imitation of a Fallen city fracturing into a dozen pieces. Instead, she howled. "FRACK. Frack. Frack that arrogant trash. That ungrateful smog. That, that." She let out a deep breath, choking on tears. "Why is this hard? Why did I see nothing?"

"Can I touch you?" Calisto asked.

Rowan shook her head. She had to get out of here: out of this tent with awful, terrible secrets. She darted out and ran, not to camp or the cliff, but to the shore. She moved across the sands to the edge of the water, glaring at the disgusting dome half a kilometer out, shining dim lights powered by smog, and small, outdated people, who somehow had taken her son from her in some twisted game she still didn't understand.

She sat there, plopping down where the tides were hitting the sands. She didn't care about getting wet, even welcomed it. Let it take her, but as the sun set and the pale light of the moon illuminated the shore, the tide waned, retreating away from her like everything else until it didn't even touch her feet. *The coward.*

"We've been looking for you," said a voice she knew, a voice she loved.

She turned to see Úna. "I want to be alone." She ordered.

"No, you don't."

"No, I don't," Rowan conceded. "Gaia, I hate that you know so much about me."

"I've been with you for decades, Grumpy Bear. I know you. The good and the crazy."

"There was so much about him I didn't know."

"Calisto told me what happened. I…" It was Úna who started crying. This was a strange development. She plopped next to Rowan and hugged her, burying her head into her shoulder. "I should've told you. It's my fault."

"Honey, how could you have known? He kept so many secrets."

"You don't get it. I knew he liked corpos," she interjected, "Like he really liked them. He talked about that nonsense all the time."

"I, honey, why didn't you just tell me?"

Úna stuttered. "I, I, I, I just thought that if we ignored it, kept moving, he'd grow out of it. But he didn't, and those polluted monsters brainwashed him," she heaved, pointing to the Eastic, her tears falling onto her moonlit skin."

"But why did you all keep this from me? I wouldn't have judged him."

A crude laughed penetrated Úna's sobbing. "Don't be serious, baby. You judged him all the time. You didn't like his purple eyes. His hobbies. Who he fucked. He probably did tell you, and you monologued at him until he shut up."

"I...maybe. I can be harsh." Rowan conceded.

"We're both pretty harsh."

Rowan wiped away the tears from her wife's cheek. "We need to stop doing that," Úna said nothing, and so Rowan then added, "There is nothing you could say that would make me hate you."

"I love you," Úna said, kissing her.

"I love you too."

The two of them held each other and then made love. After they finished, they cuddled on the sands, their suits keeping out the grit and irritation, leaving only warm bliss as they watched the shore until sunrise. Then, they headed back to camp, leaving the Eastic behind them.

TWENTY-TWO

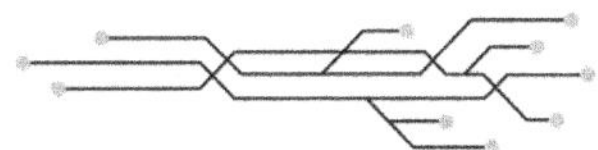

CALISTO

PUBLIC COAR DOWNLOAD/Book/The Restoration Is A Paradox/Author Hosa Liu/3-8-2094

-> In the same way the Restoration has not ended capitalism in the Americas by still allowing the baronies to lay claim to land and things, it has not stopped the sale of its fellow human beings. The baronies traffic human beings all across the Americas, and while it's easy to see these events as isolated incidents, one must naturally ask how such people are transported between large swathes of territory that do not permit slavery. There are no train stations between baronies. No great roads. No flight paths. All of these were destroyed during the Second American Civil War and continue to be destroyed by anyone so inclined to do so (and many are).

-> So how, my dear reader, does this happen? The answer is that people within the Restoration, either for resources, prestige, or simply resentment, help them. If we look at…

TIME: 10:22 AM
DAY: SUNDAY 5-22-2101

alisto was lost in the woods again. They hadn't realized how far they had strolled away until it was time to turn around. It was oddly beautiful. From their travels doing repairs from herd to herd, they were used to a variety of locals at this point: sun-burnt orange mesas, windswept plains, radiated wastelands, and bogs that seemed to teem with an untold multitude of life, but a pine forest overlooking the water, as the crackle of the waves could be heard in the distance was another pleasant memory to add to the collection.

They could see the Eastic from here. It had resumed pumping plumes of black smoke into the atmosphere: the normal activity of the barony was very much again on track. The refugees had stopped coming yesterday evening, which meant whatever fighting had occurred in that evil place had stopped for now: a problem that was outside Calisto's sphere of care. The barony was a distinctive sight, and yet, despite the landmark, it did nothing to help Calisto return to camp. They shamefully decided to send a private ping for assistance to Rowan, who was positively gleeful to rub it in how badly Calisto was at directions.

"We aren't even that far," she chided when she at last found them.

"You caught me. I'm bad at directions." Calisto joked.

Rowan rolled her eyes.

"Now, are you prepped for the interview?" Calisto continued.

She nodded. "I think so. I read your report last night. I think you're wrong about her, though. We should be interviewing Peter, not Tulip."

"Believe me, we will get to Peter. We are interviewing all Haldan's old partners, considering what we now know." Calisto paused here, still not quite used to the idea of having the bereaved so comfortable chatting about her loved one's murder. Calisto was, on the one hand, relieved that Rowan had agreed to work with them. Getting a person to help during interviews was always a boon, since it tended to soften interviewees and provide insider information that was hard to get in a report. But on the other hand, Rowan was like a force of nature they weren't sure they could control.

Remember your title, their mentor affirmed. *This is about the community. She should be involved.*

"Besides," Calisto plodded forward, "Her behavior warrants scrutiny. She was suddenly with him the night before the murder after years of separation. And she had a motive. Haldan was cruel to her."

"He was cruel to a lot of people," Rowan said, a swelling of deep self-pity, like an algae bloom emerging from the ocean floor, overtaking her for a fraction of a second. "That doesn't mean much."

Calisto thoughtfully considered what Rowan was saying. The two of them had not stopped walking, moving through the new-growth forest casually, treading over the logs and stones that had not been cleared from the footpath. "Maybe. But I've been looking into her background. Her parents didn't come with her when she escaped from the Alaskan Freehold Barony. She applied to the Restoration alone."

"Poor Tulip." Rowan gasped, and then, thinking about it more, frowned. "Wait, that's why you think she did it. That's quite the stretch, isn't it? It's not like all corpos know each other."

"Yes, but they do disclose their… smog, how do I say this, their assets in their earning statements…when they sell them."

Rowan looked horrified, and Calisto couldn't blame her. It was not easy to reckon with the fact that slavery was very common in the Americas, at least among the baronies. Roxane Chapman had delivered a rousing speech just last year about how Groundwork was close to solving the problem, but having researched the baronies' trade disclosures last night, the reality had been more sobering. The number of people trafficked seemed to be rising, not going down.

Rowan started fumbling with a piece of fabric she pulled from one of her many pockets. "Are you talking about slavery?"

"I am."

"Because," Rowan continued, practically destroying the fabric in her hands as she tried to play with it. "I may not know Tulip that well, but I can tell what kind of person she is. She may seem melodramatic because she is, but she's also a deeply kind sort. She didn't have to walk me through a panic attack or help with the Eastic refugees, but she did. And she exposed herself as a corpo to the herd in the process. Why would she do that if she were a secret human trafficker? It's ridiculous."

Rowan's breath was heavy, and everything in Calisto knew pressing too hard would be a bad idea.

Go gently, Sirius advised. *You don't actually know everything.*

Calisto remained firm but not unkind. "You misunderstand me. Her parents didn't come with her when she escaped from the Alaskan Freehold Barony, but they were sold to the Eastern Shore Trading Combine, the Eastic as you call it, several days before the murder. I have the receipt here. Baronies post information of publicly traded assets to their version of the COAR," they said calmly, swiping the information to her console.

Rowan's expression shifted as she read the information on her wrist. "Smog. That's leverage. So the motive was that a barony was blackmailing her? Why?"

Calisto shrugged their shoulders. "I have no idea. You're smart, Rowan, and you're asking the right questions. Maybe Tulip wasn't involved, but we need to interview her."

Rowan nodded. "Frack, fine, let's do this."

While the two of them chatted about possible questions to go over, Calisto quietly pinged Sirius—the droid AI, not the voice inside their own mind— for Shepherd Sam to get Tulip and ask her to wait in Calisto's tent for some follow-up questions. They didn't tell Sam to do so with urgency. They didn't know how long Tulip would stick around now that information was starting to click into place, so they wanted to be careful not to spook her.

It took Rowan no time to guide Calisto back to the camp. The footpath bled into the bustling clearing that Salem (and for the time being Calisto) now called home. They moved quickly through the half-packed tents and recently extinguished campfires smoldering from the end of the morning's breakfast.

"Now remember," Calisto cautioned as they approached their tent, "Only engage when you feel comfortable. We can always debrief afterward," and then, after a beat of contemplative silence, asked: "Shall we?" motioning to the flap of their temporary home. They held it open for Rowan to walk through, which she did without resistance. Tulip was already there, sitting on a small gray mat that had been pumped up for greater height and comfort. She was tapping her right foot anxiously.

"Rowan, it's good to see you," Tulip said warmly.

"Likewise, Tulip."

"And here comes our glorious cop of the hour," Tulip jabbed, staring at Calisto as they entered. "I heard Rowan was working with you, but I didn't want to believe it."

"I wanted to ask you some questions," Calisto said neutrally, trying their best for a smile not to leave their face.

"And if I refuse?" Tulip asked. Her voice had shifted to something more reserved.

Calisto had been waiting for this question. They tapped their wrist, and a holographic image of a document was projected toward Tulip's line of sight on the ground. "A Restorate writ. I'm afraid the Chamber strongly requests that you speak with us."

"I see Groundworks wasting no time employing its new toy. Does the law require me to?" Tulip asked bitterly.

"By consensus, actually. Everyone in the Chamber eventually agreed to it this morning, and your Head Shepherd signed off on it, which was the approval process Salem decided when passing the Peacekeeper Directive."

"I didn't vote on that law," she said, the word law dripping with hatred, "and I don't remember being included in such a consensus," Tulip scoffed. "But I see Groundwork is continuing its long tradition of twisting words until they're unrecognizable."

"Take your time to read it." Calisto deflected, feeling it would be unwise to touch such a topic.

"I don't need a document to tell me when I am being discriminated against for being born a Corpo."

Calisto noticed that Rowan looked uneasy at this development and regretted not telling her about the writ during their conversation in the woods. That had been an oversight. Rowan raised her eyebrow and gave Calisto a look, a 'why the frack did you not tell me about this' look.

"Sorry," Calisto typed on their wrist and then turned to Tulip, saying. "Please, this has nothing to do with discrimination. We just want to know the truth."

"Sure, whatever," Tulip responded, holding her tongue.

Rowan was tapping on her wrist. A message came in with a soft ping. "No more surprises," the message demanded.

Calisto nodded. They breathed and started to dig into questioning. They just needed to get to work, and the rest would follow. They pulled up a list of questions and notes they had prepared for this moment. It was always good to have something to refer to, even when interviews, more often than not, quickly spun off the rails.

Question one: "It says here in the report that you dated Haldan?"

"I've dated a lot of people. Beth from my Troupe. Even Anderson, your murder suspect, I believe."

"Representative Anderson, you mean?" Calisto clarified.

"Yes."

"So you dated both Haldan and Anderson."

Tulip sighed. "Yes, I was part of their polycule, once upon a time, with Peter too."

Calisto moved to a follow-up question: "Did you like Haldan?"

Tulip scoffed. "As much as you can like an ex that drops you." Tulip was trying to sound removed; however, her voice cracked as she said the word ex.

"Care to tell me more?"

"I don't," She said, stopping the anxious tapping of her foot.

Resistance, they would pick up on this later, but first, let it simmer. Okay, moving to question 5. "That's fine," Calisto nodded. "Let's focus on the day of the alleged murder on the Seven. You were practicing with your troupe, is that right?"

"I was practicing lines," she corrected, and with this, Tulip started to get a little animated. "For an old story called the Legend of Moshup. It's about a giant named Moshup that shaped an island near here that doesn't exist anymore because Fallen trash sank it to the bottom of the ocean."

"I thought you were practicing a comedy," Rowan interjected for the first time. "You told me so the other day."

"That's a matter of perspective, don't you think?" smirked Tulip. "I think our entire colonial history is quite funny in a sad, fracked-up kind of way. It's a dark comedy, a little more nuanced than some of your plays." She was looking at Rowan in the way a toddler does when they want to goad their older sibling into a fight.

Rowan opened her mouth to say something, but Calisto held up their hand to cut her off. "Was there anyone there to see you practicing lines?"

"No, I was alone in the woods, like half the frackin' herd from time to time. I'm sure to a budding Groundwork cop, that makes me guilty."

She was angry, prideful even. Calisto could hear Sirius lecturing them to latch onto this moment, to improvise. *See what fruits you can shake from the tree.*

"You don't like authority very much, cops or otherwise, do you?" They asked at last.

Tulip switched back to being aloof. "Perceptive," she chided. "I hate authority. The Chamber. The Fallen. The Baronies. You. You're pretending to lay claim to something you don't control, and it boils my blood just thinking about it."

"Being enslaved to a barony probably didn't help."

"No, it did not."

"You would never help them?"

"What in Gaia's brilliant green Earth is this about?" Tulip shouted.

"We received some intelligence," Calisto said, letting the 'we' imply Rowan as well. "Were you aware that your parents were transferred to the Eastic recently?"

Tulip's expression changed, not into tears or a melodramatic gasp, but one of acceptance. "By transferred, you mean sold against their will? Yes. I guess there is no point in denying it. Yes, I was. I've been monitoring the barony disclosures ever since I left, just in case."

"Tulip," Rowan gasped empathetically. "Why didn't you tell anyone?"

"Because of conversations like this," Tulip said angrily, gesturing to the room. "Say I am guilty."

"Are you guilty?" Calisto asked.

"Let me finish, you smog. For argument's sake, say I did it. You didn't get here because of your detective work, Peacekeeper Calisto," the word peacekeeper dripping with disdain. "Corpos are bad, so you assumed I must be. It doesn't matter what else."

"But did you do it?" Rowan asked, tears now running down her cheek. "Did you kill my baby boy?"

Tulip got silent for a moment. "I... frack," and then, anger bubbling up again, said, "Why would I tell you if I did?"

Calisto could see a dark thought churning in Rowan's head. The lines on her umber, reddish brown temple, deepening as they watched her. Sometimes, they saw it in their coworkers: other peacekeepers on the verge of an answer and a person frustratingly standing in their way. The thought was always the same: *Do I destroy this person today? Do I use my position of authority to make them tell me?*

"It's okay," Calisto prodded. "You can say it, Rowan."

"We could kill them easily if you don't," Rowan whispered coldly. "Wouldn't even have to be that direct about it. I know enough from story research that our internal channels are spied on by baronies all the time. They are in our systems. We would merely list you as an informant on a semi-public channel. Make the Eastic think you've turned. They'd probably execute your parents before the end of the day."

"Rowan," Tulip whispered. "Please, I would never..."

"My boy is dead," Rowan screamed. "I don't think you can possibly know what that feels like, but you could, you could very soon."

"Are you working for the Eastic?" Calisto asked again.

Tulip nodded, tears streaming down her face, ugly wails leaving her throat as she struggled to put a sentence together. "I... yes...but no. I...I was working with him." Tulip took in a deep breath, trying her best not to choke on her words. "Anderson used my parents to get me...and your son alone together on the ferry."

A million threads untangled in Calisto's head at once. It was not a surprise that Anderson had killed Haldan: that had been the most likely answer from day one, but to be aligned with the Eastic Barony made no sense whatsoever. He had been fighting to advance a directive that would make it impossible for herds to incorporate. He was the last person who would have aligned with them unless that had all been an elaborate cover.

Calm down and establish a baseline first, Sirius advised.

"How did you help him with the murder?"

"I...after Haldan and Anderson fought on the ferry, I lured Haldan to the closet under the pretext of sex, injected him with a paralyzing agent from behind, and then closed the door. Anderson did the rest."

"The Vecuronium bromide," Calisto inquired.

"I have no idea what it was," Tulip scoffed, "Anderson told me what to do, and I did what I was told."

"The Vecuronium bromide," Calisto continued, "was in his system for a long time."

Tulip shrugged. "Maybe he injected him beforehand, too, at a lower dose. I don't know. I was following orders, not asking questions."

"But why would he go with you at all?" Rowan asked angrily. "You weren't exactly his favorite person."

Tulip smiled. "I leaned into Haldan's narcissism. You have to understand, when Haldan and I were together, I found him so charismatic. Intoxicating even. Gaia, I loved him," she smiled, but just as quickly, it turned into a painful frown. "But he would always make me feel like trash. I would ask him to say sorry for the smallest of things, and somehow, the conversation would always end with me being the one at fault. He'd convinced me of being a narcissist by the end, a painful bit of projection."

"I...I know," Rowan said shamefully, opening her mouth and then swallowing.

Calisto placed a consolatory hand on Rowan's shoulder and then turned to Tulip and said, "What does any of this have to do with the murder?"

"After I started pushing back at his abuse," Tulip continued, "He convinced everyone in the polycule that I was crazy and that they should drop me, which they did."

"Tulip, I'm so sorry..." Rowan started, but she was unable to say anything else.

Tulip ignored Rowan. "Anyway, I knew all I had to do to get back into his good graces was tell him I was wrong, to apologize for resisting his abuse, and of course, it worked."

"But no one saw you there," Calisto stated.

"Because I didn't look like myself," Tulip pulled out a mask, a delicate piece of gray fabric—a holomask. She wrapped it around her face until it was completely shrouded in dark grey. She tapped on the fabric as it became enveloped in lights, which quickly filled in the details of someone else, a gaunt face they had never seen before.

"Haldan didn't even know it was me until several minutes before he died."

TWENTY-THREE

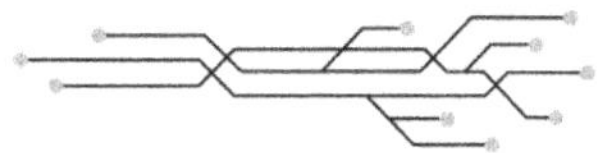

ROWAN

PRIVATE COAR THREAD Salem/Resolutions/063467/
Expulsion Debate/5-22-2101
-> *For (54)*
-> *collapse*
-> *Against (1)*
-> **Tulip Bellwether:** *My herd, I am probably not
your favorite person right now.*

*-> I wanted to explain to you why I helped Rep-
resentative Anderson murder Haldan Kramer. I
don't deny it. I may not have been the one to
slit his throat, but I was complicit. I think I
owe you not only an explanation for this behavior, but also an explanation of why I believe I
deserve not to be expelled from this community.*

*-> It would be easy to blame everything on
blackmail. Anderson had my parents' lives in
his hands, and he used that to rope me into his
scheme. I could pretend I was doing everything
against my will, but that would be only partially true. Haldan was a terrible person. He
not only abused me but also many others. If you
probe deeply, you will realize that he was quite*

manipulative. He gaslit people. He used them for favors and then did not give back to the community he drained from.

-> I regret helping Anderson, but I do not regret hurting Haldan. We are Reclaimers. We are meant to take out the bad so that new life can grow. That is what I have done. I consider it a kindness, and I hope you will agree.

TIME: 11:44 AM
DAY: MONDAY 5-23-2101

t feels wrong," Rowan exclaimed.

She and Strummer were on a stroll through an unfamiliar part of the island: a swamp nestled between two broad cliff sides. It was a canyon of muck and cattails. A bridge was here, with its floating wooden platforms that adjusted to the water level. Insects were also everywhere. Rowan had guiltily brought along a mod with a minor sonic field to ward off the mosquitoes, not wanting to deal with the buzzing that gave her a headache, and Gaia should, did, love her enough to understand that: a thought Rowan would have considered cowardly over a week ago.

Strummer had not brought any mods. She was a believer of Salem's version of the Gaiverse. While she would unconsciously swat mosquitoes from time to time, she mostly let them be without comment. Yet despite this unwavering faith, her commitment appeared to be a personal oath that, as far as Rowan could tell, Strummer did not impose on others like Rowan had. Like Rowan sometimes did, even now.

"You don't like the result?" Strummer asked, tapping away at her wrist with gentle strokes.

"No, I'm glad she was caught. It's not like I voted with her. I just." Rowan paused.

She wasn't sure how she felt. It's true Tulip had been coerced into things under the threat of blackmail, and that seemed to be forgivable to many at last night's debate, but being so unremorseful that you refuse any attempts at repair: that had tipped the vote overwhelmingly toward Tulip's expulsion. The vote was swift and nearly unanimous at 289-4. Rowan didn't know where Tulip would go next. Maybe she would live out her days as a hermit. Maybe she would voluntarily check herself into a rehabilitation center, so another herd or collective might be more inclined to take her in. Perhaps leave the Restoration forever. Wherever it was, it wasn't going to be here.

For the time being, she was being held in her own tent, unrestrained until she finished packing. Rowan had pried from Úna that an ankle monitor had been placed on Tulip, which could not be removed. Its privacy settings had been revoked, so if Tulip left the perimeter of the tent, every Shepherd in a nearby area would be notified. At their point in technological development, metal bars in a cell were redundant. She couldn't harm anyone again, not really.

Yet none of this made Rowan feel better. "I wish it did," she told Strummer. "But it just makes me feel like trash."

"What were you expecting it to do?"

"I don't know. I bullied this person into a confession, Strum. I threatened to reveal information in such a way that the barony would have killed her parents. And now we have one of the murderers, and I still feel like shit. Gaia, what was the point of any of it?"

"I don't know," Strummer responded quietly. "I don't know. But I'm glad you're recognizing that you're hurt. As well as how you sometimes externalize that hurt onto others, like with bullying Tulip. I hope you consider apologizing to her in the future, once you've processed this."

"I will consider it. And I know it's bad to hurt people. I just feel so crazy sometimes that hurting others is the only thing that makes sense. It makes me feel better."

"Not for very long, I imagine."

Rowan shook her head. It didn't: being cruel would give her a momentary bit of catharsis, but then it would make her feel like smog.

Strummer continued: "Why do you think you're crazy, Rowan? You're one of the smartest people I know."

"Well, my parents sometimes said that. And Úna. She calls me crazy a lot."

Strummer wrote something on her wrist, and Rowan was worried that Strummer would think terrible, untrue things about her relationship with Úna, and the last thing she wanted was yet another repair.

"Never, in a mean way," Rowan assured her. "It's a joke."

Strummer nodded, though she did not look convinced. "If that's your humor in your relationship, then that's your humor. I just hope you realize that you don't have to accept a joke like that just because someone claims it's love."

"I do."

She grimaced, but did not pursue the subject any further. "You've been doing your exercises?"

"I have. Five colors. Four sounds and all that nonsense."

Rowan looked away. She was not lying about that, but not every day as she had promised, and failure was, well, she didn't like admitting to it.

Not too far in the distance, Rowan spied the base for a research outpost. This area had been flagged for having a unique frog species thought to be extinct. The base was a reddish-orange square made of some new wood composite, yet right now, the only thing on top of it was a towering nanoweave, its central matter decompressor humming softly, never able to truly turn off. Rowan had to switch off some mods on her suit, as a compressor of this size was giving her strange feedback.

"That's new," Rowan deflected, pointing to the weave.

"Rowan," Strummer asserted.

"Yes, I am doing my exercises, just not every day."

"That's fine. Routines take a while to establish. Continue trying to do so, even if it's hard." Rowan swallowed, choosing not to see that as an insult because it wasn't one. Not everyone was waiting to attack her. She didn't have to hurt herself and others to feel safe.

Strummer was going through her notes on her wrist, framing a new question. "I see you haven't requested an individual or communal therapist, now that Salem's therapists have come back from their conference."

"No, you haven't fracked up yet. Why bother?"

"I see."

They walked along the path in silence for a bit. When they had reached the end of their session, Strummer excused herself, and Rowan doubled back to the base of the science station, or she should say the future science station. Herd El Paso, the Forest Sprouter herd slotted to come in after Salem, had yet to build it, but they would. Their Herd had voted to, and so her herd had begun that foundation as it had done so many times before. She wondered if the Maintainers would turn this area into a science collective after the Forest Sprouters; it certainly had the makings of it.

Rowan parked herself underneath the weave. She enjoyed its eerie hum, brooding like her, or would Strummer say avoidant? That felt more apt. She didn't want to go back to camp. People were treating her strangely, a pitiful mix of awkward guilt and obligation. She wanted nothing to do with it. She brooded there for what felt like an eternity, but was really more like twenty minutes.

Úna pinged her after a while. It looked like she had pinged her an hour ago, but the weave had messed with her signal. "Where are you?" Her wife had messaged, annoyingly, arguably concerned.

Rowan considered petulantly not telling her, but she thought better of it, walking a few feet away to send her location with a flick of her wrist, and then moving back under the weave. She liked being cut off. Rowan tried not to count the minutes, positioning herself away from the path, so Úna would have to get her attention first. Rowan practiced what she would say, crafting an elaborate monologue about the nature of grief.

"Hey, Grumpy Bear," Úna said sweetly, approaching Rowan, who had done her best not to pretend like she had noticed every second of Úna's clodding footsteps. She touched Rowan's shoulder like she was a flower, starved of sunlight, of her touch.

"Please don't be frackin' nice to me." Rowan cursed. "I'm tired of people's apologies." She said moodily, having rehearsed this line and immediately regretting it. The context was off.

"Sorry," Úna apologized. "I mean, no apologies here. Don't know her. She must have left town."

Rowan chortled.

"There's that smile I love to see."

Rowan remembered she shouldn't feel happy and willed herself to be angry. "It's smog, isn't it? Trashin' smog," Rowan shouted.

"That it is."

"I hate it," she screamed louder, punching her fist hard into the base of the wooden foundation. "Frack, that hurts," Rowan said, shaking her limp wrist.

"Easy there," Úna calmed, rushing in almost instantly, like water filling into an empty space. "Let me look at that."

"Ouch," Rowan shouted as Úna touched her hand, testing along the swollen welt that had formed after she had punched the base.

"You have to take care of yourself, crazy. I know you're angry, but by Gaia, that's not a reason to hurt yourself."

"Could you not call me that?"

"What?"

"Crazy."

"Okay, crazy," I won't." They quipped, smiling.

"It's not funny," Rowan said, punching Úna in the shoulder.

"Okay, okay." She acquiesced, at least for now.

"Anyway, I know I need to take better care of myself. I was just going over this in therapy. It takes time."

"I thought you would be happy that one of the murderers was caught. That *you* helped catch her."

"But Anderson is still out there. And besides, catching Tulip, it doesn't bring him back," Rowan said, her voice breaking.

"I know, but."

Rowan interrupted. "And for such a frackin' silly reason, too. I know she was blackmailed, but she also helped kill him because he was mean to her." Rowan was crying now, "It doesn't make sense. It's so pointless. So..."

Úna hugged her, a deep tightening that made Rowan feel almost like, however briefly, that the two of them were one being: together, complete. "I know, baby. I know. I'm angry too, but sometimes you just, just have to filter that stuff out. We can't let everything hit us like this."

Rowan unclenched herself from Úna. She wiped away the mushy snot that was forming around her upper lip. "Did you say filter?"

"Yes," Úna said, confused. "I was speaking more meta-phorically."

"Thank you, baby, I think this helped."

Rowan started to walk off. "Where are you going?" Úna called to her.

"I need to see that polluted peacekeeper," she shouted back as she walked past a blur of dark green cattails and reeds, wiping past her.

She stared backward at Úna, and, more importantly, at the nanoweave humming even now. Its three thin legs, anchored deep into the soft earth, unshifted despite the wind that swept across the reeds.

The answer, or at the very least, an answer, had been standing in front of her the entire time.

TWENTY-FOUR

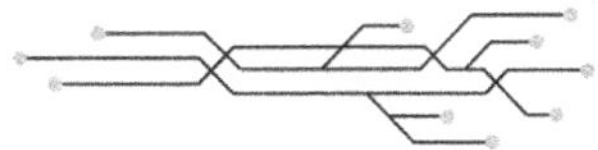

CALISTO

PUBLIC COAR DOWNLOAD/Article/The New Workers Collective/Author Garykillsfascists/5-23-2101

-> When Calisto Tremblay's Groundwork handlers sent them to the Cods to solve a murder, did such masters in their wildest dreams envision such an ideal outcome for the party? The case has not only been solved in a swift timeframe, but one of the confirmed murder suspects is Representative Anderson Leek of the Chamber, one of Groundwork's most vocal enemies, who, before this incident, pushed for an anti-ownership amendment that was really just a symbolic jab at Groundwork.

-> His anti-ownership amendment is not getting passed in the Chamber now that he has been branded an unhinged murderer who mutilated his lover over a petty beef. An outcome that feels almost too convenient.

TIME: 12:39 PM
DAY: MONDAY 5-23-2101

The table, a round metal sheet painted the same color as the concrete grey floor, was soldered to the ship's floor. It fit about six people around it, but there were only two: Calisto and Captain Felipe. Felipe had opted for a more stark look today: no paste or makeup on his sienna skin, just a frazzled assortment of anger and curly hair beneath a dramatic, oversized black hat.

Dela's face was projected in the center of the table via Sirius's holo emitter, a small metallic appendage with a white bulb attached to the end. Her face was positioned to look toward Felipe. Dela's usual mask of neutral indifference had been plastered on for the past forty minutes as the surly captain tore into her, Calisto, the peacekeepers, and the entire CRS Delegation.

Felipe should not be here. The murder suspects had been identified, and none of them were on the Shuttle. The case was well on its way to being closed, and the Northeast Seven Shuttle should have parted, resumed its rotation, and sent its remaining collective-bound to their various slots across Turtle Island. And yet, the remaining passengers, along with the ever-assertive Captain Felipe, had been so displeased with Calisto's handling of the investigation that they were now staying to officially lodge a complaint.

"We aren't leaving." Felipe balked. "You have broken our trust in this entire institution."

"And again, we apologize for the inconvenience, for the infringement, as you called it," Dela corrected.

"I don't call it anything. It is an infringement," Felipe cut in.

"Of course," Dela said, her face unmoved. "Restoratively, what are you seeking at this juncture? How would you like the Delegation to account for this harm?"

This question was the wrong thing to say, apparently. "Why should we have a solution at all? *YOU* did something wrong," he panted. "We want that on the record. That is what we want."

"And it will," Dela assured. "We, I have instructed those under me to let the complaint go through. It even has a date set. Surely, we can move the shuttle in the meantime."

Felipe shook his head. "No, Dela, we cannot. Until the complaint is lodged and debated, we aren't moving, and we don't want any of your peacekeepers on the Seven either. Leave us alone."

There was not much more to say, but Dela attempted anyway. She pushed through a few more rhetorical tacts: a written apology; even an indirect offer to provide his department with more resources. It didn't matter what she promised; the ship was not moving. Calisto said nothing. Their mere presence had probably been a bad idea, as no amount of apologizing would get Felipe to flounder. One would have to get a writ from the Chamber itself, and even then, his eyes told them not even the threat of the Restoration's Federated Forces would shake him.

When the meeting officially ended, they chose to meander along the shoreline to kill some time and process having been yelled at for over an hour. It was a windier day than yesterday. The breeze whipped at Calisto's face, causing their hair to go about everywhere. They had had a module to sort it into place, but like many of their more ancillary tech, it was now sitting in a bag in their tent to satisfy this herd's more moralistic tendencies.

Not long into their walk, Dela pinged Calisto. There was a lot of background noise, including a very aggressive flock of white and grey plovers and terns that chirped and squawked everywhere. Still, the audio quality was decent, as an audio parser was one of the few improvements Calisto had refused to part with.

"That was a lot," Calisto began.

"A disaster," Dela said in Québécois. They imagined Dela was pacing, though they couldn't tell for sure as Calisto had opted for voice only. Dela continued: "The Transportation Council will have to retool several decommissioned ships, and they are going to blame us, mark my words."

"I don't think Marx himself could have changed that smog's mind," Calisto cursed, smacking strands of hair out of their face. Their hair straightener mod needed to be re-added to their suit as soon as possible.

"Saint Luxemburg would have walked out in the first few minutes." Dela continued.

"Are you saying you're a saint?" Calisto chided.

It sounded like Dela snorted. "I have my moments. Listen, getting this ship off the Cods is priority number one, understand?"

"Understood, I'll schedule some repairs with passengers on the ship, the ones that are taking my calls, anyway."

Calisto could feel the conversation ending. They considered letting it fade into formality. The case was coming to a close, and despite this last-minute hurdle, they had done their role and solved the murder. No one could call them incompetent or say they were losing their touch. And yet, something had been bothering them: a great many things, actually.

"While I have you, did you get a chance to read my report?" They stopped walking, waiting for Dela's response, listening to the subtext behind her words.

"I did," Dela said, though it was difficult to know if this was true. She tended to never admit when she had failed to do something.

"Well, I have estimated several locations Anderson could be hiding. He may have taken refuge in the Eastic, but it's also possible he is still hiding somewhere in the Cods. With your permission, I'd like to gather a search party and...."

"No, I don't think that's a good use of your time," Dela said so softly that even with the parser, it was hard to hear. It would, to most people, sound innocuous, but Calisto knew from years of experience that a quiet Dela was an annoyed Dela: one whose patience was breaking and would view resistance as impertinence.

Yet they continued anyway: "Respectfully, I am worried about what leaving Anderson out there will do."

"It's fine, Cal. His face has been plastered all throughout the Restoration. He will probably be in hiding for the rest of his life."

"But what if there is more going on here, and it leads to an unforeseen escalation? If you could extend my tour here, then..."

"I said NO," Dela bristled. It sounded like she was barely containing her fury. She continued: "The Chamber is beside itself over this refugee crisis, one that happened during your watch. And Roxane doesn't want any more surprises. I want you back in the Party Cal, not standing in the middle of another shitshow."

By Marx, was she tabling an investigation over what, politics? Calisto ignored being blamed for the Eastic Civil War and pressed on. "So we're going to ignore finding the reason why a barony was involved in this murder because things are politically difficult."

"It's done, for smog's sake. We know who our murderer is, and you will, Marx-willing, be credited for resuming a very important transport schedule. This is good news for you."

"And if I go ahead anyway. I am not compelled to follow your orders. Not officially."

"Professionally, I would never dissuade you from exercising your rights. I'm not in charge of you, merely an advisor. As your friend, though," and here she paused for effect. "I'd warn you that you don't have a lot of bridges left here, but I won't stop you, no matter how frackin' silly I think it is."

"Understood, Dela."

"Good," Dela said, coolly. "I'll talk to you soon, Cal," she then cut the feed.

What nonsense was Dela playing at? It was one thing to be told to look the other way for a minor case involving a herd not getting an assignment it wanted or having the laying of a Transport Line delayed by a month or so to convenience the Party, and its many machinations. Calisto had been able to sleep with themselves over those trivialities, and soundly: no one was hurt having to pick up garbage a year longer than intended. This, though, was about a barony-assisted murder.

Lost in thought, they apparently had received a ping from Rowan: a location at the edge of the island. It was appended with the text: "You'll never believe what I've found. Get here now."

A part of them felt that they should probably ignore it, go back to the Shuttle, and try to get it to leave, so Calisto could go back home and rejoin the Party—to get everything they've ever wanted, but Dela's dismissal made them want to be petulant. Perhaps Rowan was rubbing off on them, too? They were angrily walking just to walk, moving vaguely in the direction Rowan had told them to. They pushed along the shoreline, and then, when a sheer cliff that they did not have the right equipment to traverse cut off their path, they turned inward, where the water flowed into a saltwater estuary. The ground, though still sandy, was hardened by decades of grounded-down shells lining its surface. It was like a man-made pathway, except humans had not been around enough to shape it, and it was lined by a brilliant, chaotic sea of purple heather in bloom.

Buried in repairs and case findings, Calisto had had few opportunities to enjoy the Cods. They turned down their audio parser, nasal inhibitor, and visual examination software and let the details of the area pour in: the sulfur smell of the sea, the way the wind beat up against their eardrums. At least in that moment, they could feel the appeal of no-mods. This felt divine. As they moved toward Rowan's location, they tried to take note of the fragments, the bits and pieces of nature that they had neglected. The texture of the tiny branches, as stalks of heather, brushed against their suit. The way the plovers and terns trailed behind them, guarding some unseen territory, their eggs sitting on the shoreline in foraged nests that any predator could happen upon, including, once upon a time, man.

The estuary channel Calisto followed led them further inland into a narrow crevice towered by two imposing cliffsides. There was a shallow swamp here that was formed by the funneling of rainwater. It had to be freshwater, or at least Calisto assumed so. Salem had set up a man-made series of wooden planks to act as a bridge, allowing them to move forward without wading through the muck.

"Oh, good. You came," said a familiar voice. I must have sent you a thousand messages." It was Rowan. She did not appear angry; in fact, there was a frantic excitement about her. She might even have been excited that Calisto had arrived, expecting them.

Rowan pointed at the massive nanoweave behind her. "It's in there."

TWENTY-FIVE

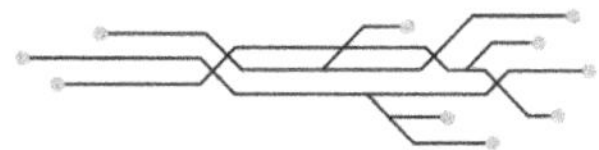

ROWAN

PUBLIC   COAR   DOWNLOAD/Manual/Nanoweave   Model
11-U/Author TechIsTheBest/10-13-2100

-> An oldie, but a goodie. The 11-U stands at a maximum of 22 feet, though its internal AI adjusts based on UV overhead. Its legs—three broad sheets of metal with the depth of a pin-prick that can stretch to 17 feet long—balance its central hub in the air. Typically made of a carbon nanofiber composite, the hub is where you toss the trash this weave then breaks down into base components.

-> Now, before newbies begin climbing the ladder, know that you can…

TIME: 1:55 PM
DAY: MONDAY 5-23-2101

owan was already heading up the ladder of the nanoweave, uniform bars that ran along the razor-thin metal to the very top of the weave's hub—a large bulbous thing humming even now.

"I got the override from Úna," Rowan said. "A benefit of being married to the Head Shepherd. And I didn't want to touch it until you arrived." Rowan got to the hub, plugged in the code, and opened the hatch, its hinges not making a sound. She started rummaging through its interior, finding what she wanted sitting at the top of a pile of decomposing electronics and other hazardous materials. "See! Incoming!" She shouted as she chucked a large object near where Calisto was standing. It was the piece of a battered, gray, and tattered Restoration techno suit.

Calisto used their suit to run a scan. "It's barely functional. Wait, is this Anderson's?" They asked.

Rowan beamed, pushing her guilt back down, letting it sink like marine snow and allowing another to take its place: pride. She had been right. "Something my wife just said reminded me that the shielding for the machine messes with signals, probably why you weren't able to find it when the pings went off." She stated triumphantly.

"What? I can't hear you from up there."

Rowan moved down the ladder, reaching the bottom with a thud. "I said that the shielding for the machine can interfere with signals, filter them out," she explained. She was explaining something! "It can scramble nearly anything. And if I cross-reference the logs, hold on one second, trash."

Rowan climbed back up the ladder. She typed into the small pad, seamlessly integrated next to the panel. "Yup, Tulip was....right, you can't hear me," Rowan repeated, going back down the ladder, panting heavily. The writer's life did not keep her in good shape. "Tulip," she panted, "was the last person to access it."

Calisto nodded thoughtfully. "Good work, Rowan!" They said, pacing somewhat as they processed what Rowan had just told them. "So the area pings go off, and Tulip throws the suit in here."

"Or it could be the result of the weave breaking the suit down," Rowan added. "We throw all sorts of junk in here. Carbon-emitting engines, lithium batteries. Really complex stuff. It takes a while, but eventually, it breaks down into its base components."

"Right, that probably makes more sense. Tulip tosses it in the weave to destroy it." Rowan couldn't help but smile. Calisto was considering this seriously. "When did she access it?" The peacekeeper asked.

"Smog, I didn't transfer the data to my suit." Rowan paused, looking back up at the tall, imposing nanoweave. "Up I go again," she sighed, moving toward it.

Calisto stopped pacing for a second. "There has to be an easier way. Here, give me the pin." Rowan did so, and Calisto typed something into their pad. "Ah ha, there it is," they mumbled, and like magic, the legs slowly retracted into themselves until the hub of the weave was at ground level.

"It makes sense," Rowan said, acknowledging the feat. It's hard to get a carbon engine up a ladder."

"Indeed."

Calisto walked toward the hub and, with a flick of their wrist, transferred the information to their suit and then, a beat later, to Rowan's suit, which they heard arrive with a ding. "...you get it?" Calisto asked, and without stopping to hear an answer, continued: "It says here Tulip's login pin accessed this around the time after the ferry had re-docked."

"Typical, dispose of your evidence shit," Rowan said.

"I tend to agree. It's just…" and here they were pacing again. "Anderson is all over this murder. He fought with the victim shortly before killing them and made no effort to conceal it. Why go through all this effort to have his lackey toss his suit at a location miles away when the ocean is right there? He could have weighed it down, and we wouldn't have seen it for weeks or years."

"Panic, maybe?"

"Suppose anything is possible. You've read the report. Why do you think he did this?"

Rowan thought back to the report, but more than that, she thought about all the times she wrote about murder. The tedious drawing out of motive, time, place, and opportunity. Turning characters into evil chess masters, then lackeys, and then innocent dunces. Fiction was more amorphous than the cold facts of reality, but the structure was the same: the reasons and ways people killed.

"It was premeditated, obviously," she said at last. "You don't blackmail an accomplice at the last minute. That takes planning. And then the fight. The location the body was disposed of," Rowan swallowed, struggling to proceed. Uncovering the suit had been so exciting, fun even, that she had briefly forgotten why she was there. Her baby. "I think the mur…" She paused. The word murder sat at the back of her throat, difficult to say and even harder to swallow. "…The murder. Trash, it still hurts to say it, you know," she told Calisto, trying not to bury her feelings. "Why is it so hard?"

Calisto stopped pacing and approached Rowan, placing their hand on her shoulder. "I'm sorry, Rowan. I wish things were different. You know I've been to a lot of herds. Most mothers are not able to solve their son's murder while processing their grief."

"Thanks," Rowan said reflexively, but this felt inadequate to the kindness Calisto was giving them. "No, not just thanks. Gaia, you are so nice to me, and I've been so mean to you."

"You haven't been..."

"Shut it," Rowan interrupted. "Yes, I have, and I'm sorry, okay? I shouldn't have organized that search party. I've been a polluted pain in your rear recently, and I'm sorry. I don't know you, and I was so angry. I simply wanted to hurt someone, anyone. It was a projection? A self-defense mechanism? Pick your psych word."

Calisto smirked. "I understand," they responded. "I lost someone dear to me not that long ago. My old mentor. I didn't react well to the information either."

This surprised Rowan. Calisto seemed like they were built in a Tinker's Collective to always be empathetic and to approach every problem with a smile. It was hard to consider that maybe, under that clinical exterior, was a person.

"What did you do?" Rowan prodded, softly.

Calisto frowned. "I don't think I'm ready to share that. Let's just say I burned a lot of bridges. So yes, I understand what you're going through, and you're handling this a lot better than I did."

Rowan smiled. "Thanks. You know you aren't a bad peacekeeper. Not really."

"That's sweet, but don't lie."

Rowan let out a loud chortle. She couldn't help it. "I think I'm starting to like you," she said, surprised.

"I'll try not to be offended...would you be okay if we got back to it. You know, the case?" They asked, their body beginning to push away from their embrace of Rowan.

Rowan nodded. They also wanted to distance themselves from this closeness, logging it as something she should probably bring up later with Strummer. That impulse was certainly a new feeling.

"So the nanoweave," Calisto deflected gently.

"Right, well, okay, so there are a million ways to get rid of something, but this weave, its signal disruptions are one of its defining bugs. There's a reason we keep them so far out from camp. At least that's what Úna tells me."

"Which implies?" Calisto prompted, appraising Rowan with a tilt and a knowing smirk.

Rowan could feel the thought forming in her head. Gaia's sea breeze nipped at her cheeks as the facts aligned and the obvious peeked forward. "Anderson," she continued, "or whoever planned this, didn't want us to find this. But I don't understand. I just don't. Why?"

"I'm afraid I don't know either," Calisto said. "But something isn't adding up. This is the second loose end."

"Second?"

"Necrosis in parts of Haldan's body set in before the time of death, remember. I still haven't explained that."

"And so they kill my baby, and Anderson and Tulip don't even have the decency to do it cleanly in a way that makes a lick of sense."

Calisto smiled, not quite laughing: "There's something we're missing."

A small part of Rowan took pleasure in the cop calling her and them a 'we.' For the first time in days, it made her feel like she wasn't alone and that things weren't so hopeless.

TWENTY-SIX

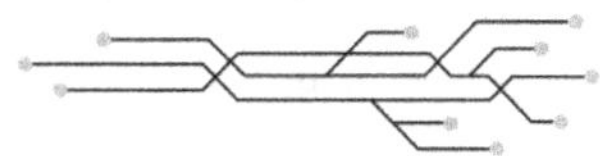

CALISTO

PRIVATE COAR DOWNLOAD/Digital Scan/Groundwork archives/Comrade Chair Roxane Chapman/Sent 5-22-2101

-> *Congratulations, Comrade Calisto Tremblay,*

-> *For years, the Groundwork Party has strived to maintain the Restoration we all love and cherish by building a faction that understands that robust processes and centralized authority in the correct hands can make a better polity.*

-> *Given your years of service as a peacekeeper to the Community Repair Specialist Delegation, facilitating difficult cases across Turtle Island and beyond, we have decided to grant your application to the Groundwork Party.*

-> *You can initiate your membership at any time. Please use your member ID, 94126, to access the relevant forums on the COAR and get started.*

-> *We are the light, held up by the collective. A beacon guiding the Restoration against both internal and external threats. May you shine brightly in this struggle.*

TIME: 7:54 AM
DAY: TUESDAY 5-24-2101

alisto examined the pinkish letter in their hands. It felt coarse and firm. Someone had pressed wood pulp into this shape and then written ink on it for it to be read a single time. It had come in a crisp white envelope that Calisto had had to rip open with their hands, nicking the edges by mistake so it could not be reused.

The subtext of the letter was clear: let's pretend nothing ever happened. We don't have to mention that you were kicked out of Groundwork. You don't have to reapply. Just come back into the fold and be a good party member. And a huge part of them wanted to do just that. They had originally applied to the Party as a teenager when they turned 14, the minimum threshold for membership. Their dads had been party members, and Calisto had fallen into the greater machinery, applying simply because it was the thing to do. Papi Dion had smiled so wide when Calisto had dropped the forms off at the admissions office.

"So what do you think?" asked Dela. She was on the line: two-way holographic projection this time, so Calisto couldn't be accused of 'avoiding her.' She had requested to speak with them the moment it had arrived, which hadn't been a coincidence by any stretch of the imagination.

"I heard they were sending it this morning," she continued.

"I thought they didn't want me," Calisto asked, confused.

"Leadership just needed to see you hadn't lost your edge, and you haven't. A quick wrap-up with this murder case, and now that the Chamber's hearing Captain Felipe's dispute this week, the Northeast Seven Shuttle will be in operation again without using force. You're probably going to receive accommodation for this."

"Ah, so, all of this was so that I could join the party... again?"

Calisto found their hands fidgeting, making circles in the dirt of their tent with a stick. They wanted to pace, to yell at Dela and ask, "What the frack was wrong with her," but they didn't want Dela to so noticeably observe their discomfort—for the news of their disobedience to ripple throughout the Party, and for their last bridge to be burned.

"Don't think of it like that," she allayed, "This case was about a lot of things. This outcome was just the best one for all of us, for you."

Calisto nodded. "Of course. "It's what I wanted, anyway." The words felt strange to say, but they were true. When this whole mess had started, this was the best-case scenario they had pictured.

Calisto had wanted to talk to Dela about the case, but that seemed pointless now. It might have always been. She wasn't going to reopen a successful case unless the evidence was irrefutable, and even then, Calisto had their doubts. The landscape in Groundwork was forever shifting, and Dela liked to add as little weight to that equation as possible. For her steps to be light and well-planned.

So Calisto merely smiled, letting his friend drone on about how good a fortune this was for their careers.

After the call died down, Rowan, who had been waiting outside the tent, asked to come in. She had very obviously been listening to the entire conversation, but politely asked: "Is it over?" It was strange to see her trying to be delicate.

"Yeah, Calisto," said. "Hey, let's go for a walk. I need to get out of here."

Rowan nodded, and the two of them headed to walk around the camp. When they had gotten a considerable distance away from their polluted tent, getting lost in the sea of hundreds of others, Rowan asked about the call, giving up the pretense of not having listened in: "And she's not going to do anything? The Delegation, I mean. Dela. They're going to ignore the evidence?"

Calisto frowned. "As far as the Delegation is concerned, or at least, my supervisor, we have our murderer. I have maybe a week to handle the situation with Felipe, report our findings to the community, and support Strummer, but then the case is over for me."

Rowan stopped walking and was silent for a bit. They were by a part of the camp dubbed 'the amphitheater.' A large stage had been set up at the lower end, and, ramping naturally upward with the hill, were a series of polished logs encased in natural resin for seating. It was one of those semi-permanent structures built by Reclaimers, but would be used and expanded by Forest Sprouters and, later, by Maintainers.

A part of Calisto wished they had held their initial meeting here that night of the search party. It was beautiful, and there was a certain calming image in them standing on that sun-beaten stage and giving out their report like an authority figure from on high, or in this case, down low. Maybe in an alternate universe where this case had not gone to trash, they had.

Yet they had wanted to go for a more personable feel. One that was less authoritative: where they were able to connect more with the herd, and be on their level. It was what had worked in the past, and even knowing everything, they were not sure they would have changed that. A million things they would change about this repair, but not that.

Rowan had sat down on one of the log benches, looking out over the empty seats. "So you're giving up?" She asked.

"I don't know what else to do. I know it's silly, but I got my membership back. I don't want to lose it again by making trouble."

"That's trash, you're supposed to make trouble. Your whole job is unpacking the messy shit people ignore. Do you even care about that?"

Calisto found themselves angered by the comment, almost screaming at Rowan to shut the frack up, but they dug their thumb under their fingernail to distract from the moment instead.

"Yes," they said, breathing so deeply they felt like they might choke on the air itself.

"Sorry," Rowan apologized profusely. "That was uncalled for."

"A little bit," Calisto affirmed, and then added, "But not by much. I am being cowardly here. You're right to call that out."

Rowan smiled weakly. "Well, as far as I see it, you have a couple more days."

Calisto couldn't help but crack a smile as well: "You don't give up easily."

"No, I don't. So, interviewing people for the time being is probably out. It will draw too much attention. How do you feel about following up on old locations? See if we can shake anything new from the trees."

"We only have to lose our chains," Calisto joked.

"You were saying that the other thing that doesn't make sense was the necrosis in Haldan's body setting in the evening before his murder on the ferry. Well, we know where he was the night before. Let's start there."

Calisto followed Rowan into the trees, their footsteps light against the sun-warmed earth. The morning air was thick with the scent of damp leaves and fresh pine, the last traces of dew still clinging to the underbrush. Sunlight filtered through the dense canopy, casting shifting patterns across the forest floor as birds flitted between branches, their songs filling the air with restless energy. They had arrived at the clearing where Haldan had played with Anderson that night before his death, or maybe even the night of his death. The sun's golden light streamed through the trees, illuminating the meadow in soft hues, making it seem too beautiful for anything bad to have ever happened here.

Yet Calisto could still see it—the laughter shared between Haldan and Kramer, their play, and the moment before everything had gone wrong.

TWENTY-SEVEN

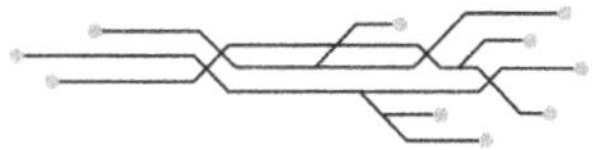

ROWAN

PUBLIC COAR DOWNLOAD/Interview/DW/Interviewee Representative Anderson Leek/05-01-2101

-> The following transcript has been translated from German to English and edited for clarity.

-> *REPORTER: You're plotting against your own government?*

-> *ANDERSON: No, there is no government. Gaia, I am trying to explain it to you. We have a de-centralized network of groups that occasionally coordinate. Listen, I want to stop a political faction called Groundwork from forming a centralized authority that will eventually turn the Restoration into a nation-state, don't you get it?*

-> *REPORTER: [Silence]*

-> *ANDERSON: A centralized, hierarchical authority needs a stake in the land to do anything. Otherwise, how do you enforce laws? If the land is not yours, why are people compelled to even follow the rules you make for them?*

-> *REPORTER: This is very philosophical.*

-> ANDERSON: Spoken like someone who doesn't understand that laws are violence...I'm getting off track. My directive is to amend the Restoration constitution to say that, without a shadow of a doubt, no one can own the land and that no authority can be imposed on another, anywhere, even from Groundwork's precious cops. It's foolproof.
-> REPORTER: If you say so.

TIME: 12:04 PM
DAY: TUESDAY 5-24-2101

Rowan and Calisto waded through the forest clearing, their boots brushing against tall grasses that swayed in the gentle breeze. The sunlight filtered through the surrounding trees, casting patches across the ground and illuminating wildflowers scattered among the greenery. The air was thick with the earthy scent of moss and the occasional sweetness of blooming asters and goldenrods.

They had decided to return to the last place Haldan and Anderson had been noted to be before their big fight: the clearing. Rowan did her best not to picture her son playfully torturing Anderson, tied to a tree branch. Hours later, that consensual act would lead to a fight that would result in her son's death. Or maybe it was unrelated. There was still so much they didn't know.

They were combing across the surface of the clearing, their backs bent as they scanned the ground for anything out of the ordinary. So far, they had found several used condoms, a torn suit, and a woven dildo already biodegrading. No trash that was out of place for a sex party.

"I'm not detecting any DNA, that's particularly surprising. Anderson. Tulip. Sam. And many other people whose testimony indicated they were here."

"This was a frackin' silly idea," she bemoaned. "It feels like we're trying to hit a target in the dark."

"It's daytime," Calisto countered.

Rowan gazed at them scornfully.

"Kidding," Calisto smiled. "Just giving you shit." There was a pause as Rowan could see them turning over new topics in their head. "How do you feel about your wifee's support of Peters' resolution at the upcoming meeting? Revoking the Restoration's Charter. Sounds like it's going to be...well, not fun exactly, but interesting."

Rowan sighed. She was in mid-motion, picking up a stained metal ball that had been lying on the ground. "It's another thing she didn't talk to me first before doing it, so I'm thrilled." She sniffed the brown stain on the ball, realizing very quickly that it was caked on shit. "That's not dirt," she said, chucking it in a pile they had placed all the other trash they'd found so far.

"Gross."

Rowan shrugged, squirting antiseptic into her hands. "Living in nature has you dealing with shit a lot. You get used to it."

"Charter meetings happen in Salem a lot, too?" Calisto said, clearly not wanting to stay on the topic of fecal matter, and also probably curious about the subject of Charter Meetings, too. Their little collective sounded a bit too rigid to allow casual debates about withdrawing from the Restoration.

"All the frackin' time. It's how we express our displeasure with a bad directive."

Rowan smiled with pride. Every time a directive—a law—manifested in a way that people in Salem didn't like, someone would introduce a proposal to revoke Salem's Charter of Membership to the Restoration. The matter would be debated, and eventually, a cooler head would prevail and raise the subject that was actually annoying the person. This would then be talked about instead. Sometimes, that led to a repair. Other times, another unrelated directive would either be amended or revoked by direct vote.

"It's mostly bluster, though," Rowan tacked on, seeing the concern on their face. "We eventually move on to what's actually bothering us. I think Úna's backing Peter because she's upset about the refugees. In fact, I know that's why. We've argued about it constantly. Why? Has a herd ever left the Restoration?"

Calisto shook their head. "Not for very long. The Fallen forced people to follow their laws, or they tortured them. I think sometimes people forget that all of this is voluntary. There's not much incentive to leave a body that doesn't require your community to listen to any of its directives. Herd Wichita did so for like a year or two, but then they came back."

"Well, hopefully, it doesn't take us that long to find something here," Rowan said, gesturing wide to the clearing.

"There might not be anything here," Calisto counseled with all the optimism of a dead fish. No, that wasn't fair...a person exhausted and wanting to go home. "But here's hoping."

When they finished going through the clearing, they expanded the perimeter slightly outside of it. Work, Calisto sheepishly admitted, they had neglected to focus on party business.

"Sorry," they said meekly. "I was so focused on getting the Seven to depart, I didn't do this."

Rowan considered cursing Calisto out, but let the thought go and breathed instead. "I get it. Like it still makes me angry, but I get it."

And with that, they resumed their work. The two of them pulled all the various pieces of trash they could see with the naked eye, and then they started using more advanced methods: geothermal scans to detect anomalous energy outputs, ground-penetrating radar to reveal hidden debris beneath the soil, and ultraviolet light to identify residues, though that was mostly ejaculate and pollen. It was here that some interesting stuff started to pop up.

"Is this medical equipment?" Rowan asked as she pulled out a used vile buried several inches below the surface. Fresh dirt crusted her hands.

Calisto opened the vial's top and scanned its interior. "Isopropyl alcohol. It's a fast-acting antiseptic. Was anyone that night engaged in knife play? That's a kink where users enjoy being cut open and..."

"I know what it is," Rowan interrupted. "And, what folder did you keep the interviews in?"

"Interviews-The Cods-2101."

Rowan retrieved the information with a few taps and then had a rudimentary AI scan the entire folder for kinks performed that night, a process that took mere seconds. "There was impact play. Pet play. Nova engaged in an intense form of sadism where her domme kicked her so hard that she bled. The aftercare was apparently extensive. Oh, here's something: Sam noticed that Haldan caused Anderson to bleed a little, but they didn't think it warranted enough concern to mention it to the monitors. No one else noticed it, though, and then Sam found a pup handler and was distracted for the rest of their time."

"No one noticed knife play?"

"Anderson wasn't making much noise, apparently."

"Hmmm, that is something. Let's keep looking around."

They found more medical equipment buried throughout the clearing. Some of it was wrapped in decayed fabric, hinting at makeshift attempts to conceal it. There were scattered syringes, rusted scalpels, and shattered glass vials everywhere. Their labels were partially readable, with technical words like 'Phosphate-Buffered Saline,' 'polyethyleneimine,' 'magnesium chloride,' and 'vecuronium bromide.'

"Most of these are used for biohacking, and that last one's a paralyzing agent," Calisto stated. "Explains the lack of screams. It's so obvious. The biohacking responsible for the necrosis could have happened here."

Rowan couldn't help but cringe a little at this fact being realized. He had been violating himself till the end, transforming his body into the opposite of what Gaia had intended. She felt ashamed for thinking such a thought. A part of her knew that Gaia wouldn't want her to judge her dead son for wanting to modify his body, and yet it clung there in the back of her mind all the same.

"Wait," Rowan interrupted, thankful for an interruption to her self-hatred. "This would have happened to Anderson, not Haldan. He was the one seen hanging from this tree. Unless their suit IDs were spoofed, maybe?"

Calisto shook their head. "Not that I could tell. I had the Neo-Boston Techno Collective double-check my work. Strummer, too, for that matter. Haldan and Anderson's suit

IDs were there in those positions. I guess it's possible that they might have switched suits. It was after sunset, so a holo-mask would have been easy to pull off. Quite frankly, I don't know what else it could be."

"So my son, wearing another man's suit, was chained to this tree and operated on while a paralyzing agent masked his screams? And everyone else just...what assumed they were having kinky fun?"

The thought caused a lump to form in Rowan's throat. How could they not have known? How could an entire camp full of supposedly watchful, tight-knit people have over-looked something so horrific? Rowan's breath hitched as she stared at the tree, at the holes in the bark where cuffs had been mounted that night. The tree stood silent, indifferent, bear-ing no trace of the nightmare it had witnessed. The weight of it settled like iron in her chest.

"That's what this information is telling us, yes," Calisto stated firmly, allowing for a beat to pass to see if Rowan need-ed a moment to process that. When Rowan said nothing, Calisto continued: "But that would imply Haldan would need medical stabilization to get to the ferry the very next day, at least, if your testimony is right and you did drop him off."

Calisto stared at her guiltily, and Rowan knew what they were implying with their knowing stare. The same question that had haunted them from the very beginning. *Are you sure that your memory is correct? Are you positive you really saw him that afternoon?*

Rowan's jaw tightened. She wanted to snap back, to tell Calisto that, of course, she remembered, but given everything she now knew, that defensiveness felt unreasonable. She breathed, doing her best to respond from a place of objectivity. "I'm sorry," she said at last, "I know it makes no sense, but I swear to you that I did. It was the middle of the day, and besides, he acted like my son. He ignored me like he always does."

Calisto nodded, accepting her truth. "There's something we're missing. Well, if that medical stabilization did happen post-surgery, there should be some traces aboard the... Frack, we're going to have to get aboard the *Seven* to check, aren't we? And Felipe told me yesterday to frack off and not bother him."

Rowan smiled. "Leave that to me, Cal. We're not going to let some smog stop us from learning how my baby died."

TWENTY-EIGHT

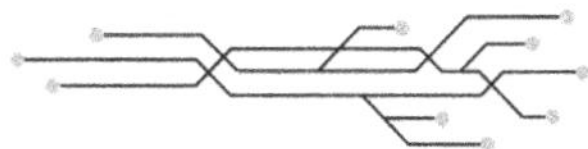

CALISTO

PRIVATE COAR THREAD/Communication/Haldan-Anderson/5-11-2101

-> message chain:
-> Haldan Kramer: It's like you cannot understand reason at all. I confided in you, Andi. I told you everything, and you threaten me like this? That's really frackin' manipulative, you know that?
-> Haldan Kramer: I'm giving you one chance to stop this nonsense and apologize.
-> Haldan Kramer: Do you hear me?
-> Anderson Leek: …
-> Anderson Leek: …
-> Anderson Leek: … You aren't going to bully me into agreeing with you. I'm not trying to pass this directive because of your weird political beliefs. This is bigger than you. Groundwork needs to be stopped. I know you disagree with this directive, this amendment. But if you love me, you'll respect my decision to advance it.
-> Haldan Kramer has left the chat

Calisto was standing on the wooden floor of the Northeast Seven Shuttle, their boots pressing against the worn planks that creaked softly with the ship's gentle hum. They had snuck onto the Seven in no small part due to the bluster of Rowan, who was currently giving Captain Felipe a piece of her mind in the angriest, most long-winded way possible. Loud enough for her voice to echo through the halls.

"This is unacceptable," she shouted, hoping to give Calisto enough time to snoop through the ship. "I need you to tell me where exactly the authority comes to kick me off this ship because under Section 7, Paragraph 31 of the Restoration Constitution that clearly states..."

Calisto smiled, doing their best to sneak quietly through the Seven's interior. If their theory about biohacking were correct, some equipment would have had to have been brought here to stabilize Haldan. He would not have been able to walk around with the level of injuries he sustained the night before, and somehow showed up to fight Anderson the following day, without it. There should be something here, even if it were only a cracked vile or the lingering DNA or chemicals of the stabilization procedure.

The *Seven* was one of the few places they had not thoroughly analyzed, as Felipe had been a consistent roadblock to their efforts. It was like one of Rowan's tacky morality plays where the hero had to return to the scene of the crime to discover the final piece of the puzzle was there all along. Calisto was hurriedly scanning everything they could, searching for something their investigation had yet to find. Their fingers grasped tightly on their handheld scanner, the device pulsing faintly as it tried to detect traces of something—anomalous energy signatures, broken equipment, anything that would indicate what had happened the afternoon of the alleged murder. They walked through the narrow hallway on the second level where Haldan and Anderson had fought, barely able to see what was ahead, the light outside unable to penetrate this interior hallway. The witnesses had claimed to have seen Haldan fight Anderson, but at best, they would have only gotten a partial view.

They would have heard them fight more than see them, Sirius interjected.

The hallway was connected to several storage closets, including the one Haldan's body had been dumped in hours later, but also the crew's rec room and, further down, the office of Captain Felipe himself. Calisto had surveyed it that first day and found it to be unremarkable, a simple room, with a cramped wooden desk and a built-in bookshelf behind it, with books so dull that Calisto had not retained them. This time, however, their scanner pulsed as they moved past the door—something was waiting for them on the other side.

The door was locked, but Calisto had not worked for years solving cases across the Restoration without learning how to pick a few locks. They crouched in front of the slim metal door, their breath steady as they reconfigured one of their suits' finger coverings into a lockpick. The keyhole was significantly rusted over, but they had worked in worse conditions. With practiced precision, they slid the interface into place, feeling for the slightest resistance as they twisted it ever so slightly. Their fingers moved quickly, each movement deliberate as they worked the pick along the tumblers, listening for the telltale *click* of each one falling into place. The cold metal vibrated under their touch, every minuscule shift sending a whisper of feedback through their fingertips. A final, satisfying *click* echoed in the quiet hallway as the lock gave way. Calisto hesitated for half a second before gripping the handle and easing the door open. The hinges groaned softly, revealing a significantly changed office.

Holomasks were everywhere. On the floor. On the desk. There were no books on the bookshelf anymore, just piles of masks, like discarded pieces of paper-thin gray silk. Some of them appeared unused, still rolled up in their original positions, but others were torn and frayed beyond repair. These were being used a lot, and given the hundreds scattered about, by way more than one person.

Calisto frantically began snapping photos of the room, then used their droid to perform a 360-degree scan that they could analyze in more detail. They weren't quite sure what they were looking at, but it had to be related to the case. It implied a level of organization that was beyond a mere murder. This was a conspiracy.

Suddenly, a ping came in on their wrist. Colibri had been pinging them every day this week about when they were coming home, and like every moment before this one, they sent a non-answer, in this case, 'can't talk right now.' Then, another ping came in, and another, until Colibri sent an image of a crashing wave, their symbol for calling them back immediately.

"Frack," Calisto mumbled under their breath.

It was not a symbol they used lightly, and even though this was the worst possible time for an emergency, Calisto knew they had to answer it. They made the instinctual decision to grab a bunch of masks and stuff them in their pockets before ducking out of the office and hallway onto the deck of the ship, where reception appeared to be better. They took a call, praying it would be worth it. Only a voice one, though.

"Hello, Colibri," they whispered as quietly as they could.

"That's it. You haven't talked to me in over a week." Her voice was strained, annoyed.

"Sorry, I've been busy. Listen, now's not a good time."

"Busy," she scoffed. "Where are you right now?"

"Somewhere I'm not supposed to be. I will call you back."

"Ping me your location," she commanded.

"Colibri, I…"

"Your location. The tracker you gave me is off by several hundred feet."

"What?" Even in disbelief, Calisto complied, and although Colibri didn't hang up, she stopped talking for about a minute. "Hello?" Calisto said. Are you there?"

"Turn around."

Calisto looked out into the water. Their heart fluttered a little at the sight of Colibri's familiar stance, weight shifted to one side. Her narrowed eyes. She was standing on the dock, glowering. Their two children, mirroring their mother's discontent, shot wary glances at Calisto, making them feel even more like an intruder in this moment. The huge sack on Colibri's back looked heavy, suggesting she had been carrying it for a while, which probably added to her irritation. Calisto cleared their throat, searching for the right words to defuse the tension, and then, remembering she couldn't hear them from across the water, whispered into the phone: "What are you doing here?"

"Kids, go play," Colibri instructed. She watched them go off into the distance. "Don't go too far," she called back to them. When they were far enough away, she continued: "I am here on vacation," she said calmly as if it were the most normal thing in the world. "I'm coming up."

"No, don't."

But she was already marching up the ramp of the ferry, and Calisto could only cringe as she did so, not attempting to hide herself. They could hear Felipe noticing the disruption, but whatever Rowan was doing kept him at bay. When Colibri finally reached them on the deck, Calisto found themself still trying to pretend they could keep everything a secret. "Why are you here? I told you that I am working on a case." They whispered.

"Well, you told Dela you were wrapping up this case, and I bragged days ago about coming here. She started to get suspicious that I wasn't planning to go on vacation."

"What did you tell her?"

"I told that pitchy soprano that she never gets the material prayer correctly."

Calisto chuckled, almost forgetting that they had uncovered a fracking conspiracy aboard the Seven.

"No, I obviously told her that we would meet you here, later. It's now later."

"Colibri," Calisto chastised. "Why didn't you tell me earlier?"

"I tried. I don't like lying to her, Cal. You haven't been answering your calls, so there was no way to coordinate. Now, Dela just thinks you're a bad partner and not directly defying her."

"Great," Calisto said, rolling their eyes. "So that's going to spread like wildfire all over the collective."

"You should be thanking me. Not many partners are willing to be this supportive. Anyway, I have to go and monitor the kids. We will be at the beach."

"Of course, I will see you later." They said, moving in for a kiss.

She let them wait. "I will literally have your balls if you don't," she said, before giving them a smooch and then cooly sauntering off.

Colibri passed Captain Felipe as he angrily stormed onto the deck wearing an oversized Charcoal Gray beanie that stretched to the back of his face like he was concealing something, because he was. It was starting to make sense now why he always had a hat on. That was probably not Captain Felipe.

"Ah ha," he shouted triumphantly. "I knew you were up to something," he said, pointing at Rowan and then to Calisto. "I told you not to come on the ferry until the Chamber finishes listening to our complaint."

"Your ship is at the center of a crime scene," Calisto countered.

"One that is closing, or so I was told. Shall I dial Coordinator Dela up? Perhaps she can clarify this?" He asked facetiously.

"There is no need. We were merely being thorough," Calisto stated as calmly as they could manage, which was little. They were losing their shit right now.

"You understand that, don't you, Captain?" Rowan inquired. "What it takes to get the job done."

The Captain stared at Rowan with a bitterness Calisto could not quite understand, a resentful cruelty that felt familiar. "More than you know," he stated smugly. "I'll see you tomorrow at the Restoration Charter Meeting. Now get the frack off my ship."

TWENTY-NINE

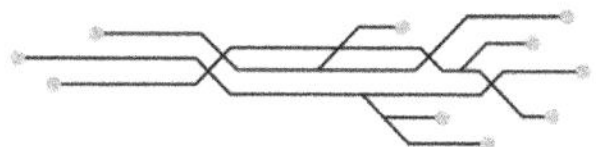

ROWAN

PUBLIC COAR DOWNLOAD/Book/The Restoration Is A Paradox/Author Hosa Liu/3-8-2094

-> *The Restoration has no standing armies, and we do not patrol our borders. A citizen of a nation-state would ask how we defend ourselves from invasion. What is stopping the baronies from reclaiming Turtle Island and the rest of the Americas? Or the surviving nation-states of Asia and Europe, for that matter?*

-> *The answer is simple. Our population is heavily armed, and we have hundreds of thousands of self-organizing militias. When threats do arise (and there have been plenty in our short history), these militias kick into gear. We call them the Federated Armed Forces, and while some militias do merge into a single army for the war effort, the name implies a level of organization that does not exist. Like a swarm, federated forces employ thousands of different tactics that a centralized authority cannot combat. We overwhelm our enemies with guerrilla warfare, terrorism, industrial sabotage, worker upris-*

ings, and, in the case of the baronies, the fermenting of slave revolts. So far, there has not been a single theater of war that the Federated Armed Forces have lost in. If someone wants to take down the Restoration, they have to be much smarter than engaging in a direct confrontation. They have to…

TIME: 7:28 PM
DAY: THURSDAY 5-24-2101

The frogs chirped among the reeds and other tall grasses in the dusk light, their rhythmic calls blending with the gentle rustling of the evening breeze. The fading sun cast long shadows over the water's edge, where fireflies had begun their slow, flickering dance above the rippling surface. The low trill chorus of the frogs was deafening, so much so that Calisto, Rowan, and Three-Seven had to stand face to face just to hear one another, which was intentional. They were terrified of being overheard.

The nanoweave stood not too far away, towering above the marsh. Its three thin legs, anchored deep into the soft earth, barely shifted despite the wind that swept across the reeds. The structure shimmered in the dim light, its woven, metallic fibers adjusting and realigning with every passing breeze, almost as if it were breathing. The machine disrupted any signal that might be spying on them, and that, too, was purposeful.

While Three-Seven watched them with amused indifference, Rowan argued with Calisto to take the only sensible course of action. "We need to contact the Delegation," Rowan angrily whispered. "The Chamber. Anyone? This is an invasion."

"That sounds a little dramatic. "

Rowan punched Calisto on the shoulder hard and un-forgivingly. "Gaia, you're so frustrating. You showed me the number of masks in Felipe's office, if that's even his real name. There could be hundreds of people on that ferry. What else do you call that?" She realized that touch wasn't something Calisto was necessarily comfortable with, at least not from an acquaintance, and added, "Sorry for punching you...with my hand."

"It's fine. When's your person getting here?"

Rowan pointed at the nanoweave behind them. "I don't know exactly. A couple of minutes. Three-Seven, tell them what you told me."

She nodded. "I saw him. Lord Manager Benison is here as one of the people on the ferry. It was only for a moment. The holomask he was wearing broke at dusk yesterday, only for a second, but I saw it."

"I'm sorry, whose Benison?" A confused Calisto asked.

"If what Three-Seven's told me is true, the current leader of the Eastic." Rowan clarified.

"You sure?" Calisto asked, disbelief hanging in their voice.

"I wouldn't forget that man's face," she shuddered. "He's the reason my kids are dead."

"See," Rowan said, gesturing frantically toward Three-Seven. "We're being invaded."

"I agree with you that something is happening," Calisto affirmed, "but I think it's sneakier than that. Unless those troops are hiding some sort of super-weapon, and we don't know that they even are troops, a surprise attack would be starting a war they couldn't win. The barony is standing in the middle of the ocean. One well-placed rocket, and they're dead."

Rowan considered the argument. Nothing Calisto said was false. "That's true," she said, fiddling with a piece of string in her pocket. The baronies are dying. Three-Seven, you told me they're falling apart."

Three-Seven nodded. "I didn't realize it until coming here, but the Eastic's tech is old, and most of the new stuff appears to be things they stole from the Restoration."

"Didn't stop us," Calisto said. And then, seeing that Rowan and Three-Seven were confused, asked: "What do you know about the collapse of the United Corporate States of America?"

Rowan laughed. "You're really making me recall my studies." She paused, staring off in the distance at the water in the direction where the Eastic lay, trying to remember. "It was inevitable. The United Corporate States of America was unsustainable, and more and more people were moving to the Restorate way of life."

Calisto shook their head. "That's what we like to say, but, well, have you read about the revolutionary militias?"

"Everyone has, but I think those were unnecessary. It might have taken longer, but the Restoration would have formed, or something like it."

"Disagree. Those battles were, a, bloody. The first herds had to fight inch by polluted inch through Corporate territories. We practically razed the Greater New York Holdings to the ground. And then, UCSA forces scorched the land as they retreated. Revolutionary forces hunted them for months until they capitulated. It's taken generations to get em to be small specks on the map that can now be treated with, a, embargoes rather than federated forces."

Rowan stared at Calisto, their face twitching uncomfortably. "What's this have to do with anything?"

"We've lost sight of our history, I think. We assumed that the baronies would die, because they are small and dying, but that was us too at one point. Early herds were small and dying, and we fought back, but we didn't do so head-on. We played dirty. Blew up supply lines. Poisoned crops. Maybe the barony is playing dirty, too?"

Rowan, who had frayed the string in her hands completely, tossed it to the ground. "So you agree with me then," she stated triumphantly. "They will start launching an invasion, just a protracted, sneaky one."

"It has to be smarter than that. I think...we need to talk to Tulip again. We know she's lying. It's the only thing that makes sense."

"I agree," Rowan said. She had been thinking about this ever since they figured out the conspiracy was more than simply two people with a grudge. "Her confession had been a cover of sorts to protect whatever was happening from going public. She knows something. But she's at a rehabilitation center. I don't know how we will be able to talk to her without Groundwork..."

There was the sound of a branch snapping underneath someone's feet, cutting off Rowan's thought.

"Trash, that has to be your person," Calisto said. "Three-Seven, let's go hide just in case Rowan needs support."

Three-Seven nodded, and Calisto walked off, fading into the night, leaving Rowan to wait and stew on the wild events of this week: her son's passing, the machinations of the barony, the potential invasion. She had trouble believing so much had happened, that her world had unraveled in such a short span of time. The weight of it all pressed against her ribs, making each breath feel heavier than the last. So heavy.

Then she remembered her exercises. She counted the sights, sounds, and smells around her. The ripples along the stagnant brown water. The rush of the water as insects buzzed above the surface. The sulfur-like smell of dimethyl sulphide, a byproduct of bacteria waging an eternal war against the nearly invisible phytoplankton all around her. She thought about Gaia's network of life, and her breathing steadied, allowing her to wait for her wife as though no emotion had thrown her off her feet.

When Úna finally arrived, Rowan had almost managed to be thinking of nothing at all, staring off into the distance.

"There you are, my crazy, grumpy bear," her wife said as she trudged onto the science station platform, kicking a bit of muck as she did so. She was wearing a hat with netting that protected her from insects, something she had worn before but not for some time.

"Can you take that hat off?" Rowan said, not bothering to say hello.

"But you know I hate bugs, grumpy bear. And if we aren't going to use sonic modules, and no, I am not rehashing that argument, then what else can I use?"

"Take it off."

"Rowan, you're acting crazy."

"Úna, please," Rowan begged. "It's been a long day. Can you just take it off, please? I promise I will explain."

Úna complied, holding the hat in her hands. "Gaia, I hate bugs," she complained as she swatted some mosquitoes from her unchanged face.

Rowan approached her, examining the pores and crevices of her peach face, watching for the slight distortions of light that would come from a holomask, but none appeared. It was her. Rowan hadn't let herself think through the possibility of what would happen if her wife had been a replacement. Of the violence that would need to be done to defend herself, but now that she didn't, the relief came rushing in.

"I had to be sure." Rowan cried, breaking down as she told her wife everything.

It took some convincing, and the word 'crazy' was thrown around more than once (Úna was always trying to doubt her), but eventually Rowan was believed.

THIRTY

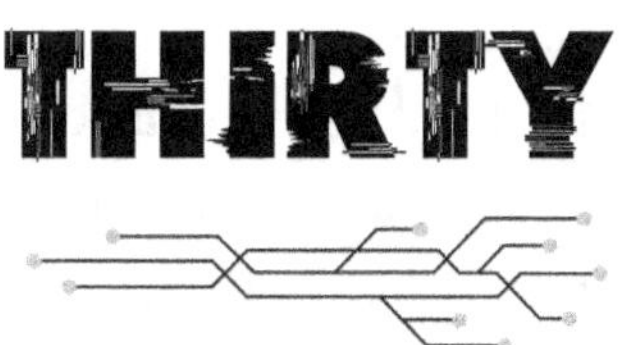

CALISTO

```
PRIVATE COAR THREAD GWP/Communication/05400/De-
la-Daniel/5-25-2101
```

-> message chain:
-> Daniel Young: Hey Dela, Groundwork member Daniel from Eden. I figured you should know that your little pup is working behind your back.
-> Daniel Young: **Sends File**
-> Dela Feinberger-Wu: I'm going to kill them.

```
TIME: 10:37 AM
DAY: WEDNESDAY 5-25-2101
```

Dela's face was red; her voice hoarse and frayed. "You dare go behind my back like this?"

Calisto hadn't shared with Dela that they had secretly booked a meeting with Tulip at the Eden Rehabilitation Center. They had needed to interview Tulip, and they were hoping the news wouldn't reach Dela until well after the case, but somehow Dela had learned the truth. A

Groundwork member somewhere in the Eden Center had slipped information to her behind the scenes.

"You'd better have a good frackin' reason to resume a repair that is officially closed." She continued.

Dela glowered at them. Calisto considered telling her why they had done this. She had a right to know about the conspiracy unfolding here, but every bone in their body was screaming at them not to trust her anymore. Maybe a part of them never did. They certainly didn't trust Groundwork with that information. They were afraid that Dela would not only refuse to listen but also add more barriers in their way, and then it would be too late. So Calisto had resolved not to say anything important, and because of this, they were at a loss for words as Dela peered into them, utterly disappointed. They had to lie, but no words felt adequate.

"I...Dela."

"Don't Dela me. Don't try to manage me. When you broke down in the Boulder Collective, I went to bat for you, and you betray me like this?"

"I'm sorry." There was nothing else to say. At this moment, they were starting to realize just how spiteful and incompetent Dela really was. What do you say to someone who doesn't listen to anything you have to say? Not really.

"Well, thankfully, I learned about your little call to the Eden Center first. If you cancel now, no one will be the wiser."

Calisto cleared their throat. "I'm not going to do that. Tulip has important information that I need for the case."

"The case I told you to drop?" There was an icy moment of silence as Calisto said nothing in response. "So you're ignoring my counsel then?"

"As is my right."

She sighed. "Fine. Get results, Cal, for your sake."

Dela cut the feed, and it felt like a punch to the face. They were, had been friends before this all started. Maybe that wasn't true. Dela would deny it, but there had been a hierarchy between them, as she delivered to Calisto whatever plan Roxane had deemed necessary, with the expectation that they would follow it. A flow that was less a conversation, and more like water dripping down into its appropriate receptacle. A relationship so simple and easy to follow, and here they were, refusing to do even that.

Calisto found themselves pacing around their tent frantically, their breath shallow, thoughts tangled in a mess of frustration and regret. The weaved walls felt too tight, the air too thin, as if the very space around them was collapsing under the weight of what had just happened. Dela had cut the feed. Just like that, as if their history meant nothing. As if the trust, the unspoken understanding—however uneven it had been—had never existed in the first place. They ran a hand through their hair, fingers catching in knots they hadn't had the time or energy to comb out. Everything was a mess, and desperately, they wanted more than anything for Sirius to be here. He would know what to say. He always had before, and yet he was gone.

"Calisto, friend, things alright in there?" It was Rowan. She was on the other side of the tent flap, mucking about as always.

"No." Nothing was right. Everything about this repair had been an utter disaster.

"Can I come in?' Calisto didn't say anything, but Rowan came in anyway. She took a few tentative steps inside, her gaze darting around the room before settling on Calisto. "You're crying. What's wrong?"

Calisto hadn't realized that they were crying. They touched their cheeks and felt them wet with salty tears. The realization seemed to shock them even more. In all the chaos and turmoil, they had somehow detached from their own emotions, keeping everything at arm's length. "I fracked up, Rowan. My supervisor found out that I'm still on the case. She found out about our upcoming call with Tulip, and she's upset with me. And after Boulder, I don't know how to make any of this better."

They hadn't meant to say that last part. It had just slipped out, too fresh after Dela had bandied it about as a threat during their call. They could see the memory of Boulder in their mind: the corpse of Sirius on the ground as the color started to drip from his face. The angry herdspeople, furious about the murder of one of their spiritual figures, the prime suspect in the case.

Rowan looked puzzled. "I don't understand. What happened in Boulder?" She walked closer to Calisto, her outstretched hand hovering in the air, uncertainty clouding her eyes.

However, Calisto didn't want touch. They felt themselves clamping up, and so they stepped back. "Don't touch me." They cried out.

Rowan stopped in her tracks. "Okay, I won't touch you." And then, after a pause: "Calisto, what happened in Boulder?"

Calisto wiped the snot dripping down their nose with the back of their hand, trying to regain some composure. The raw directness in Rowan's voice weighed heavily on them. Taking a shaky breath, they responded. "It was a repair. I was helping an old friend named Sirius. And I fracked up, and people died. He died."

Rowan's eyes widened in sympathy as she realized that she'd touched on a deeply painful memory. The silence that followed was thick with unsaid words and emotions. "I'm so sorry, Calisto," she finally whispered.

Calisto shook their head, fighting back tears. "I should've been better. Sirius trusted me, and I let him down."

Rowan once again took a hesitant step forward. "I'm sorry, Calisto, but you have a hard role. Surely, people wouldn't hold that against you."

"I pushed someone too hard. I assumed they were guilty, and my faulty reasoning led to an improvised firefight. CRS aren't allowed projectiles, but I thought I knew better because I... the people I was pursuing were leading a sex trafficking ring, and I didn't want to wait to get the proper clearance."

He remembered how Sirius had argued so passionately about how they needed to be armed for this repair. That 'these people' would be armed, and so 'they should be too.' His approach had seemed so right at the time: until the shooting started, and everything went to smog.

Rowan gasped and then stifled it. "It's not as simple as you make it sound," Rowan said slowly, choosing her words carefully. "You made a judgment call. Maybe it wasn't the right one, but in high-stress situations, we often have to make split-second decisions and..."

Calisto looked up, their eyes rimmed red, "Peacekeepers always say that when they don't want to reckon with their mistakes, but it was the wrong call, Rowan. People are dead because of me. And the worst part is that I can never truly know whether those people could have been reformed. Even if they were doing heinous trash in the present, I robbed the world of the people they could have been." They wheezed at this, imagining the people they had killed, and then continued: "I'm on such thin ice with so many people, Rowan. And this case was Dela's attempt to get me into Groundwork's good graces again, to secure my future candidacy in the GWP, and I couldn't even do that right."

"Frack that. Was there a repair with the herd you hurt?"

Calisto nodded, their tears so bitter it stung, "I'm not allowed back there, ever."

Calisto shrugged. "So you're facing the consequences. People frack up all the time. I raised a literal monster."

"You didn't," was all Calisto had the energy to say.

"All I am saying is that the actions of others aren't because of a single person; that's why we do repairs."

"But I..."

Rowan cut in. "Smog, do you think somehow you're uniquely so awful that you don't deserve redemption. That you alone should be thrown into some Fallen prison. Get over yourself, Cal. Pity isn't a good look on you, and this case is more important than your ego. We're dealing with an invasion, or whatever you want to call it, and leaders too incompetent to rely on for help." She shook her head, frustrated, and then took in a deep breath, collecting herself. "Listen, I can't say this situation will turn out okay. Maybe we will frack it up too, but you don't have to do it alone," Rowan said, reaching her hand out for the second time.

Calisto took it, frack it. Things couldn't get much worse. "Thanks," they said. They could do this, or at least they could try. They spent a couple of seconds saying nothing, breathing, and centering.

"We're so close to catching this trash," Rowan said after they had a solid beat of breathing. "We confirm this with Tulip, and that's it. We have everything."

"Okay, I'm ready. Let's do this interview before I think better of it."

Rowan smiled, allowing Calisto to type in the call details a member of the Eden Rehabilitation Council had sent them. They used a holoprojector to display a screen onto the tent's wall. It took them a bit to connect with Tulip because, according to a facilitator, she was in meditation class. And as the facilitator said, "Her autonomy wouldn't be violated, not even for a murder investigation."

They had to wait awkwardly for her to finish. Rowan sighed, crossing her arms as she leaned against the tent wall, watching the faint flicker of the holoprojection. Calisto tapped their fingers impatiently against their knee, the wait stretching on longer than either of them would have liked.

By the time Tulip's earthen face came onto the screen, Calisto felt much calmer. Tulip was in a minimalist, but clean room, with relaxing meditation music playing in the background. "Welcome to my cell," she quipped sarcastically, but also with some warmness, as if she was not angry with them at all; an act, Calisto was sure.

"Haven't lost your flair for drama, I see," Rowan quipped. "You should check out the COAR to see what a real prison is."

"I grew up enslaved; of course, I know what a real prison is," she clapped back, an edge of bitterness in her voice, revealing that the warmness before had just been a performance. "You can't leave a real prison."

Calisto, who felt confident enough to speak now, edged in. "Fair enough. Apologies for the remark. I heard you officially logged your confession with the Delegation."

Tulip, who was sitting behind a sleek metal desk, tapping her hands listlessly on its surface, didn't change her cocky expression. "Are you calling me to simply state the obvious?"

"No, I'm calling to tell you that you're going to retract that confession."

Tulip laughed, and not a small one either, but a loud one that was too melodramatic to be real. "You all really need to make up your mind. Do you want the murderers for this or not?"

It was then that Rowan broke in, laughing. "We know Tulip."

"Yeah, because I told you. I'm the murderer, me and Anderson..."

"No, we know about the conspiracy," Calisto interjected. "About the dozens of infiltrators, maybe more, on the Seven. We know this is about much more than just you and Anderson."

Calisto watched as Tulip's face drained of all warmth, and in an instant, they knew it wasn't acting. She was *shocked* that they had found out. Her lips parted slightly, but no words came at first. The serene, composed mask she had worn just moments ago cracked, her eyes darting off-screen as if searching for some unseen anchor. When she finally spoke, her voice was quieter, more fragile than Calisto had ever heard it.

"How did you know?" She whispered.

Calisto continued triumphantly: "Now, tell us who *was really* blackmailing you?"

THIRTY-ONE

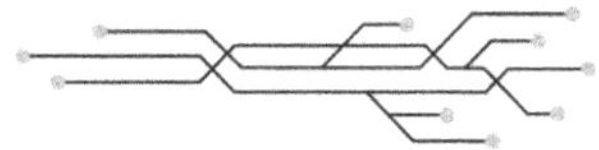

ROWAN

PUBLIC COAR DOWNLOAD/Interview/DW/Interviewee Representative Anderson Leek/05-01-2101

-> The following transcript has been translated from German to English and edited for clarity.

-> *REPORTER: I still don't understand. How can you have laws that your localities just ignore?*
-> *ANDERSON: [Groans] What is so hard about this?*
-> *REPORTER: You don't have to be rude.*
-> *ANDERSON: [Scoffs] I'm in hell. Our directives, our laws, are not top-down. Each herd or collective, 'locality' as you call it, has to approve every directive that is passed by our highest legislature, the Chamber. Half the directives in the Restoration barely get 50% adoption, and even then, the individual herds rework them to fit their local circumstances.*
-> *REPORTER: [Horrified] That sounds like anarchy.*
-> *ANDERSON: Now you're getting it. And wait till you hear that nothing keeps us together. People can leave the Restoration at any point.*

My herd threatens to do it all the time. The weather goes badly, and someone files a motion to revoke Salem's charter of membership to the Restoration. It's very funny, I assure you. We all have a good laugh about it afterwards.

TIME: 7:13 PM
DAY: THURSDAY 5-26-2101

The herd meeting was held at the amphitheater for once. The midday sun cast long beams of light through the canopy, illuminating the stage where Úna and Calisto stood, their expressions unreadable. The amphitheater, with its polished log seating and resin-coated supports, had an air of quiet dignity, a space reclaimed and reshaped for moments like this. It had taken so long to build that there had been no chance to use it before now; there often wasn't time for fancy meetings for Reclaimers. They were too busy fixing the world.

Not too far away sat Captain Felipe, dressed in one of his standard oversized hats. He was not alone today, in this respect. He was sitting with a contingent of about forty people from the *Seven*, all wearing similarly ridiculous hats. Wide brims, floppy crowns, even a few adorned with feathers or woven beads—each hat was more absurd than the last. Felipe, as always, wore his with complete seriousness, but the others stole amused glances at one another, the occasional smirk breaking through their otherwise composed expressions. None of them was probably the person they looked like, a thought that sent a shiver up Rowan's spine.

Úna cleared her throat, her cough booming for all to be silent, and for the most part, everyone did, letting their heated conversations die off mid-sentence. "We're here because of

Peter's request that we leave the Restoration, as is his right to propose," Úna affirmed.

There was a groan from several in the audience.

"What's this really about?" Someone shouted.

"Now, we'll get to that, but I wanted to give Peter a chance to speak." She gestured to him to come to the stage.

He walked forward, broad-shouldered with the kind of strength that came from years of hard labor. His braids, thick and sun-bleached at the ends, framed his face, falling just to his neck in a way that made him look both rugged and deliberate.

"Thank you, brothers, sisters, comrades. I know we all propose these charter resolutions whenever we're angry, and I am angry. Look at what's become of Salem. We were prevented from continuing our path up the coast to heal the environment, to heal *Her*. Refugees have flooded our shores. And rather than helping us, the Restoration sent cops to police us instead." They gestured to the small contingent of about 15 peacekeepers, sitting apart from the rest of the herd in the front row. "I'm not proposing that we leave because of some tantrum. I genuinely believe that we don't need the Restoration, and I'm not alone."

The tension hung in the air in a way it had not moments before. This was not a performance. Peter was genuinely serious about leaving the Restoration, which killed the joking atmosphere that had prevailed only a moment ago. This wasn't just a debate—it was a tipping point.

Other people filed up to speak. One by one, members of the herd took their turn on the stage, their voices rising and falling with passion, frustration, and conviction. Some of them had undoubtedly been arranged beforehand by Peter to speak, but some of them were swept up in the moment. If Rowan hadn't been prepared for this outcome, she might have been one of them. They spoke of the broken promises of the Restoration, of how its biggest proponent in the herd, Anderson Leek, had murdered someone, and how their efforts to heal the land had been stifled by bureaucracy and force.

"We were promised coordination, not cops," was a common chant thrown about from the crowd.

The peacekeepers initially sat motionless in the front row, their expressions carefully neutral, but the tension in their shoulders betrayed them. They weren't here to listen; they were here to contain. Rowan watched them closely, noting how their eyes flickered between speakers and how their hands rested just a little too close to their weapons.

One of them finally got so frustrated that he stood up to speak. "We're here to protect you," a young twenty-something yelled earnestly, too close to his perspective to understand how other people could hate it. "Don't you get that?"

There were boos at that, and the young peacekeeper reddened so much with shame that he eventually sat back down.

It was not all arguments of support, however. There were people worried about what a separation would mean. They were worried about survival—about dwindling supplies, about whether cutting ties would mean isolation rather than freedom.

"Do we really want to be treated as some barony?" One person asked.

It was here that Captain Felipe came on stage to speak: "Some of you know me as the captain of that ship that just won't leave." There were chuckles at this, and Felipe seized on the opportunity to make his pitch. "We also aren't happy with the Restoration and want to leave it too. And we would be happy to work with you all. The good news about a ship is that we could connect you to people all along the coast, both inside the Restoration and out. You wouldn't be as alone as you might think."

This had probably been his trump card to get Salem to leave the Restoration and unknowingly become a little barony in the making. The reassurance that there would be someone to look after them, even if that someone was a barony just off their shores. She imagined him practicing this monologue, rehearsing it over and over until it was perfect. That was how he liked to do things.

Úna had been told to wait for this moment for Felipe to speak because, of course, he would. He had always had a flair for the dramatic, even as a kid. At least if he was the person she now suspected him to be.

When he finished his calm, practiced lie, Úna asked him to remain on stage. "I believe my wife has a point you will want to address directly."

He smiled and agreed to wait. Rowan made her way to the stage. She must have looked unhinged as she almost ran up to him. Felipe smiled, opening his mouth to say something, only for that expression to turn to horror as Rowan grabbed hold of his face and pulled. His chestnut skin shifted in a blur as the holographic projection degraded. His deep purple eyes came through first, and then the rest of her baby Haldan's face as she wrestled him to the ground for all to see.

THIRTY-TWO

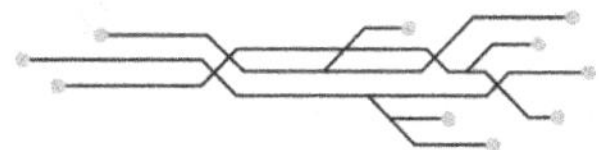

CALISTO

PUBLIC COAR DOWNLOAD/Book/The Restoration Is A Paradox/Author Hosa Liu/3-8-2094

-> *The Restoration is a paradox. It is not a nation-state but a contradictory mass of competing organizations bound together by an ideal. It distrusts any attempt to tie it together. Tens of thousands of herds and collectives across the Americas have contradictory governing structures, values, and organizations, yet so far, it has worked.*

-> *Yet that doesn't mean it always will. The forces of reaction never went away, and they continue to chip away at the Restoration's contradictory cohesion. Time will tell if they succeed.*

TIME: 7:46 PM
DAY: THURSDAY 5-26-2101

There was a ripple of shock through the crowd as people settled into the bitter reality that the man they had buried, the person they loved, was not only alive but had been lying to them this entire time.

"Don't be alarmed," Úna reassured the crowd.

Salem's shepherds had surrounded the Seven's contingent, yanking the holomasks off their faces while the shock of the moment hadn't yet pushed them to flee. The disguises flickered and died, revealing faces that had no business being there— spies and infiltrators from the barony, including His Royal Majesty, CEO Benison, his pale face scowling. Gasps rippled through the gathered herd, a mixture of outrage and vindication, as if this revelation had confirmed every suspicion they had ever harbored about the Seven's true intentions.

The peacekeepers, still seated in the front row, tensed, hands drifting instinctively toward their control panels to configure their suits' weapons. But no one moved—yet. The shepherds were firmly holding the intruders in place, not needing to shoot first to make their message clear: a point Calisto had stressed tonight as they went over the plan with all the other shepherds.

"Don't be alarmed," Úna repeated. "There's an explanation for this. Peacekeeper Tremblay," they said, looking for Calisto to say something.

Calisto stepped forward, happy to oblige. They turned to the crowd, savoring the reveal. "Yes, Haldan Kramer is alive. He has been pretending to be Captain Felipe this entire time."

There were more gasps. Murmurs spread like wildfire through the crowd, but Calisto held up their hand, continuing to talk so no gap allowed for confusion to take root. "You may have seen people on the Seven wear these overly large hats," Calisto said, holding Captain Felipe's hat, Haldan's hat in their hands. "It was to diminish direct exposure to sunlight so the holomask's image wouldn't have small artifacts in the projection, flickers like in an ancient Fallen TV; it's the same reason you darken the spaces around you during a performance. You don't want to ruin the show."

Calisto paused, letting the fact sink in for a fraction of a second before continuing, bellowing: "This case was confusing from the start. Haldan's supposed body was so badly damaged when we recovered it, and some of that damage had set in before his fight on the ferry. I was convinced that these facts meant that he couldn't be on the ferry that afternoon. That someone else was pretending to be him. So convinced, in fact, that I disregarded the testimony of his mother for far too long."

Calisto glanced briefly at Rowan, who was smiling—not a smug smile or one of triumph, but something quieter—a knowing, bittersweet expression that carried the weight of everything she had fought to make them see.

Calisto pressed on, their voice unwavering. "Rowan told us from the beginning that I was wrong. And I, in all my certainty, ignored what should have been obvious. Because Haldan *was* on that ferry, but he didn't die that day. The person whose body we laid to rest was someone else entirely." The murmurs didn't stop this time; they swelled, the amphitheater vibrating with unease. Calisto exhaled, rolling their shoulders back. "Now the question remains: Who was it that we buried? And why did someone go to such lengths to make us believe it was Haldan? Care to answer that, Haldan?"

Haldan, whose arms were pinned behind his back by his mother, Rowan, didn't answer them; instead, he spat at Calisto's feet.

"It's okay, you don't need to answer." Calisto turned back to the crowd. "You see, the night before Haldan and Anderson's so-called 'fight,' the two were actually engaged in a rather... intimate performance in the forest clearing near camp—one that involved ropes, trust, and, oh yeah, a syringe full of Vecuronium bromide to paralyze Anderson Leek. Why? Because Haldan needed Anderson to be completely silent while he played scientist. What followed was an ambitious—some might say unhinged—surgical masterpiece where Haldan rewrote Anderson's DNA to match his own. Fast forward to the next morning: Anderson's body, now a near-perfect genetic doppelgänger of Haldan, was conveniently stashed in a ferry closet, ready to be 'discovered.' Was this plan risky? Absolutely. Overcomplicated? Painfully so. But let's be real—everyone involved in this fiasco has the theatrical instincts of a Shakespearean villain. You already know Haldan, who that day mostly played himself. Tulip, perhaps you can explain your real role."

The petite Tulip emerged from the backstage, where she had been waiting quietly for this reveal. She looked tired, as if she had been carrying the weight of this secret for far too long. Her usually bright eyes were dulled with exhaustion, and she smoothed down the front of her suit with a nervous energy that did little to hide the tension in her shoulders.

"My real role?" she echoed, her voice light but edged with something bitter. "Well, if Haldan was the star of this little tragedy, I suppose that makes me the supporting role. I was being blackmailed, that part is true, but it was by Haldan, not Anderson."

"Traitor," Haldan snapped, his voice sharp with venom, but Tulip barely flinched. She tilted her head, regarding him with something that might have once been pity but had long since curdled into hatred.

"Oh, please," she sighed, crossing her arms. "Let's not pretend you ever had any loyalty to me either, Haldan. You used me. Just like you used Anderson, just like you used everyone else. The only difference is that I finally stopped playing along. "So," she continued, turning to the crowd, her voice steady. "The plan was never just about deception—it was about spectacle. Haldan didn't just want Anderson gone. He wanted him ruined. And to do that, he needed the whole camp to watch." She exhaled sharply, then pressed on. "I was the decoy, the illusion. I put on Anderson's suit to fool people's sensors and masked my face with a holomask so that I would look like him. We weren't worried about the mask degrading—no sun on the second floor of the Seven, no interference, just shadows and staged violence. And then, right on cue, I stepped into that hallway, into the spotlight, and started a fight that was never mine to begin with."

"Must have been cathartic telling Haldan off."

Tulip smiled bitterly. "You have no idea. After that, all I needed to do was to disappear." Here, she dramatically used a holomask of her own to change her appearance. "I disappeared into the crowd as someone else, and then I just waited for us to return to the Cods."

Calisto smiled. "Where you got rid of the most incriminating piece of evidence, Anderson's suit, by tossing it into a nanoweave at the edge of camp."

Tulip nodded.

"Which brings us to our final actor of this performance. Peter, would you like to explain your role in this whole affair?"

Peter bolted within seconds of his name being announced, but he wasn't fast enough. A shepherd lurched forward, tackling him to the ground before he could make it more than a few steps. Peter hit the dirt with a grunt, twisting furiously beneath the weight of his captor, but the shepherd had already pinned his arms behind his back. The crowd parted, eyes locked onto him like a pack of wolves smelling fresh blood as he was dragged to the front of the stage.

Calisto stepped closer, towering over Peter like a storm cloud about to break. "Running already?" they asked, voice laced with sharp amusement. "But you haven't even had your moment in the spotlight."

Peter sneered up at them, his chest rising and falling with ragged breaths. "Frack you."

Calisto smirked. "Charming. But don't worry, I'll do the talking." They turned to the crowd, letting their voice carry through the amphitheater. "Peter's role was simple—he was here to turn you against the Restoration. And let's be fair, we peacekeepers have done a stellar job making that easy," they added, glancing toward the front row, where the uniformed officials were shifting uncomfortably. "But what you may not realize is that this wasn't just about grievances. This was a performance, and the final act was secession. Peter and Haldan—well, they aren't just angry citizens. They're devout fans of the Fallen. They want to return us to debt servitude, to the Old Ways, and they weren't alone. The Eastic Barony was more than happy to lend a hand," they said, gesturing to the Seven's contingent, all now revealed to be barony spies. "They snuck in during the refugee crisis, taking advantage of our open borders to insert instigators among our midst. Leave it to corpos to take advantage of our humanity."

The crowd murmured in shock, but Calisto pressed on. "But why the murder? Well, Anderson was a problem. A loud, insufferable problem. He was pushing for a directive that would make the formation of a new barony much more difficult. Let's see," Calisto said, pulling up Anderson's amendment on their wrist. "'If such a centralizing force were to ever arise from the ground of the Restoration, it shall be our work to destroy it.' It was a not-so-subtle jab at Groundwork, but it would have made this cession plan grounds for war, and that simply wouldn't do. So Haldan killed him. And because our conspirators love efficiency, they didn't just want him dead—they wanted to weaponize his death. If Anderson were framed as a monster, as someone so vile that he killed his lover over a petty beef, then his proposed amendment would be soured by association. When the vote on secession came up tonight, they were hoping his example would dissuade you all from voting no. It was a murder designed to move the masses."

They turned back to the accused, their voice thick with mock politeness. "Did I leave anything out?"

Haldan and Peter said nothing.

It was Úna who finally broke the silence, stepping forward with an air of forced calm. "I think we're all still processing this, but given that tonight's Charter meeting was advanced under false pretenses, perhaps we should table the conversation for now? All opposed?"

No one objected. The discussion had already begun to shift—from politics to justice, to the repairs between Herd Salem and Haldan, Peter, and everyone else who hurt them.

THIRTY-THREE

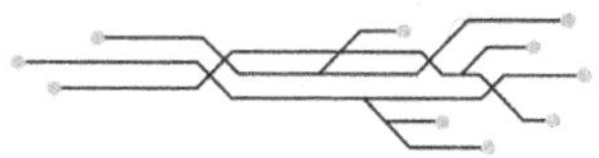

ROWAN

```
PUBLIC COAR DOWNLOAD/Poem/The Toast of Despair/
Author Voltairine de Cleyre/1892
```

-> God is a lie, and Faith is a lie,
And a tenfold lie is Love;
Life is a problem without a why,
And never a thing to prove.

-> it adds, and subtracts, and multiplies,
And divides without aim or end;
Its answers all false, though false-named true —
Wife, husband, lover, friend.

```
TIME: 10:41 AM
DAY: FRIDAY 5-27-2101
```

Rowan let go of Haldan's hand as he walked up the ramp onto the Northeast Seven Shuttle, which was now being captained by someone who wasn't a barony spy attempting to destroy the Restoration. Haldan scowled at her and Úna, bitter and resentful at their efforts to stop him. He was not headed to Bangalore this time, truth be told, he never was, but to the Eden Rehabilitation Center, where he would voluntarily check in until he satisfied the conditions of his repair, or left, whichever one came first.

"We will always love you," Rowan told him, meaning it despite everything he had done.

Úna said nothing, silent as she choked on words unable to escape her throat.

Haldan didn't respond to this statement. He hadn't talked to her since she had wrestled him to the ground during the charter meeting. He merely paused walking for a second, as if he intended to say something but must have thought better of it, and continued walking toward the ferry. She wondered if he would actually go to Eden or if he would duck out beforehand to some barony stronghold to live out his fantasy of being a rugged individualist. Nothing was keeping him from doing so, except for the knowledge that few herds would accept him if he didn't do this: didn't show that he was willing to admit he could be wrong, and even then, many wouldn't. Salem might take decades to forgive him, if it ever did.

As the two of them watched him leave them for the second time, the ferry disappearing into the wideness of the ocean, she found herself turning to her wife, still uncertain of everything that had happened, but not how it had happened.

They walked into the woods to the cliffside overlooking the water. The Eastic's smockstacks were still spewing black smoke, but perhaps not for much longer. There was talk about declaring war on the barony, though it was still too early to tell what would come of such talk.

They stared out into the sea until Rowan broke the tension. "You know he got it from us," She said wistfully. "That refusal to listen, that sense of superiority. That was learned from a little of both of us."

"Row, I..." Úna sounded like she was about to disagree, but merely swallowed her unformed words. "Maybe," was all she managed to say.

"How long did you know?"

"About his corpo sympathies? I told you already, it's been a while."

"No, how long did you know that Haldan was up to something in the Cods, specifically?"

Úna didn't skip a beat. "You're sounding crazy."

Rowan still felt like a part of her was crazy, but not about this, not when it came to the truth. "The night he killed Anderson," Rowan continued, "and I heard that scream, a scream that was probably Tulip reacting to his death, and you told me it was a coyote. That I was imagining things. Did you know then?"

Úna looked down, unable to meet her wife's gaze. "No."

"And when he came to us that night to establish what was undoubtedly an alibi, if his little plan backfired, and there was blood on his hands. What about then?" Úna tried to avert her gaze, and it made Rowan want to howl. "Look at me." She said firmly.

Úna feebly raised her head. "I...yes...he told me he wanted to kill Anderson weeks ago, but I didn't think he was going to actually do it. You know how crazy that sounds?"

Rowan shook her head. "No, if I had known everything you knew, I wouldn't have thought it was crazy. He was an abuser. He was a narcissist. And he hated the Restoration. People like that don't have a limit." Rowan said cooly, letting the implication hang in the air.

"Well, we can't all be as smart as you." Úna quipped bitterly.

Rowan nodded slowly, taking the insult. "Don't be so modest. You figured it out well before me."

"I thought it was just talk, Row," she repeated. "And then when I saw the blood on his hands that night, I panicked."

"His death threats probably didn't sound crazy then."

"It would ruin me. Ruin us. I would never be able to run for Head Shepherd again if my son had killed someone. I couldn't let anyone find out."

"Not even me?" Rowan asked.

Úna turned away in shame.

"Gaslighting," Rowan continued, "The denying of someone's reality. It's learned. His stubbornness, his refusal to listen to others' perspectives. He got that from me. But this, he got from you."

"I didn't know that he was trying to get us to secede. That he would fake his own death. I thought...I don't know what I thought."

Rowan gave out a small, cruel laugh. "Trash, you didn't know? You were helping Peter with his resolution this entire time. You may not have been told, but you knew. When did you piece it together?"

Úna tried to pivot once again. "Baby, it's not like..."

But Rowan was not receptive in the slightest. "When." Rowan barked deeply. "I've placed you under review, dear. You're not recovering from this. Don't lie. Just tell me."

It was here that the mischievous light left Úna's eyes, and she gave up trying to win.

"It was the way Peter and Felipe talked to each other. Their chemistry. It was too quick. Too much like Peter and Haldan. That's when I put the final pieces together."

"And you just went along with their scheme until, what, the night I came forward, and you knew Haldan wasn't going to win."

Úna nodded. "I did. His plan was too complicated to survive the truth. I pivoted."

"They'll be coming soon," Rowan said, squeezing Úna's hands. "Your former shepherds. I told them to give me a few minutes. Sit with me until they do?"

Úna did so. The two of them sat down on a flat boulder overlooking the waters, sitting quietly as the sun set and the embers of their love died.

THIRTY-FOUR

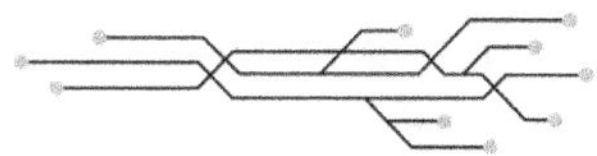

CALISTO

PUBLIC COAR DOWNLOAD/Essay/Why I Left the PSL...
or the DSA or Socialist Alternative or whatever/
Author a filler kid/2021

-> *Anarchy, on the other hand, is a flawed and centerless constellation of relationships, which is to say anarchy is built on affinity, trust, and reciprocal knowledge...It is true that 'we' do struggle to sustain coordination and momentum, beyond the intermediate term. Like every movement, anarchy waxes and wanes. I couldn't care less. Any communist or anarchist who believes that revolt in the united settler-states actually depends on the strength of 'the Left' is deluding themself. Revolt happens with or without us. So rather than waste my time obsessing over the strength of some organization or ideology's influence in a given region, I'd rather learn more projectual approaches that might contribute to conflictuality. I know some of you reading this are studying this framework as well, and I look forward to discovering your projects, wherever they may incite or strike.*

TIME: 12:02 PM
DAY: FRIDAY 5-27-2101

Calisto was half-packing, half-listening to their supervisor, Dela. She hadn't stopped apologizing. It was one thing to be wrong about a murder, but to be so corrupt that a barony could count on that corruption to try to coup a portion of the Restoration was a major frack up. Groundwork had had thousands of members resign in protest. Already, hundreds of herds had withdrawn from the CRS Delegation, and over a dozen had left the Restoration completely, threatening not to return until Groundwork was completely dissolved. Dela needed Calisto now more than ever: the one member of Groundwork who had done anything about the conspiracy she, and by extension, Groundwork, had neglected.

"Your initiative is truly impressive," she applauded. "I've been telling everyone that you were a genius during this repair."

Calisto had to stop themselves from rolling their eyes. Their supervisor, for all their disagreements with her during this case, wasn't malicious; she was merely a tool. In another world, she might have channeled that energy into squashing authoritarian organizations rather than building them up; it just wasn't this one.

"I thought you were going to have my polluted ass under review at one point." Calisto joked in that not-really-joking kind of way.

Dela squirmed. "What can I say, I was wrong. I only hope you don't hold it against me."

"Never. I appreciate your support," Calisto lied, at least partially.

They hadn't told her that they would be leaving the Party and the Delegation—although leaving one naturally required leaving the other. There was no point in their honesty. They knew they could not reach her. It had taken a conspiracy theory and the entire Party turning against them for Calisto to have changed their perspective. They weren't expecting lightning to strike the same place twice. They would be here if and when reason ever seeped into her core. They owed her that much. Dela had made a decision based on what she had thought was true, and, in her own way, she had given them support. They could forgive her for that.

Rowan poked her head into the tent, making a motion for wanting to talk.

"That reminds me, I have some final CRS work to do. If you'll excuse me, boss."

Dela started to make more inane small talk, but Calisto cut the feed. They were so very tired.

Rowan walked in. She was tapping her feet uneasily, looking over at some notes on her wrist. "You asked me to remind you when…"

"It's time then? Calisto asked.

Rowan nodded.

A buzz came in for a call. Calisto projected a video feed onto their tent wall: the face of a wiry man sipping coffee from a mug, with perpetual bags under his eyes fading into his dark brown face.

"Garykillsfascists?, I presume," Calisto asked.

"Gary Russo is my non-pen name. I was surprised to get your message, Peacekeeper Tremblay."

"That I am, at least for the next day or so, that is. I'm not going to resign from the Delegation or the Party until your article goes out. Don't want to give Groundwork any ideas." Calisto said, smirking, sitting in the unreality of the moment.

"Trash, you really are doing this, then. Can I ask why?"

"Because I'm tired of pretending that building back up a police state is okay."

"Can I quote you on that?"

"Yes, please do."

EPILOGUE

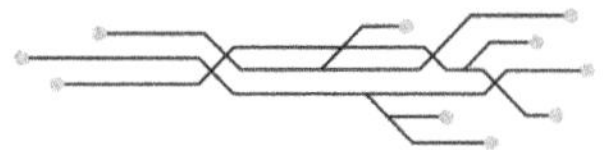

Three-Seven had been fascinated by the Chamber ever since coming to the Restoration, reading everything she could get her hands on about it. The first herd, one that had started out of necessity to find food, and later, to be one step ahead of Corporate Forces as the Greater American Civil War exploded.

Like then, it was a collection of wagons and tents, but now some of them were so massive that Three-Seven doubted they would be able to escape the raining bombs of corporate forces, if the baronies still had an air force anyway. The largest of these buildings was the central Chamber, the namesake of this self-hating legislative body. It was opulent by Restoration standards. It had a large ceiling covered with a painting of the Restoration's founding mythology: various factions on the decaying highways of this Fallen hegemony coming together to fight the United Corporate States of America. The walls were adorned with more art, historical moments captured in vivid colors: Ojibwe guerrilla fighters partnering with internally displaced refugees of the fallen

Americas, forces toppling statues of corporate icons, buildings with smiling arches and arrows on fire.

Three-Seven was sitting on a plush chair, facing a group of politicians. She had received a formal invitation to speak before a cadre of Chamber members. There were no standing committees in the Restoration, as that would (to them) be considered an alarming concentration of power, but there were cadres: groups of like-minded individuals who met and convened meetings, which sounded a lot like Board Members if Three-Seven was being honest. She had read on the COAR that this cadre was one of the oldest in existence. Its membership always fluctuated, but as far as she could tell, Roxane Chapman, the lean woman sitting before her, had always been a part of it, before she had even started the Groundwork Party. And so, while she could have turned down this invitation, cadres had no formal authority; she had decided not to. She had things to say.

"Thank you so much for joining us," the excitable Roxane stated. "I am Roxane Chapman. These are my comrades, Lu and Alvarez."

"Hello," Three-Seven said.

"We wanted to get your perspective on the recent Eastic incident." The Chamber Representative, Lu, stated.

"Am I compelled to?" Three-Seven asked, amused.

Roxane frowned. "No, of course not. We're interviewing all former... all the former members of the Eastic, who have escaped. You understand?"

"To what end?" Three-Seven stated bluntly.

Roxane all but ignored this question. "For the record, could you tell us how things proceeded in the Eastern Shore

Trading Combine, the Eastic, in your own words? You were there when the Eastic Civil War broke out, correct?"

At first, Three-Seven attempted to do this, but there were too many interruptions to get her points across. These were not clarifying questions but political theater over what had happened. Three-Seven would say something, and then Roxane Chapman would smile and ask her to pause and resay something with more charged language and maybe a speculation or two.

"That sounds horrible," she would smile. "Would you say that the Eastic is dangerous?"

And then later, a comrade would interject. "My heart goes out to you. It sounds like they denied you all autonomy. Would you say that this barony is capable of similar actions in the future?"

"What about other baronies?" Alvarez would join in.

Three-Seven had no interest in defending the Eastic. The Restoration had every right to bloviate about it, but then the conversation shifted to something she wanted to discuss. Roxane smiled and said. "And when the peacekeepers stopped this plot..."

"They did no such thing." Three-Seven interrupted.

This caused Lu to bluster. "I see, but Peacekeeper Tremblay..."

"Calisto has resigned from the Delegation, and they were only able to solve this case because they went behind Groundwork's back. You were more interested in resuming the operations of a ferry than solving this case. Corruption, the barony exploited. I know because I was there, and Tremblay told me."

"The witness has every right to..."

"Three-Seven," they corrected. She considered it rude that they hadn't referred to her by her name this entire time, but realized immediately that it had nothing to do with her: they felt awkward about it. About her once being property, and what that meant for the Restoration they felt was so perfect under their aspiring stewardship.

Alvarez broached the subject tactlessly. "Surely you don't want to be referred to by a number. After everything this barony has done..."

Three-Seven gave him a withering glare. She had thought about this a lot recently. She'd been referred to as Three-Seven her entire life. She'd never been bothered by it until coming to the Restoration: since being free, freer, that is.

"I do," Three-Seven said at last. "You'll just have to get used to that. The Restoration still has blind spots it doesn't acknowledge: slavery it still tolerates; bureaucracy it has built up bit by bit, inch by inch, that it refuses to see. I'm one of those blind spots. You're that bureaucracy. Have a good day."

And with that, Three-Seven stood up from her seat and walked out of the Chamber.

ACKNOWLEDGMENTS

Publishing a novel is frackin' hard. I have been trying to get this work off the ground for years. I completed the first draft all the way back in 2023, and have been slowly whittling away at it ever since. I had hoped to publish it last year, but you will notice that there was a whole gap between April of 2024, when I published my first novel, *The Bubble We're In*, and now with *Policing Utopia*. To say life got in the way is an understatement. In 2025, I moved, prepared all my documents for the incoming Trump administration, placed myself at the center of a lot of activism, healed from burnout, and continued writing, not just this book but a blog as well. It was probably one of the most challenging years of my life, and I would like to thank everyone who helped me get through it.

I would like to thank my wonderful partner, Arty, who helped build this world alongside me, through our many many late night conversations. He had to struggle through the early drafts, when my characters were not nearly as developed or nuanced as they are now. You have the patience of a saint, my love.

I would like to give a shoutout to my sisters, and my parents, both in blood and law. Family is a huge part of this novel, as characters struggle to figure out where they belong, and you shaped this world's conception of family as much as you shaped me. I love you all.

I would like to thank the wonderful Norah K. Dick and Shauna Gordon-McKeon, who both beta-read this novel and provided detailed, exhaustive notes. I appreciated these so much! I would also like to thank Fay for her developmental edits and designers David Colón and Brady Moller, who helped with the book's cover and layout.

All of these people helped make the work you have read today possible. I am grateful for their assistance. A better world is possible.

ABOUT THE AUTHOR

Alex Mell-Taylor is a trans, nonbinary writer who reports out from the digital trenches on pop culture and politics, often with an intersectional, queer bent on their blog *Alex Has Opinions*. They are also the founder of the futurist magazine *After the Storm*, which has accepted stories from around the world. *Policing Utopia* is their second novel.

READ MORE FROM ALEX MELL-TAYLOR

WHEN THE WORLD GRINDS TO A HALT BECAUSE OF A deadly pandemic, two men move in together way too quickly to avoid being alone. Sebastian is a workaholic straining to escape his modest roots. Christian is a trust fund kid who can provide Sebastian with the life he craves. As they struggle to adjust to the new normal, class and political differences begin to poke holes in their uneasy relationship.

Both men soon expand their COVID bubble and their relationship to include a group of strangers they meet on Grindr. Between raucous underground parties and a last-minute vacation to the Bahamas, Sebastian and Christian's newfound bubble seems to thrive, despite challenging conditions. But as troubles on the outside slowly find their way in, the group—and Sebastian and Christian's relationship—threatens to implode. Both men are forced to weigh their options and decide what scares them more, being together or being apart.